Intolerable!

He removed his hat and drenched great coat as he hurried to climb inside. "Thank you. I was afraid I'd have to walk for miles—" He stopped, obviously as surprised to see her as she was shocked to realize it was *him.*

The Duke of Colster sat across from her. The line of his mouth flattened. He stood, reaching for the door handle, but at that moment the coach lurched forward, throwing Colster off balance and on top of Charlotte.

He practically leaped to the other side of the coach to get away from her. It wasn't a far distance. Their knees still touched and would have to. There was no way to avoid him.

Colster pounded on the roof. "Driver, stop this coach immediately!"

But his order must have gotten lost in the sound of wind and rain, for no one responded.

All the anger she'd been carrying inside, the indignation, fear, and humiliation, rose to the surface. He didn't want to be in the same coach with her?

She didn't want to ride with *him!*

"You could jump," she suggested.

Cathy Maxwell

IN THE
BED
OF A
DUKE

AVON BOOKS
An Imprint of HarperCollinsPublishers

This is a work of fiction. Names, characters, places, and incidents are products of the author's imagination or are used fictitiously and are not to be construed as real. Any resemblance to actual events, locales, organizations, or persons, living or dead, is entirely coincidental.

AVON BOOKS
An Imprint of HarperCollins*Publishers*
10 East 53rd Street
New York, New York 10022-5299

Copyright © 2006 by Cathy Maxwell
Teaser copyrights © 2002, 2003, 2004, 2005 by Cathy Maxwell
ISBN: 0-7394-6771-9
ISBN: 978-0-7394-6771-8

Avon Trademark Reg. U.S. Pat. Off. and in Other Countries, Marca Registrada, Hecho en U.S.A.
HarperCollins® is a registered trademark of HarperCollins Publishers Inc.

Printed in the U.S.A.

For Kathy Jorgenson.
Thank you.

I am wealthy in my friends.

Acknowledgments

I am grateful for the assistance and insight of Glennis Pleasants and her son Brandon, who have been blessed to live with twins. I also appreciate Catherine Solari, who offered a number of great resources for my research.

Chapter 1

London, 1807

*P*hillip Maddox, Duke of Colster, walked through the crowded halls of Parliament not meeting the eye of anyone he passed.

They made way for him.

He was a duke, after all, and one with enviable power. Here and there, someone would nod, and murmur, "Your Grace," but for the most part, they waited until he'd gone by to speak—and when they did, he knew they were talking about *him* and how Miranda Cameron had jilted him at his own betrothal ball. She'd run away with her lover while her sister Charlotte, a brazen, unprincipled woman, had openly defied him when he'd attempted to stop her.

For eight months he'd had to put up with this. He'd tried to carry on, certain some other scandal would come along to occupy idle tongues. After all, what had happened was his private business. But London was a town of gossips and, unfortunately, of matchmakers. They didn't show any sign of letting this matter go.

Apparently, his offer to Miss Miranda Cameron had surprised everyone. His wife Elizabeth's death had been an emotional pivot point in his life, and, in his grief, he'd vowed not to marry again.

However, now that money-hungry mothers and fathers with marriageable daughters knew he *could* bring himself to marry again, they were determined that he *should*. Every acquaintance had a daughter, sister, cousin, niece, and perhaps even an aunt or two, who would make a perfect duchess. Phillip could paper the walls of his house with the invitations he'd received, many of them hiding a scheme to see him wed.

And he didn't want any of it.

Miranda Cameron had been a grave miscalculation on his part. Perhaps the only one he'd ever made. People thought he'd been drawn to her because she was beautiful, but that wasn't quite it. Miranda had reminded him of Elizabeth, who had died in childbirth. Seeing the resemblance had made him long to try and right a wrong, something he now realized he was powerless to do.

He didn't need an heir. His cousin could inherit the title. He'd make a good duke, and Phillip could maintain his stoic existence. There was peace in that decision, a peace he'd longed for since Elizabeth's death.

"I say, Colster, wait up," Lord Heaton's voice said from behind him.

Phillip paused. He knew Heaton from school and rather liked the man. Their fathers had been good friends and had served on numerous diplomatic envoys together. Heaton had a good head on his shoulders. Phillip enjoyed listening to his arguments and valued his counsel in the House of Lords. Here was a man who, like Phillip, didn't put up with nonsense. Furthermore, Heaton had no daughters of a marriageable age.

"How are you, Your Grace?" Heaton said in greeting.

"Fine, and yourself?" Phillip asked, nodding for Heaton to walk with him toward the Members' Entrance ahead. "My coach is waiting outside. May I offer you a ride?"

"That would be kind. I'm to my club. Perhaps you will join me?"

"Would that I could," Phillip answered. They were of two different political spectrums and Phillip could not politically afford to be seen in a liberal club.

The assessing look in Heaton's eye told him he knew the reason behind his refusal. "Is there anyone you trust?"

"No."

Heaton raised his brows. "Be careful, Your Grace, you are in danger becoming a hermit, hair shirt and all."

The observation was a bit too apt for comfort. Nor could its ring of truth be denied. Phillip hid his uneasiness by changing the subject. "What did you think of—?" he started, but Heaton's hand on his arm interrupted him.

"Damn, there is Monarch." Heaton glanced around. "It doesn't appear as if we can dodge him."

"Monarch?" Phillip scanned the men crowded by the entrance, uncertain which one Heaton meant.

"You haven't met him yet?" He dropped his voice. "You don't know how fortunate you are. No man has ever been more misnamed. He's an out-and-out reformer who's new to the Lords. Down from Edinburgh. Inherited his title last summer and is determined to do something with it. He's been anxious to meet you."

Phillip let his step slow. "Me?"

"Was not your father one of the prime supporters of the Clearances? Monarch is keen to see us do something about them and has been talking about how your support is vital to any legislation."

Phillip had to consider a moment what he was talking about. "The Clearances? You mean where landowners evict tenants who can't pay their rents?"

"Something like that. It's a Scottish issue," Heaton answered breezily just as young Lord Monarch approached.

Monarch had a shock of orange-red hair that fell over one eye. He couldn't be older than four-and-twenty and had that earnest puppy air Phillip associated with the true crusader of social justice. The jaded denizens of London would gobble him up in two bites.

"Lord Heaton," Monarch said, his voice cracking on the second syllable as if it was taking courage for him to approach them. He cleared his throat, obviously embarrassed, and Phillip couldn't help but feel a touch sorry for him.

"Hallo, Monarch," Heaton said, and would have marched right on by without pause except for the young Scotsman's placing himself squarely in Phillip's path, forcing both him and Heaton to stop.

"May I beg an introduction?" Lord Monarch asked without preamble. "I've heard much of the great Duke of Colster." He held out his hand to Phillip. His *ungloved* hand.

He truly was a republican.

"It's a pleasure to be introduced to you, Your Grace," he said, his voice again in danger of cracking. Interestingly, Phillip didn't hear an echo of a Scottish lilt in it. This young man was English-educated . . . and fighting for the Scottish cause. *Interesting.*

Heaton was not pleased with Monarch's forwardness. "I don't like being forced into matters," he informed the Scotsman coolly, and would have walked on except Phillip reached out and shook the offered hand.

"Colster," he introduced himself. "I hear you are new to London."

Monarch had the good grace to blush. "I am."

"Then welcome," Phillip said genially, aware that by now, everyone within listening distance was attending to their conversation. They had all registered Monarch's social blunders. Phillip wouldn't be surprised to learn the man had not followed any protocol at all with anyone—and he rather liked him for it. Protocol and the "rules" of polite society had been drummed into Phillip's head since birth. However, now that the Duke of Colster had recognized the man, society would keep their criticisms to themselves. Sometimes, power was a good thing.

"Thank you, Your Grace—"

"Ah, well, that's done," Heaton cut in. "Shall we go, Colster?"

"Let me have my hat," Phillip announced, looking over to the attendant who handled such things. The servant stepped forward with his wide-brimmed beaver hat, bowing when Phillip slipped a guinea in his hand from the leather purse of coins he kept for such occasions. He liked being thought of as generous.

The beadle attending the door leading out to St. Margaret's Street opened it for them, but Monarch wasn't ready to conclude the interview. "I need a moment of your precious time, Your Grace. Please."

Damn, he was going to make a request, and Phillip didn't want to talk about something as old-fashioned as the Clearances right now.

"Not here," he counseled Monarch in a low voice. "Later. Arrange an appointment with my man Freedman."

"I *can't* later. I've been called out of town, and I must leave. My wife's mother is ill."

"Sorry to hear that," Heaton said cheerily. "Your conversation with Colster will just have to wait."

Phillip turned to the door, but Monarch would not give up. He raised his voice. "There are people dying, Your Grace. Women and children. Whole families are starving over the Clearances. You must use your influence to help."

The conversation in the hall stopped. Annoyed, Phillip silently amended his opinion of Monarch. Heaton had been right. The man was an idiot.

Aware that all listened, Phillip answered in a calm, steady voice, making his decision on the matter in that moment, a decision his father had once explained to him. "This is a private matter between tenants and landowners. It's not the business of the Lords."

"Who better to censure us than our peers?" Monarch argued. "The situation is desperate. You are of Scottish descent, Your Grace—"

"But I don't own land there."

"No, your father was one of the first to sell out."

"Precisely because my family has no interests there. We're English. Not Scot. And I mean no offense," Phillip continued smoothly, "but that is the true reason why my father sold."

He would have walked out the door save for Monarch's bold, "And not to line your family's coffers?"

Phillip's indulgent attitude toward the new lord evaporated. "My family does not need its coffers lined."

"They don't," Heaton agreed, obviously pleased that his prediction about Monarch was proving to be correct. They should have avoided him. "If you knew anything, Monarch, you'd know you are speaking to one of the wealthiest men in Britain."

"Wealth gained at what price?" Monarch asked. Jaws dropped. The men standing around them were the leaders of the realm. These were not accusations to toss around lightly.

Phillip faced Monarch. "I take my honor seriously," he said.

Realizing the insult he'd just paid, the pup started to stammer an apology, but Phillip wasn't letting him off that easily. "It's true my sire was a hard man—some have even called him ruthless, and I would not disagree. However, he also served his country well. As do I. Accusing the line of Colster of the deaths of women and children is not something I will allow."

The young lord opened and closed his mouth like a fish gasping on dry land. He glanced around, becoming alarmed at exactly how large an audience they had attracted. "I—I," he started and then froze, words finally failing him.

Heaton's dramatic sigh filled the void. "I don't believe I've mentioned to you, Monarch, that the Duke of Colster is a crack shot and a well-regarded swordsman. You aren't, by chance, one of those two things yourself . . . ?"

"I am not." Monarch paused a moment, and then confessed faintly, "I just want to do what is right."

"As do we all," Phillip answered. "As do we all." He took a step away before turning. "I'm not unsympathetic in your concerns, my lord. Prepare a paper on your position and send it round. I'll read it. It's all I can offer until I am better educated on the matter."

Monarch appeared ready to collapse with relief. "I shall, Your Grace. Thank you. I shall."

"And, Monarch," Phillip said, couldn't resist adding, "don't be so blunt with these others." He nodded to the lords and statesmen gathered round them. "They lack my tolerance."

"Yes, Your Grace. I shall remember that."

His point having been made, Phillip left the building, Heaton beside him. They'd barely made it out the door before Heaton almost doubled up with glee.

"'Pon my soul, I do believe Monarch has learned a lesson," Heaton said. "What a moment! You had him quaking in his shoes. He's a hopelessly knotty head. Imagine leaving London because your wife's mother had taken ill?"

Phillip smiled. "He's not such a bad sort. He's what you said—a reformer. We were all starry at one time."

"Not me. And you were far gentler with him than any of the others have been. With his attitude and lack of manners, he belongs in the Commons, not the Lords."

The arrogance behind his comment stopped Phillip. "Why do you say that? Are we not also tasked to see to the common good?"

Heaton made a dismissive sound. "We see

after our interests, just as they are to fight for theirs. It's fair. The best man always wins."

"Or the one with the most power."

His companion smiled. "There is that, too. But then, power, like the land, was given over to us for safekeeping. Could you possibly believe it fair to order Scottish lords to give up rights that have been theirs for centuries?"

"I don't know. I've never thought of Scotland or visited it."

"Not even to hunt?"

"I don't have time for such pursuits."

"You should take time. You work too hard."

But before Phillip could answer, a lad ran up to him. "Message for Your Grace, the Duke of Colster." He held a letter in his filthy hand.

Phillip looked the boy's bare feet and thought of Monarch's accusations. He flipped a guinea toward the boy, who caught it in midair before handing over the letter.

The envelope's expensive vellum was marred by the lad's dirty fingerprints. There was no seal. Colster's title was written in a spidery handwriting on the back. "Who gave this to you?"

"A man at the Old Ship. It's a tavern by the docks."

"Did you know the man?" Phillip asked, knowing what the answer would be before the boy shook his head.

"No, Your Grace."

"You can solve the mystery by opening it," Heaton suggested.

Phillip's coach pulled up to the walk. Before the vehicle had completely stopped, one of the two footmen accompanying the driver jumped down to open the door for Phillip.

"We're taking Lord Heaton to his club," Phillip informed the driver.

"Yes, Your Grace."

While Heaton gave the address, Phillip climbed into the coach and opened the envelope. All of his correspondence went through Freedman. He had no idea what this was about or why someone would make the effort of bypassing his secretary.

He read the first lines—and his world came to a halt.

Few knew that he'd had a twin who had died at birth.

He reread the opening paragraph again, thinking his mind must be playing tricks. It wasn't.

> . . . *I have been party to a most grievous crime, a sin so black the Almighty may not forgive me. Your twin brother did not die.*

Heaton joined him in the coach, the footman shutting the door after him. "I can't believe even in the city you travel with two outriders—" He broke off. "Is something the matter, Your Grace? You look pale."

Phillip looked up, not truly comprehending what he was saying. He needed a moment alone to think. He forced a smile. "Nothing's wrong." He sat back against the seat, folding the letter.

"You appear upset."

"I'm not."

Heaton noticed he'd opened the letter. "Distressing news?"

"It's from my childhood nanny. She's dying. Wanted a last request."

"And she's a regular at the Old Ship down by the docks?"

Phillip wasn't in the mood for his probing. No one must know what was in the contents of this letter. It was probably a hoax. A cruel one.

He hid his alarm behind a smile. He was a skilled diplomat. He could hide every feeling. "It's sad. That's all," he heard himself answer.

Heaton accepted his explanation without question—because, as it turned out, he had his own interests in mind. "Actually, I did want a moment to discuss a matter with you."

"Your agricultural legislation? I have every intention of supporting you."

"No, something a bit more personal." Heaton

shifted his weight on the soft leather seat uncomfortably. "I have a niece I believe you should meet—"

Dear God, not Heaton, too.

"—She's a lovely girl, fluent in French, her manners impeccable, a true English rose—"

"I don't want to marry. I'm done with it. Losing Elizabeth tore me apart." Especially having childbirth claim her life. It was the same death his mother had suffered. They said she'd died of grief over losing her baby. His brother. His *twin.*

No wonder he didn't want to marry. Subconsciously, Elizabeth's death had triggered an overwhelming sense of remorse that he'd kept bottled inside . . . until this moment.

He longed to crush the letter in his hand. He didn't. He didn't move even so much as an eyelash.

"But your title, Colster. You have a responsibility to your title."

Mutiny welled up inside him. He tamped it down. "I know my responsibilities, Heaton."

"Very well then. You should marry for yourself." Heaton sat back. "You live like a monk. It's not healthy for a man to hold himself off from women."

"Now you are calling my manhood into play? Forget Monarch. I'm closer to calling *you* out."

"I mean no insult," Heaton hurried to declare.

"I'm speaking as a friend, and I've been thinking. We are both two-and-thirty. It's a good age for a man to start a family. Alicia is such a comely girl. Delightful even. And, differing political views aside, it would be an advantageous marriage for both of us—"

"I won't marry again."

Heaton remained unconvinced. "I remember you telling us all that once before, and then you met Miss Cameron."

"And I damn the day she ever crossed my path, both she and those fortune-hunting sisters of her. They've turned me into food for scandalmongers."

"The gossips talk about each of us from time to time."

"Not I."

"Yes, they did," his friend told him gently. "You were just less sensitive to it."

The coach rolled to a stop. "We're at your club," Phillip said pointedly.

The footman opened the door, but Heaton didn't budge. "So you won't even come round for a peek at Alicia?"

"No, Jack."

Heaton studied him for a moment. "Elizabeth's death wasn't your fault," he said with startling insight.

The letter was a heavy weight in Phillip's pocket. Heaton didn't know what it was like to have a person ripped out of one's life by death. Phillip had lost everyone close to him. Mother, brother, father, wife . . . and even the fickle and silly Miranda Cameron. It was easier to shut it all out. "My cousin will make an excellent duke. Introduce Alicia to him."

Heaton knew he'd been dismissed. He climbed out of the coach. "Thank you for the ride."

"My pleasure." Heaton closed the door, and Phillip was finally free to unfold the letter and read the deathbed confession.

. . . Your twin brother did not die. He was stolen by the Laird MacKenna, whose sister your mother unwittingly hired as a midwife. 'Twas on my recommendation. I told Her Grace that Rowena was a cousin. She was nothing of the sort. She paid me well for my hand in the foul deed, and I was greedy and foolish enough to agree.

The duchess, may God have mercy on her soul, was in pain and so trusting of us who had the care of her. When the first babe was born, she didn't see the drops of tincture Rowena placed in his wee mouth that caused him to fall into such a deep sleep he appeared as if dead.

'Twas a blessing Rowena had already left the room with Justin when we realized there wasn't

one babe but two, or who knows what she would have done to you?

Later, I had no choice but to help her. We placed a dead dog in the casket that had been prepared for your brother. Everyone was so consumed by grief, they trusted us to do what was right, and we betrayed them.

I do not know the fate of your brother. However, if Justin Maddox is alive, he is in the hands of Laird MacKenna and his blackhearted sister Rowena. I have heard no word from any of them since she disappeared with the baby.

Father Nicholas is helping me write this letter. He serves as my witness.

By the time you read this, I may no longer be on this earth. I can't ask for forgiveness for I have never been able to forgive myself. May God have mercy on my soul for what I've done.

The letter was signed by Meredith Frye and witnessed by Father Jean-Pierre Nicholas.

Phillip sat very still.

He *wasn't* alone.

He had a brother.

One who was in the hands of his family's enemies.

Phillip frowned. He knew the tale of the feud between the MacKennas and the Maddoxes, but it had taken place close to two hundred years ago. It could not be important now. The tale was impossible to believe—*save that his brother might be alive.*

And if he was, Phillip was not the rightful Duke of Colster.

The thought sucked the air out of the coach. He couldn't breathe.

Colster was more than a title; it was Phillip's very being, his purpose. He looked out the window at the expensive stone houses of the quiet, elegant neighborhood and told himself his whole life couldn't have been a lie. The letter was nothing more than paper and ink. It would burn in a blink, and no one would be the wiser—except for himself.

And if Phillip Maddox believed in one thing, it was honor.

A sense of destiny stirred within him. A twin. Another half to himself. The light to his darkness.

And the reason why he'd always felt alone.

Before his coach reached his front step, he knew he'd be leaving for Scotland.

But he'd not take servants and outriders. This matter was too personal. If he was being played for a fool, he didn't want the gossips to know.

And, if Nanny Frye's claim was true?

He might not want that known either.

Chapter 2

Scotland

*G*ale-force winds of a sudden Highland storm pounded Charlotte Cameron's coach, accentuating the desperateness of her situation. But she would not turn back. Indeed, she would have traveled to meet the devil himself if marriage could undo all the harm her ambitions had caused her family.

For that reason, when Laird MacKenna had invited her to visit his Highland home, Nathraichean, located on the northernmost coast of Scotland, she'd accepted. Granted she didn't know him well; but the two of them had one thing in common—they were both enemies of the Duke of Colster. With the duke as one's enemy, friends were few and far between, as were marriage offers.

And besides, she told herself repeatedly, although Laird MacKenna was really quite old, he didn't *truly* have horns and a tail. Marriage to him would provide respectability, which was what she needed to find a suitable husband for Constance.

Nor was Charlotte in a position to be choosy over choosing a husband. At seven-and-twenty, she was beyond the pale for the marriage market. An old man is all she would have caught anyway. It was her penance to put aside her romantic dreams and ensure that Constance's were fulfilled.

Or would be, Charlotte amended, if she survived the fury of this storm. She rode in Laird MacKenna's own coach, an old, heavy vehicle that was no match for the force of wind, hail, and lightning Mother Nature threw at them with all her might.

Charlotte gripped the leather seat and anything else she could grab and tried to think positively. Everything would work out. *It had to—*

A particularly strong gust of wind hit the side of the coach, interrupting her fervent prayers. The motion was like being slapped by the hand of God, and she could have sworn she felt the wheels on one side of the vehicle lift off the road. She caught her breath. The last time she'd dared to look outside the coach, there had been a huge drop off the side of the road into a rocky gorge. They'd all be smashed to pieces.

Her fears were confirmed as the laird's men, Klem and Fergus, cursed the horses. One yelled, "Weight on the other side, weight on the other side."

Charlotte grabbed her precious knitting bag and scrambled as best she could toward the opposite door, bringing every ounce at her disposal toward the task of preventing the coach from flipping.

For one horrifying second, the vehicle heeled, suspended over disaster.

She thought of her sisters, whose lives she had ruined by insisting they leave the Ohio Valley and come to England. She'd wanted to reclaim their birthright as granddaughters of the Earl of Bagsley. As the oldest, she'd assumed she'd known what was best for the three of them. She'd been mistaken. Terribly mistaken.

Every wrong thing that happened since their father had died almost two years ago had been her fault. It was because of *her* that Miranda and her husband Alex were fugitives from England. *She'd* encouraged them to defy the powerful Colster. She had even stood up to the man himself and had pushed Miranda to jilt him—no, to jilt him *publicly*.

She now knew how heinous a crime that was amongst the *ton*, the leaders of polite society.

In that one moment, Charlotte's dreams of her and her sisters being the Toast of Society had turned to dust. The *ton* had been scandalized by her audacity. They'd made both her and her youngest sister, Constance, pariahs in society. The only invitations they had received were to children's musicales and church suppers.

In response to these disastrous circumstances, Charlotte had sent Constance to a boarding school for young ladies in Scotland, where she could safely stay until Colster's terrible temper and society's condemnation had been expended.

And then Laird MacKenna had come into her life, begging an introduction through mutual acquaintances. His unusual introduction had caught her interest.

He'd said, "So, we have a common enemy."

"I have no enemies, my lord," she'd answered.

"Not even Colster?"

Charlotte had attempted to dissemble, but Laird MacKenna was well aware of her troubles. He'd understood, and Charlotte had been in need of sympathy.

For two weeks, he'd called on her daily before abruptly returning to his Highlands. Charlotte had assumed that was that, until she'd received the invitation to visit, giving her a second chance to bring him up to scratch.

But now, she'd never succeed in any of her dreams because she was going to die a horrid death in a coach accident. The coach and all were going to be blown off the side of the mountain, not ever to be seen again. Miranda and Constance would wonder what had happened to her and never know that she'd given her life trying to exonerate their family name—

The coach gave a violent jerk, and the wheels hit the road with a teeth-jarring bounce.

Once again, the horses had saved the day. Klem and Fergus gave out a shout as the coach rolled to a stop.

Charlotte didn't move.

She was too busy thanking God that she was still alive.

The small door in the roof that served as a means of communication between the driver and the passenger slid open. Rain splashed in as Klem asked, "Did that give you the frights, miss?" His brogue was so strong she had to listen hard to understand him. He had a broken tooth right in the middle of his mouth, chubby cheeks, and deep circles under his eyes as if he spent too much time up at night plotting dangerous deeds. Fergus was half a head taller and a bullyboy with a high forehead and a belligerent attitude. If she hadn't met Laird MacKenna, and could only judge him by his servants, she would have thought him a perfect scoundrel instead of a sophisticated gentleman in search of a wife.

"It did, Mr. Klem," she responded.

He cackled his pleasure. "Scared me, too. Fergus told me I couldn't make it through the pass at that speed, but I was out to prove him wrong. I should have listened to him."

"You should indeed," she agreed, fighting the urge to throttle him for his stupidity. "Where is Mr. Fergus now? I don't hear him gloating."

"He fell off."

Shocked, she asked, "Good heavens, is he all right?"

Klem grinned at her. "He splashed around a bit in the mud, but he's climbing aboard." The coach gave to one side, proving the truth of his words.

"You could have helped me up," Charlotte heard Fergus complain.

"You're fine," Klem said, dismissing him.

"I told you to slow down," the other Scotsman said, but Charlotte had had enough.

These two had bickered all the way from London.

She cut through any retort Klem was preparing to make. "We must pull over and wait this storm out."

"And sit on the road twiddling our thumbs? No, can't do that, miss," Klem assured her. "Although, there are better places to wait."

"The laird wants her at Nathraichean as soon as possible," Fergus reminded him.

"He'd understand a storm and a man's need to see a bit of his family," Klem argued.

"I don't know—" Charlotte started.

"You don't need to," Klem said cheerily. "I'll handle the laird. I know what to say to keep him happy." He shut the trapdoor, leaving Charlotte with a very bad feeling about the questions forming in her mind.

The coach jerked, and then went forward. They were on their way again.

Charlotte sat back against the seat. What had she gotten herself into?

Thankfully, the storm settled into a steady, miserable rain. Her fingers trembled as she pulled out her knitting needles and wool and set to work. The murky afternoon light inside the coach was not good for handwork, but she needed something to put her fears at bay.

Isabel Severson, who, along with her husband, had invited the Cameron sisters to live under their roof, had urged her to hire a maid to travel with her, but Charlotte could not spare the expense. Besides, she was long past the age of needing to hire a lady companion for the trip, and Laird MacKenna had assured her he had maids on his staff she could use.

Instead of fears and doubts, as she worked the wool around her needles, Charlotte focused on what she did like about the laird. In spite of being well close to the age of sixty, he'd had little gray in his dark hair, had been soft-spoken, and well mannered—*in fact, Colster had more gray at his temples than the laird*—and she'd liked his musical accent. It gave him character.

Looping the wool around her needle and finishing a row, Charlotte allowed herself to imagine what it would be like if Constance were to marry a Scottish fellow, too, and they could live close to each other. There was a certain charm to being a Highland lady. Or so she'd thought until she'd had a taste of the miserable weather—

Her thoughts were broken when the coach came to an unexpected halt.

Now what?

This time, the door in the roof didn't slide open. Instead, she heard a man's voice outside the coach. "I need a ride to the next village." It was an English voice, one with a note of authority as if he were a soldier or accustomed to being in command. He must have waved her coach down. "My horse lost his footing on the road and fell. Can you help me?"

Charlotte waited, expecting Klem to say yes. He didn't.

The man, too, must have been vexed by Klem's reluctance because he said with a note of exasperation, "I'll pay handsomely for the ride and not trouble you once we reach an inn or village where I can hire a mount."

The rain had let up a bit, but it was still a wet, uncomfortable day. The man was probably knee deep in mud. She waited for Klem or Fergus to answer.

They didn't. They seemed perfectly content to make the stranger stand in the rain and beg.

She'd had enough. She'd been raised on the Ohio Valley frontier, where a person didn't hesitate to help another in distress. She reached up and knocked on the trapdoor.

Klem slid it open. "Yes, miss?"

"Give the man a ride."

He stared at her before drawling, "Are you certain, miss? The laird might not like this."

Charlotte couldn't understand why he was challenging her. "Of course I'm certain, and I'll be happy to explain all to the laird."

"Aye then." He closed the door, and she heard him say to the stranger, "The lady says you can join her in the coach."

That wasn't exactly what Charlotte had said, and she was irritated that Klem had phrased it that way.

However, the gentleman was grateful. "May I put my saddle and tack in the boot?" he asked.

Klem must have nodded because a moment later, Charlotte felt the lid lift on the storage boot located on the wall behind her seat, then slam shut. His footsteps squished in the mud.

The horses were restless to get moving. They took a step or two forward, and Fergus shouted at them to quiet.

The door opened. Wind and rain swept in. Gathering her knitting into its bag, Charlotte moved her legs to make room for him to take a seat on the bench across from hers.

The man had manners. He removed his hat and drenched greatcoat as he hurried to climb inside and shield her from the storm. He slammed the door shut and settled back saying, "Thank you. I was afraid I'd have to walk for miles—" He stopped, obviously as surprised to see her as she was shocked to realize it was *he*.

The Duke of Colster, as wet as a drowned rat and still looking every inch The Duke, sat across from her.

The line of his mouth flattened. He stood, reaching for the door handle, but at that moment, the coach lurched forward, throwing Colster off-balance to land on top of Charlotte.

Her immediate instinct was to push the wet

man off of her and scramble as far away from him as possible. But she didn't get a chance.

He practically leaped to the other side of the coach to get away from her. It wasn't a great distance. Their knees still touched and would have to. There was no way to avoid him. He was a tall man with broad shoulders and a presence that filled every corner, every crevice of the vehicle.

Colster pounded on the roof. "Driver, stop this coach immediately."

But his order must have gotten lost in the sound of wind and rain, for neither Klem nor Fergus responded.

All the anger she'd been carrying inside, the indignation, fear, and humiliation, rose to the surface. He didn't want to be in the same coach with her?

She didn't want to ride with *him*!

"You could jump," she suggested.

He eyed the door.

"Oh, don't be a fool," she said crisply.

His Grace moved to the corner on his side of the coach, placing his wet hat and folded coat on the seat beside him as if warning her not even to *think* of getting close to him. *As if she would.*

It was only then she realized she'd just called the Duke of Colster, confidant of kings, statesman extraordinaire, chosen god of the *ton*, a fool.

For a moment, she tasted panic, before willing herself to be brave. After all, he *was* one.

And from Miranda's jilting, she knew better than to offer an apology. He wouldn't accept one; and she wouldn't have meant it.

She pulled her knitting out of her bag and started her needles working. She was knitting a pair of warm socks for her new brother-in-law. Practical socks. She'd wager the duke had never made anything practical in his life. She just wished her fingers didn't tremble. It ruined the impression she wanted to give of ignoring him.

She tucked her needles back in the bag.

More minutes of stony silence passed between them.

Colster appeared to be sleeping, but Charlotte doubted that he was. There was too much tension in his body.

It really was a sin to have so much power and waste it on a petty vendetta against her and her sisters. He was no better than a worm in her estimation. A squirming, sightless, fish bait worm—although he didn't resemble a worm. Not by any stretch of her very capable imagination.

No, the Duke of Colster was a finely made man. Charlotte could understand why half the female population in England fawned over him. His shoulders were broad, his nose straight, intelligence clear in his eyes. Add to the mix his devotion to his late wife, and he became the tragic hero. What woman could resist that?

Secretly, Charlotte had to admit that when she'd first met him, she'd been jealous of Miranda for having attracted his attention. Charlotte even liked the premature hint of gray at his temples.

He appeared younger now, and less well groomed. He must have been on the road for some time. A shadow of a beard was forming along his jaw. There was an intensity about him, something beyond the force of his normal personality. She wondered why he was traveling through Scotland . . . and why alone? Dukes rarely went anywhere without fanfare. Or so she had heard.

Certainly when she'd first met Colster at his home even the servants had servants.

One thing, she was glad she wore her best day dress, which was a forest green high-necked dress with a triangle of let-in work at the bodice. When they had started out this morning, Klem had thought that if they pushed hard, there was a possibility they could arrive in Nathraichean by nightfall. Consequently, Charlotte had chosen her finest clothes including her kid leather slippers, of which she was inordinately proud. After years of wearing moccasins or going barefoot, these shoes and her white silk stockings with their red ribbon garters were a potent symbol of all she hoped to achieve.

Outside, the rain hit in sheets. The coach seemed to slow down to a crawl. She tried not to think of what further dangers lurked ahead for them.

Nor was it in her nature to sit silent.

"How is your horse?" she asked civilly.

He didn't open his eyes.

She'd not be ignored. Not by him. She repeated her question.

The duke still didn't open his eyes, but he said, "I put him down." Terse, clipped words that belied the emotions she sensed behind them.

"I'm sorry," she replied honestly.

At last, the duke opened his eyes and looked right at her, evaluating her sincerity—just as he appraised everything, and everyone, around him.

Refusing to be cowed, she met his gaze with a level one of her own.

His jaw tightened. "I'm sorry, too. He was a good horse. A companion. He deserved better than to be left at the bottom of that gorge. When I get to a village, I'll send someone back to bury him."

It was a simple admission, but heartfelt. She'd known men who valued the friendship of their four-legged beasts more than that of humans. They were the sort of men accustomed to being alone.

She would never have considered Colster one of their number.

Against her better judgment, a crack formed in her shell of anger toward him.

Was it possible their paths had crossed for a reason? Maybe that was why Fate had thrown them together on the road to Nathraichean. After all, she did owe him an apology. Miranda would have married him, at considerable misery to herself, if Charlotte hadn't interfered and stopped her. At the very least, Miranda should have cried off earlier *and* in private. Perhaps if she explained that Miranda had only wanted to help her sisters, Colster could forgive all of them . . . even just a little.

Charlotte cleared her throat, gathering her courage. Apologies didn't come easy to her. She decided to ease into it. "You are fortunate that we came upon you," she said, wanting to remind him gently she was doing him a service. "Few travel through a storm like this."

He'd settled back, once again pretending to sleep, ignoring her.

Stubbornly, Charlotte continued, "And the Laird MacKenna's coach may be old, but it is dry and sturdy—"

"MacKenna?" He bolted across the coach at her, moving so quickly she barely registered his movement before he was on top of her. He pinned her against the hard leather upholstery, his forearm pressing her windpipe, cutting off her air. His weight held her down. "MacKenna owns this coach? What the devil are *you* doing with Laird MacKenna?"

Charlotte couldn't answer. His arm across her throat was cutting off the flow of air to her chest. If she didn't act quickly, he'd kill her.

Chapter 3

He had her frightened, and that was what Phillip wanted because then he'd hear the truth.

Certainly he was being no gentleman, but he'd been on the road for two days and the trip had been one frustration after another, culminating with Dynasty's death.

Nor did he believe in coincidences. Miss Cameron's presence on the road to Nathraichean, MacKenna's family seat, had a significance, possibly a sinister one, and he wanted answers.

It also felt good to finally have a flesh-and-blood target for his temper. What had seemed a simple undertaking had already cost him dearly.

"Answer me," he demanded.

But instead of obeying, he caught a movement out of the corner of his eye a second before she attempted to stab him with what appeared to be a knitting needle.

He raised his elbow and deflected the blow. He'd heard these Americans were little more than savages. She was proving the point, and he was too damn tired for nonsense. He squeezed her wrist until she was forced to drop the needle, but that didn't stop her from fighting.

Charlotte Cameron was taller than her sister and surprisingly strong. Instead of listening to reason, she bucked and twisted like a madwoman. Her strength was no match for his. He leaned all his weight upon her, using his legs to keep her from kicking him. She arched, attempting to throw him off—and he found himself settled intimately against her.

Just as he realized where he was, what position they were in, she froze, also aware.

In spite of himself, Phillip went hard.

She felt the movement. Her expressive eyes came alive with shock. She opened her mouth to scream. He clamped a hand over her lips. "Don't," he warned in her ear. "Answer my questions and I'll let you go. Untouched."

Her response was to attempt to take a bite out of his hand. He yanked his hand back, her teeth skimming his skin. She got one wrist free to knock the side of his head with the heel of her palm with enough force to hurt.

The thin hold he held on his temper snapped. "Damn you and damn your sister," he said. He grabbed her wrist and forced it back. His life had been peaceful until he'd run into Miranda in the lending library that summer afternoon. Ever since that moment, everything had gone to hell. The Cameron sisters had made him appear weak, and he couldn't let one of them escape unscathed.

Still, he did not strike women.

And so Phillip took the only course open to him. He kissed her.

It wasn't the path he wanted to take, but it was either this or strangle her . . . and strangely, he really had no choice. Instinct guided him, even as his conscious mind said no.

Her mouth was open when he brought his down over it. He was not gentle. He didn't want to be. This kiss was punishment. His intention was to break her to his spirit, to overpower her into submission.

It became a war of wills.

But only for a moment.

Phillip was many things—duke, diplomat, legislator . . . but he was first and foremost a man. A man whose desires had not been slaked in years of self-imposed celibacy. His secretary Freedman and others had warned him it wasn't wise for a man to be alone. Phillip hadn't agreed. He was a rational man. He'd never had difficulty controlling his lust.

Until now.

His body responded to this woman with a force that was staggering. His brain went blank. He no longer cared about questioning her. Instead, his interest shifted to lips that God had fashioned to be kissed . . . and the knowledge that only the leather of his breeches and thin material of her dress and undergarments separated his sex from hers.

Her skin smelled spicy sweet and inviting. His thumb rested over the pulse point of her wrist. He could feel the rushing, anxious beat of her heart. It mirrored the rapid pounding of his own as if they pulsed together, and he was lost.

He shifted his hold, capturing both her wrists in one hand, freeing his other to explore. He'd forgotten the feel of a woman's breasts crushed against his chest. Or the pleasurable curve of her waist to the flare of her hips designed for a man's pleasure.

Freedman was right. There was a thing a man *had* to have. Although Charlotte Cameron was the first to inspire this overwhelming, primitive drive inside him.

The nature of their kiss changed. There was an unexpected connection. Desire sparked into a flame. She was hot, and moist, and suddenly very willing.

He released her wrist and moved his hand to cover her breast. Her nipple was hard and begging. There was fire in this woman. Spirit. He longed to feel her naked, to have her tighten around him.

His fingers found the bare skin of her thighs. He traced the ribbons of her garters, which held her stockings in place, before moving upward toward a more intimate place—

The coach rocked violently as if a wheel had come off the road. The movement brought Miss Cameron to her senses. The magic of the moment disappeared. The kiss broke just as she bucked, catching him off guard, and throwing him toward the floor.

Phillip managed to catch himself. He moved over to the opposite seat, leaning back against the hard leather. He never lost control. Ever.

And yet, he had with this woman.

Miss Cameron scrambled back into her corner, pulling her skirts down with shaking hands. She appeared as stunned as he felt.

Charlotte was not as lovely as her sister Miranda. Both sisters had blond hair and clear, ocean blue eyes. But there, similarities ended.

Miranda was a goddess, a woman with the sort of looks that stopped a man in his tracks or would make him gloat to have her on his arm.

This older sister was more human. She had hair

that was more the rich color of honey than the golden radiance of sunlight. Her nose was shorter than Miranda's, too. It lacked aristocratic straightness, and yet it, along with her arched brows, gave her face character. Here was a woman who did not hold back on her thoughts or emotions.

Her curves were less generous than what Phillip would have liked in some places and more in others, though he had no complaint. She'd felt good, *womanly* beneath him.

A man could easily picture himself in bed with her.

Phillip was doing that right now.

Nor had he ever kissed Miranda, or even his late wife, the way he'd kissed Charlotte.

His gaze went to her lips.

Of all her attributes, he was attracted to her mouth the most. It was generous and inviting. He'd liked the way she'd opened to him.

He *didn't* like the way her mouth was frowning at him right now or the snap of anger in her eyes.

She noticed the knitting needle on the floor and swooped it up to point at him with trembling fingers. "Come near me again and I shall gut you."

Gut you. He marveled at her choice of words and her bravery. A proper miss would be in hysterics, but not Miss Cameron. She was threatening to use her knitting needle to split him open like a hare. She'd probably use it as a spit to roast his heart, too—and therein lay the danger.

Her threat reminded him that there was nothing proper about any of the Cameron girls. The laws of polite society held no sway inside this coach.

"Why are you so dramatic, Miss Cameron? I thought you and your sisters were selling yourselves to the highest bidders? Or," he said with sudden insight, "have I been replaced in your money schemes by MacKenna?"

Her jaw tightened, and her eyes burned bright at his challenge.

Phillip decided that, for once, he was wrong—she *was* more beautiful than her sister. In spite of her mussed hair and lips still swollen by his kiss, she appeared as regal as a queen—until she reached up and with a very deliberate movement, wiped his kiss off her lips with the back of her hand.

The insult was surprisingly effective. A shot of temper whistled through him. She'd been a willing partner, and he was tempted to kiss her again to prove it, but Phillip sensed he'd best not push his luck.

Charlotte had been the first woman who'd made him lose the careful control he kept over himself. He told himself it was because he was tired. Under normal circumstances, she'd mean nothing to him.

"What was that?" he asked. "Some sort of *frontier* slight?" He shook his head. "I hate to think what my life would have been like if I *had* married Miranda. Oh, put your knitting needle away. I'm done with you."

Heat rose to her cheeks, emphasizing their high bones and the blueness of her eyes. He forced himself to focus on what had first started the clash between them.

"What are you doing with MacKenna?" he repeated, this time, keeping his voice civil.

"That's my business," she replied, equally cold, her fist still holding that damn knitting needle as if she would come at him.

"Miss Cameron, I'm not accustomed to people not answering questions when I ask them."

"You can go to the devil," she said.

She was so graceful in her curse that instead of being offended, Phillip caught himself chuckling. "It seems I already have," he admitted, reaching for his beaver hat, only to discover it had been crushed during their tussle. He slapped it into shape, put it on his head, and pulled the wide brim low over his eyes. It was an effective way to shut her out.

So what if he'd wanted to bed her? He stretched out his legs, uncaring if he took up all the foot room in the coach. He needed sleep. Hours ago he'd stopped in an inn to snatch a nap, but his busy mind had prevented him from relaxing. However, the swaying of the coach and a sense that he was closer to his destiny eased his fevered brain a bit.

As he had done a hundred times, perhaps thousands since he'd started this trip, Phillip reached inside his coat and touched Nanny Frye's letter. He needed the physical reminder of why he was making the journey. He was tempted to unfold it and read it again. He knew the words by heart, only now, after repeated readings and his being closer to his goal, they took on legitimacy.

He rode in MacKenna's coach with a woman who had just cause to hate him. Could it be possible that she knew the contents of the letter? That she was in league with the devil?

Phillip knew Miss Cameron still watched him closely. He could feel her scrutiny. Good. He wanted her wary of him.

As for him, the answers would come soon enough. They were both traveling the same road. Right now, he needed a few moments' sleep.

But God help her if she was part of the machinations behind this letter.

The last thing Charlotte expected the duke to do was fall asleep in a blink.

He was snoring after a feel, a pat, and a jolly good kiss.

Whereas *she* was tense, angry, and ready for a fight. If his goal had to been to completely humiliate her, he'd met it.

Hot tears burned her eyes. She forced them back. She wouldn't cry. She wouldn't give him the satisfaction. Besides, if she hadn't let herself cry over Thomas all those years ago when she'd been younger and more innocent, she wouldn't do so now over this arrogant, selfish, spiteful *worm* of a duke.

She was *glad* Miranda had jilted him.

And to think she herself had once dreamed of marrying a duke. She'd imagined them to be the noblest of the noble.

Of course, that was before she knew how the *ton* treated those it felt were inferior. Growing up, listening to her mother's stories of her "come out" and the parties she attended, Charlotte had believed there was no greater place on earth than London.

Now, she knew differently. The *ton* looked down their noses at her, and always would. They laughed at her accent, her ingenuousness, and every one of her family's misfortunes.

Her one saving grace, as far as she was concerned, had been that she'd stood up to Colster. All of London, of England, bowed and scraped to him, but she had faced him in front of everyone of importance. No matter what they said about her, she'd reclaimed a bit of her own.

She wasn't so confident of that now. Convinced he truly slept, she picked up her knitting bag from the floor where it had fallen and started to put the needle back. Her hand shook . . . but not from fear, or even from anger.

No, what unsettled her was his kiss. It had shaken her to her core. Her legs still felt weak and, in the deepest, most secret female recesses of her body, something had been awakened. Something that she'd not known had existed.

That wasn't true. From the first moment she'd laid eyes on him, Colster had made her edgy and too aware of him—and she didn't know why. She seemed to understand his drives and motivations better than she comprehended herself. He was angry she had responded to their kiss. He'd meant to punish her, but it hadn't worked as he'd planned.

Nor could she believe she'd responded as wantonly as she had.

Charlotte had always guarded her virtue. It was the only thing of importance she owned that was truly hers to give. She'd been ten when her mother had been murdered, old enough to receive and remember her advice about men. There had been those who had tried, but only Colster had breached her defenses, and she didn't like it.

She thought about knitting, but knew it wouldn't relieve the tension inside her. Her lips still tingled and she remembered too clearly the way their mouths had melded together.

Charlotte had to stay away from the Duke of Colster. She didn't want to understand his faults or forgive his temper. She wanted him angry and distrustful.

Unfortunately, that didn't mean that she wasn't wildly attracted to him.

"He is your enemy." She spoke aloud, quietly, needing to impress the words on her rebellious senses. "Don't be a fool."

A heavy murmur as if answering in agreement escaped him.

She started. What if he'd heard her?

The cynical curve of his lips confirmed her worst fears. He raised the brim of his hat. His gray eyes were sharp, focused as he said, "You're right, Miss Cameron. Don't be a fool."

For a second she feared he knew exactly what she was thinking, and then realized he couldn't. She hadn't given away anything, or so she thought until his gaze dropped to her breasts.

She didn't know what emboldened her to say, "My face is farther up, Your Grace."

He smiled lazily at her, completely unrepentant. Another insult. Then again, who would have thought the reserved, always refined duke of Colster could be so— Her mind searched for a word. *Male.* He was very male.

And she was female enough to be secretly thrilled that she'd attracted him. However, her voice was icy when she said, "Your arrogance doesn't impress me, Your Grace."

"Was I being arrogant?" he asked with mock sincerity. "I beg your pardon. I assumed I was being rude."

Charlotte closed her hand into a fist. That was it. Her lustful thoughts toward him vanished. She had her equilibrium back. "Please, don't assume, Your Grace. Let me assure you, *you are.*" Now, it was her turn to smile.

"Cheeky, Miss Cameron. And very American. They have no respect."

"You're right, *Colster,*" she said. "We Americans don't know how to handle ourselves at all around dukes with wandering hands. Then again, that does allow a person a certain familiarity, don't you agree?"

He gave her a grudging smile, free of any of his earlier hostility. "Very good, *Cameron.* Let's be republican. You and I." He paused a moment before adding in softer tone, "You have a good head on your shoulders. You'll need it. I am a worthy opponent . . . however, I am starting to believe you are, too."

It wasn't the most flattering compliment, but

Charlotte found herself pleased. She folded her hands in her lap, realizing that it might be the moment to offer an olive branch. "I understand your anger. I admit my sister treated you poorly—"

"You encouraged her to do so."

"Are you purposely trying to make this difficult?" she demanded, all thoughts of a conciliatory tone fleeing. "Yes, I spoke up for her but only after I realized it was in *your* best interests, too. She loved another man. She would not have been happy married to you."

"How pleasant of you to say so."

"How *honest*, you mean," she corrected.

"I like you better when you are being rude."

His dismissive tone sparked her temper. "Why? Because it gives you license to return the rudeness?" She shook her head. "No, I won't be angry. I have something to say. It deserves to be said. Your Grace—" she started, but he cut her off.

"Colster," he interrupted quietly. "I think I like you calling me Colster. It reminds me that we aren't friends."

"You can call me *Miss* Cameron."

His smile was genuine and quick. "*Touché.*"

She plowed on with the determination for which she was known. "Miranda meant little to you, and she has the right to be happy. I'm only apologizing because I know that a man with your *excessive* pride and *overbearing* sense of consequence suffered greatly at being jilted." There, let him chew on that.

His smile hardened. "You're right," he agreed. "She meant nothing to me."

Charlotte's sisterly defenses rose. "Then I am glad she married Alex. They were meant for each other."

He leaned back, his expression inscrutable. "That's good because that is *all* they have."

"Alex is very capable of making money. You don't control the world, *Colster*."

"I do in England, *Miss* Cameron. He's not making money there."

Charlotte crossed her arms. "Well, we aren't in England anymore, are we?"

"We are," he assured her. "The king's reach certainly covers the Highlands."

He was so smug in his own sense of omnipotence. "Laird MacKenna may be of a different opinion," she answered.

"Then I shall set him straight," was the curt answer, but Charlotte had caught the flicker of doubt in his half-hooded eyes.

Suddenly, she understood. "You are on you way to meet Laird MacKenna. Why? He doesn't like you. Not at all."

Instead of answering, he said, "If you are wise, Miss Cameron, you will turn on your heels and go running back to London as quickly as possible."

"And miss this meeting? I think not."

Grimly, he warned, "Beware of involving yourself in business that is none of your concern." He started to pull his hat down over his eyes again, but Charlotte's curiosity had been whetted.

"It *is* my concern, Your Grace," she said. "You made it so when you accepted my hospitality for a ride in this coach and in return manhandled me—or is that some sort of medieval feudal right you were exercising?"

His brows came together. "You have a sharp tongue, Miss Cameron."

"And a sharper wit," she informed him.

Was it her imagination, or, in spite of her insolence, did she see a ghost of a smile on his lips?

She had. And with his humor, the stiffness seemed to leave him. He appraised her a moment before sitting forward, his manner changing. Without the earlier animosity, he asked, "Why are you visiting MacKenna?"

"Because he invited me," she said simply, and couldn't resist adding, "and because you have made it very difficult for me to feel comfortable in London. I'm welcome on very few doorsteps. Which I can handle," she hurried to assure him, "except that my friends the Seversons are also being forced to share my guilt. They have done nothing save extend the hospitality of their home to me and my sisters. In return, they have been practically shunned by polite society."

The line of his mouth flattened. "Not because of me. I've done nothing."

"You don't have to. People are so anxious to please you they anticipate what they believe you want."

"I can't control what people imagine—" he started, but was interrupted when the door in the roof slid open. Wind blew rain into the coach's compartment. Caught up in the furies between herself and Colster, she'd forgotten about the storm outside.

"We'll be stopping," Klem said. "The rain's letting up, but the horses are spent."

Charlotte couldn't hide her disappointment. "This morning you had hoped to reach Nathraichean by nightfall."

Klem frowned down at her. "This morning I did not expect such a storm. We're done, miss. The horses and us have had enough. I have a cousin with a small inn not far from here by Loch Airigh. We'll stay the night. It will also give us a chance to let him off," he added, nodding to Colster. "Malcolm will be happy to see us. He doesn't get much decent custom." He slid the door shut, the matter closed before Charlotte could question what he'd meant by "decent custom."

Colster sat up, apparently fine with the arrangement. Charlotte wasn't. After two days of travel, she really was sick of being in this coach. Before she was tempted to bang on the door in the roof and demand Klem keep driving, His Grace removed his hat and pushed his fingers through his hair. Every hair fell back into place, giving Charlotte a new concern to worry over.

She must appear remarkably untidy. Turning away from him, she repinned her hair the best she could and reached for the hatbox on the floor that held her straw bonnet trimmed in a matching green for her dress.

Having finished with his own hasty toilette, he watched her. It made her self-conscious and her fingers clumsy. She feared the bow she tied under her chin appeared lopsided, but she wasn't going to fidget with it. She pulled on her gloves and picked up the hatbox, intending to take it with her, and placed her knitting bag inside it.

The coach leaned as they pulled off the road. The ride was rough. It was as if they weren't traveling on a road at all. The shades were down over the windows because of the weather, but she sensed they drove through a forest. After half an hour of this, the coach came to a halt.

Klem and Fergus jumped down from the driver's box with a call of greeting. A man's voice answered in a thick brogue.

There was a moment of almost unintelligible conversation as the cousins exchanged greetings, and then the coach door opened. Charlotte moved forward, her hatbox in her hand, waiting for Fergus to put down the step.

With a flourish, Klem said, "Welcome, miss, to Loch Airigh. The water is over beyond. You can tell where it lies by the fog, but you wouldn't want to be wandering around at night or you might fall in. This is my cousin Malcolm, who owns the inn."

He nodded to a man about five feet tall with a balding head, a straggly beard, and a nose that appeared to have been broken several times. A man who Charlotte would wager had been up to no good more than once in his life. "Good eve to you, miss." He kicked aside a chicken that had been pecking too close to his feet. The bird issued a protest and took a few quick steps out of the way.

Charlotte hung back. Something wasn't right.

The rain had turned into a mist. Fog drifted along the ground, swirling around the crumbling stone walls of what appeared more a run-down cottage nestled beneath the boughs of overhanging fir trees than an inn. In the gloominess, the light in the small, narrow windows seemed welcoming until a burst of rough male laughter coming from inside punctuated the air.

"Malcolm makes a mutton stew that tastes better than anything that could ever grace a king's table," Klem offered, as if to entice her.

Her stomach rumbled loudly.

She wished it hadn't done that, not with Colster listening. Still, she was hungry. Her last meal had been breakfast, and she'd been so anxious about arriving at Nathraichean she'd not taken the time to purchase anything to take with her for the road.

"Malcolm, go dish Miss Cameron a bowl of that stew," Klem ordered with the familiarity that made her uncomfortable.

"That I will." Malcolm turned and left. He walked with a pronounced limp. Charlotte shifted the hatbox to her right hand and offered her left for Klem to help her down. Her shoes sank into a bed of wet pine needles almost as deep as her ankles. "Not many coaches stop here, do they?"

"Malcolm sees to a local custom, miss," Klem said, moving around to the back of the coach. Charlotte followed.

"I really wish we could reach Nathraichean tonight," she said. "Do you not believe that we could push on?"

"We're hours away," Klem answered, "and the horses need a rest. It's been a hard drive through that storm. Yes, I could have stopped sooner, but then I would not be seeing my cousins." He opened the boot to bring out her bag packed with her personal items. Her trunk was tied to the roof. "Malcolm has a room with a cot. It's not fancy but good enough—" The tone of his voice changed to mild surprise. "Well now, this is a fine saddle." He'd had to move Colster's saddle to get to her bag and now took a moment to rub the leather with an appreciative hand.

Colster, who had been left to his own devices, had come around to join them. He took the saddle from Klem. "I need to hire a horse."

Klem lifted his gaze from the saddle, his expression speculative. "The only horses here are my coach horses."

"Name a price, and I'll pay it."

The coachman gave another appraising look at the fine quality of the saddle, and Charlotte decided it was about only fair Klem knew the identity of the man he'd been carting around. At the very least, both her drivers deserved a more than handsome tip for rescuing His Grace.

It was also a way to pay the duke back for all the difficulties he'd caused her and her sisters.

"He means what he says, Mr. Klem," she said. "The Duke of Colster has *plenty* of money to spend on whatever he pleases." She hadn't meant to sound quite so bitter, but it didn't matter because Klem's reaction was completely unanticipated.

"*Colster?*" The word seemed to explode out of him. "You are the Duke of Colster? The Maddox?"

"I am the duke," Colster said impatiently, shifting the weight of his saddle while he reached inside his coat and pulled out a heavy leather money purse. With a world-weary sigh he said, "And, yes, you should receive recompense for your aid—"

Klem knocked the coins Colster was about to offer out of his hand. "I don't want Maddox money. It's blood money. If I'd known it was you by the side of the road, I would have run you over." He turned and walked up to Fergus, who had unhitched the horses and held them by lead ropes. "It's the Maddox. The bleeding Maddox."

"Nah," Fergus said with disbelief, and then looked past Klem's shoulder, eyes wide in disbelief. "Are you certain?"

"Told me his name himself. Wait until the others meet him," Klem predicted darkly. He marched into the inn without a glance even to Charlotte.

Fergus's behavior was equally strange. He backed away from the horses, his gaze not leaving Colster until he turned to run inside the inn.

Charlotte had a very bad feeling—and knew it was her fault.

She'd seen men react this way before. Her father and his friends had this same urgency whenever they set out to deal frontier justice. "Take one of the horses while they aren't looking," she advised Colster. "Get out of here."

"You want me to steal a horse?" he answered, puzzled.

"I want you to save your skin," she responded. At the same moment Klem, Fergus, Malcolm, and four other men came pouring out of the inn door as if to confirm her worst suspicions. They were big men with barrel chests who rolled up their sleeves and doubled their fists. Malcolm pushed to the lead, an ugly cudgel in his hand that could crack a man's skull with one blow.

"*Run*—." She turned to urge Colster, her earlier grievance forgotten in her anxiety that he escape what was coming his way.

However, her warning caught in her throat when she saw the small pistol the duke aimed at the angry party of Scots.

"Hold it right there, gentlemen," he commanded. He cocked the trigger.

Chapter 4

The pistol had been stored in a hidden holster attached to Phillip's saddle. He had used it to put down his horse Dynasty. His skill was equal to putting a hole through a pheasant's eye at ten paces with it; but he had never dueled, had never aimed a gun at another man. He was relieved his hand was steady and prayed that the powder cap was dry.

Malcolm pulled up short, as did the others.

"I'm not here to quarrel," Phillip informed them.

"Then you shouldn't have come at all," Malcolm answered.

"You've the wrong man, mate," Phillip said. "I've done nothing to you. I've never set eyes on you."

"*Nothing*?" Malcolm questioned. "My great-great-great-grandfather and his brother hanged because of your scum of ancestors."

"Great-great-great-grandfather?" Miss Cameron repeated as if confused. "What is this all about?"

"Go inside, Miss Cameron," Phillip ordered. "You're safer there."

But Miss Cameron wasn't one to listen to good advice. Especially from him. She stood her ground. "You want to kill him. Why for?"

"For what I said," Malcolm snapped, his patience at an end. "For the lives of five good MacKenna men. Men who had served their rightful king while he and his were more interested in titles."

Miss Cameron took a step toward Phillip. "Pretend I know nothing—because I don't—and explain what is going on." When Malcolm started to protest, she said, "If you all want me to docilely wait inside, you'd best give me a reason."

"The reason is the Battle of Worcester when his ancestors sold out all of Scotland *and* the MacKennas," Malcolm said.

"When did this battle take place?" Miss Cameron asked.

"Sixteen fifty-one," Phillip answered grimly.

"Aye," one of the Scots said. "And it is time to settle the score."

"His family name was Maddoc then, miss," Klem explained. "They changed their name when they sold out to the *Sassenachs*."

"The what?" she asked, sounding lost again.

"The English," Klem interpreted. "There was always a rivalry between the MacKenna and the Maddoc, but it turned sour during that battle. Their chieftain sold his pride for an English title. He betrayed our plans to Cromwell, and Charles barely escaped with his life. We helped him, and, for aiding him, five men paid with their lives."

"But that was a *long* time ago," Miss Cameron said reasonably. "It doesn't have anything to do with any of you."

"It has *everything* to do with us," one of the Scots said, stepping forward. He was almost as tall as Phillip but stronger, meaner. "When Davy MacKenna was hanged, our ancestors swore vengeance, and none of us will rest until it's done. We were robbed, and that's why so many of us live dirt poor now."

"What about Laird MacKenna?" Miss Cameron said, shifting the weight of her heavy portmanteau from one hand to the other. "Would he want you to do this? Why, he probably itches to mete out justice himself. I would if I were the head of a clan."

Her common sense fell on deaf ears.

"The laird's wishes don't matter here," Malcolm said darkly. "Not in this glade."

"Aye, and he'll be happy we did it," Klem answered, and the others nodded agreement while

Phillip decided which man he should shoot. He had only one shot. Would it be Malcolm or the tall young man with the hulking muscles?

Miss Cameron turned to Phillip, her exasperation clear. "Say something to dissuade them," she ordered under her breath.

"Such as?" he asked.

"*You* are the diplomat," she reminded him. "Negotiating tense situations like this is rumored to be your strength. Don't you believe you should be negotiating now?"

"Would it do any good, Malcolm?" Phillip asked the innkeeper.

"No good at all, Your Grace. We've a score to settle, and we are doing it now. Come along, lads, he can't shoot us all."

Malcolm and the other men started forward. Now was the moment Phillip should shoot. He must. He took aim, knowing he needed his mark almost on top of him for the shot to be effective.

However, before he could act, Miss Cameron swung back her heavy leather bag, and brought it with full force right into the big hulk's groin.

The man was not expecting the attack from this quarter. She'd caught him completely off guard and, just like any other man who valued his "jewels," he dropped to the ground. The others stopped, confused, since Phillip hadn't fired a shot.

Miss Cameron didn't miss a beat. She stepped over to Phillip, placed her hand over his holding the pistol and fired. The shot hit Malcolm in the shoulder. He cried out in surprise.

"Run," she said calmly Phillip. "And this time, don't diddle around."

He was as stunned as the men, but he knew good advice when he heard it. The saddle would only slow him down. He dropped it and went for the nearest coach horse. The animal balked as he grabbed its lead rope and leaped onto its back. Holding mane, he whirled the horse around, grabbed Miss Cameron beneath the arms, and pulled her up in front of him.

"What are you doing?" she said in alarm.

"Saving your life," Phillip answered, and kicked the horse into a gallop, just as the cry went up to stop them.

The Scots came after them but the poor coach horse was now out of his mind with fear. He went charging through the thick woods as if the hounds of hell followed, which was exactly what Phillip needed.

Of course, it would help matters if Miss Cameron were a touch more appreciative.

"*Stop* this horse. *Let me off*," she said.

Phillip was too occupied riding through the forest to answer.

"I thought to save your haughty neck, not *escape*

with you," she confessed. "Please, leave me here."

The ribbons of her bonnet, which had been knocked off to hang around her neck, came undone, and the hat blew away. She made a soft sound of distress.

"I'll buy you another one," he said.

"I don't want another. I wanted *that* one," she said.

Phillip didn't bother to answer. They'd come up on a road. Fog lingered in the low places, but the rain had passed, and the clouds were clearing. A much-needed full moon made an occasional appearance. It would provide light to guide their way.

However, he reasoned, if it helped him, it would also help the Scots. He pushed the horse off the road at a trot, cutting across a boggy pasture. The grass was tall and wet. Their pace slowed to a walk. He moved toward the sheltering darkness of a forest.

"I don't like horses," she stated. "I don't like riding."

"I can tell. You have a death grip on my arm."

She released her hold immediately, and he tightened his on her lest she slide off the horse. The animal was actually not a bad ride. He was no stranger to being ridden and comfortable going off Phillip's leg.

They continued onward. Within an hour, the

clouds had completely drifted away. The blue light of a silvery moon lit their way down a shadow-dappled path through the trees.

At last, Phillip decided they were safe. However, the moment he relaxed, Miss Cameron shoved all her weight against him. Phillip let her go. She slid down to the ground in a flurry of skirts.

Most women in her circumstances would either be in tears or making demands. She started walking back in the direction they'd come.

He watched her a moment, both amused and irritated. He'd never witnessed such a purposeful stride. One would think she planned to walk all the way to London by the way she moved. He was tempted to let her go . . . and yet couldn't.

With a heavy sigh, Phillip nudged the tired horse in her direction. He had no problem catching up with her. Nor was he surprised that she ignored him, her head down, her face frowning in concentration. Dismounting, he walked with her for a pace, waiting.

He didn't have to wait long. As if she could contain herself no longer, she rounded on him, the words exploding out of her. "How could you do that? You've *ruined* me."

"Ruined you? I was under the impression that I may have saved you from death or something worse."

She stopped. "*You* saved *me?*" The last of the

pins fell from her hair as she shook her head in denial. It tumbled down her shoulders in a golden mess of curls. "I beg your pardon, Your Grace, but if I hadn't intervened, you'd be minced meat right now."

The truth of her statement pricked his pride. "I was the one holding the pistol."

"And I shot it," she answered, a statement that seemed to remind her of something else she wanted to say. "You don't point a gun at a lot like that unless you are prepared to pull the trigger, even though such a little gun wouldn't stop the likes of them."

She was right. He'd thought the same.

He didn't want to admit it.

But, for once, Miss Cameron wasn't in the mood to argue. "How shall I explain this to Laird MacKenna?" she asked, looking around at their surroundings as if expecting the trees to answer.

"You won't be telling him anything," Phillip answered. "You are returning to London."

Miss Cameron rounded on him, her spirit returning. "I am not."

"You are," he assured her. "I'm hiring a vehicle to take you back first thing on the morrow."

Her nose wrinkled with distaste. "You don't like the fact I was the one to fire the shot, do you? I've wounded your male vanity, and you want to rid yourself of me as quickly as possible."

"What nonsense. I'm not vain—"

She interrupted his claim with a definitely unladylike snort of disagreement.

Phillip was perilously close to losing his temper. "Listen, Miss Cameron, I am worried for your safety. If you believe that is vanity, so be it. However, do you truly think MacKenna would welcome you with open arms after you shot one of his clansmen?"

That gave her pause.

"I didn't *kill* him. I only wounded him," she admitted in a somewhat contrite voice.

"An action that could be interpreted as your siding with me. I'm certain MacKenna will not be pleased."

She raised her hands to her head as if wishing to hit herself for such an error in judgment, and then dropped them to her sides. "I only helped because I felt somewhat responsible for what they were about to do to you. In hindsight, I should have let them beat you into a pulp."

"I'm fond of you, too," he said dryly, surprised to find he was thoroughly enjoying himself. She had quick wits and a cool head in the face of danger.

But she wasn't paying attention to him. "I *am* going to Nathraichean," she said with a determination. "I will explain to Laird MacKenna. He knows I don't like or trust you. He'll understand my concern, and I'm certain he will be as distressed over his clansmen's behavior as I was—"

"Why were you going there anyway?" Phillip demanded, cutting through her verbiage.

"Are we back to this again?" She made an exasperated sound that she released in a sigh of resignation. "I met Laird MacKenna at a garden party. He called on me and, since I am a woman alone in this world and the security of a husband would not be unwelcome—" She said this as if blaming *him* for every single wrong in her life. "—I encouraged him. Naturally, when he invited me for a visit in Scotland at his estate, and I accepted. Can I be more clear for you?"

Phillip shook his head, satisfied.

She wasn't. Hands on hips, she said, "Now, since it is obvious you will not be welcome, why are *you* going there?"

He grinned at her. He couldn't help himself. She was not afraid of him or showing the smallest desire to toady up to him. She was also the one person who didn't seem to want something from him.

But he wasn't about to tell her why he was in Scotland. "It's none of your business. Come along," he continued, overriding any protest she could make. "We'll keep walking and eventually find a place for the night. I'll pay for your passage to London, and no one need be the wiser about what *either* of us was doing this night."

Leading the horse, considering the matter settled, Phillip walked over a hundred feet before he realized she wasn't following him. Instead, she was walking off in the opposite direction.

"Damn it all," he muttered to the horse, his earlier admiration vanishing. "She can't do one thing I ask her to." He started after her. The horse lowered his head and dragged his back feet, a sign he wanted to rest but had no choice other than to follow.

She heard Phillip approach. Her step quickened. He stretched his legs and had no trouble catching up with her.

Phillip walked alongside Miss Cameron for a bit before saying, "Homer."

Her chin came up. She didn't ask about the word, but he sensed she wanted to.

He waited.

There was a long moment filled only with the sound of their footsteps and their breathing.

"Homer what?" she asked at last.

He smiled. He'd gambled on her curiosity, and won. "The name of the horse. I believe I shall call him Homer."

Miss Cameron shot him an irritated look out of the corner of her eye. "Why should you name him at all? What gives you the right?"

"I have no right," he said. "However, the old boy has carried us well and deserves to be called something other than 'the horse.' Do you not agree? Or do you believe it better to ignore his hard work and courage?"

"Is that a slap toward me?" she said, her back still stiff and unyielding, her eyes on the road ahead. "Are you saying I ignore you?"

He didn't answer. He didn't have to.

And then, when he least expected it, she murmured, "Homer is as good a name as any."

"I thought so," he quickly agreed. "Unfortunately, I believe Homer could care less. He's exhausted. The poor old boy's tail is dragging."

Miss Cameron couldn't resist glancing at the horse to see if what Phillip said was true, and her gaze met his. The tension eased in her brow. Her proud, stubborn chin lowered enough for her to say, "He should be. It has been a long day."

"It has," Phillip answered, slowing his step. Miss Cameron slowed hers also.

And a truce, however unacknowledged, existed between them. One Phillip credited himself with negotiating although not even the Spanish ambassador had ever made him work so hard.

This time, when he turned back in the opposite direction, she followed—but not without a dramatic sigh of resignation. They were both accustomed to being in charge, and he counted it a victory that she gave him this small trust.

They walked a ways in silence. Phillip thought

of her, of her stubbornness and her pride. Finally, he could no longer contain his curiosity. "Why did you do it?" he asked. "You didn't have to, and you'd be a more welcome guest at Nathraichean than you would be now."

She pulled her hair forward, her fingers quickly weaving into a long braid that she let hang loose. "Have you ever seen a man beaten? I have. A gang like that beat my brother-in-law Alex until he was close to death. Your sex goes a bit mad in large groups like that. You can't be trusted to use reason. I couldn't stand by and let it happen again."

"You are talking about Haddon, aren't you?" he said. *The man Miranda had jilted him over.* "Some men deserve their beatings."

"Not Alex." She knew what he was thinking. "They *belong* together," she reminded him quietly. "They would have been together years ago when they were younger. However, my father hated Indians, especially the Shawnee. You know Alex is a half-breed?"

After his curt nod, she said, "He came to ask Father for Miranda's hand. Alex is truly more white than Indian. His father was an English officer. He'd been raised with privilege. He understood how to ask for Miranda properly. However, all Father could see was the part of him that was Shawnee. He and three of his friends beat Alex to the point where I feared they'd killed him. I helped Miranda cut him down from the tree where they'd tied him."

"Perhaps your father had just cause," Phillip said, not wanting to empathize at all.

"He did. The Shawnee killed my mother and my baby brother Ben." She said this as a statement of fact, completely devoid of emotion.

Phillip stopped, shocked. "That *is* a good reason," he answered. "I'm surprised Miranda doesn't share it."

A shadow passed in Miss Cameron's eyes. He sensed she wondered the same . . . but would never admit such. Her stubborn chin lifted. In a voice laced with pride, she said, "And be like you and your clan and carry a grudge for two hundred years?" She shook her head. "*Men* are ridiculous."

"*Some* are. I have no grudge with anyone—"

"Except me," she swiftly reminded him.

This woman never knew when to leave well enough alone. He swallowed his sharp retort, not wanting to give her any more fodder against him—and failed. "Tell me, then," he challenged. "What is your secret? How can you put aside the deaths of those close to you so easily?" Elizabeth's death haunted him, and he had no one to blame, save God . . . and he'd blamed Him for years. "How can you accept anyone connected with your family's killers?"

"Because life goes on," she said flatly. "Because, sad as it is, death is a part of life. Especially on the frontier. The Shawnees in that war party were not Alex. To hold him responsible would be the same as equating you to Klem and Fergus. Did you not inform me moments ago that you were not like them?"

She was right.

"Well put," he murmured.

"And I know about blaming oneself," she continued. "Father did that for years. He'd left us that morning to go with some trappers to look at furs they had to offer. He'd seen the Shawnee but had thought it was a hunting party." Her hands balled into fists as she walked. "We hadn't even known the Shawnee had gone on the warpath. Often something could happen miles away, and then war would spread before anyone could warn us. I was away from the trading post collecting kindling with Constance when Miranda came running to us in the woods. She'd seen them murder Mother in the garden. The three of us girls buried ourselves under a pile of leaves beside a fallen tree trunk. The braves came searching for us. They looked *in* the trunk but didn't anticipate us hiding *outside* of it. We held each other's hands all night long. I've never been so frightened and, with Mother gone, I had to make the decisions."

At last, Phillip understood. The bonds between the Cameron girls were stronger than those of ordinary siblings. Would he and his twin experience this same need to unite together?

"But we survived," she said firmly. "The three of us have held together over the years, and we shall continue to survive."

In that one moment, Phillip felt such a desire to believe his twin was alive. He didn't want Nanny Frye's letter to be a hoax. He refused to believe it could be. "I still don't know if I could marry someone from those who killed a family member," he said. He would not forgive MacKenna if he'd stolen his brother. He'd kill him.

"I don't know if I could either," Miss Cameron confessed. She noticed her fists were clenched and spread her fingers as if wanting to release the tension in them. She didn't look at Phillip as she said, "It has caused a great deal of conflict in Miranda. It was the reason she sent Alex away all those years ago. She couldn't choose between him and her family." She stopped, facing him. "That's why, Your Grace, *I* made the choice for her the night of your betrothal ball. My intention wasn't to humiliate you. I just couldn't bear the thought of Miranda's giving up someone she loved, someone she was meant to be with for us. Not a second time. Her happiness is very important to me."

"I didn't want her unhappy either," he agreed. "But could we not have had the discussion in private? Did half of London have to be a witness?"

"That wasn't good," she admitted. "My only defense is that if I hadn't spoken up, she would never have told you herself. Once the betrothal had been announced, neither of you could, or *would*, have backed out."

She was right.

"Perhaps," she continued thoughtfully, "the reason you are so angry—"

"I'm not angry," he assured, and he wasn't. Not any longer.

"You had to be," she pressed. "Especially if your heart was involved. Miranda had assured me it wasn't—?"

"It wasn't," he interjected. "But my pride was. There," he said, "complete and brutal honesty. It feels good. I haven't had the opportunity to practice it that much in London."

"And there is no one to witness it?" she said, her voice light.

"There's you, Miss Cameron. There is you."

She studied him a moment, her intelligent eyes alive with speculation.

"But don't," he warned her, "push your luck. I only have so much candor to spare in a day."

His admonishment startled a surprise laugh

out of her, and he was transfixed at what a smile could do to her. No one had a more glorious smile than Charlotte Cameron.

And the idea that it was he who brought it to her lips pleased him greatly. More greatly than it should.

She started walking.

He could only follow.

They came out of the woods into another field. Here the land was rolling pastures. The clouds had parted to reveal a full moon that gave off a light almost as bright as day.

Phillip noticed a three-sided hayrick with a thatched roof on the other side of the field. He started toward it. Here was shelter for the night.

Miss Cameron skipped a step to stay even with his since Homer was eager to reach the hayrick.

"So, what *are* you doing in Scotland?" she asked Phillip. "Especially since you are apparently risking your life to be here."

"We've already had this discussion," he said, brushing the question aside. The grass was short but very thick. His boots were soaked. Her kid slippers could not be better. He reached for her hand to help her over a muddy gully time had eroded in the field.

She jumped it, almost landing in his arms. She pulled away immediately without looking at him. "Several times," she agreed. "You haven't answered my question yet."

"Because I don't wish to," he reminded her.

Exhibiting a remarkable tenacity, she pressed, "Is it because of the feud?"

"After almost two hundred years?" Phillip shook his head. "Please, Miss Cameron, give me some credit. I have few thoughts about Scotland. My family considers itself English."

"But you have Scottish roots?"

Phillip stopped, realizing she would pursue her line of questioning until she had answers or discovered the truth—and he had no desire for her to know about his twin Justin. It would be best if he gave her something to occupy her nimble mind. "We held land up here at one time," he said with undisguised irritation, "but my father sold it—and at a good price, too. Perhaps that is what has them all foaming at the mouth."

Miss Cameron wrinkled her brow in puzzlement. "Has anyone ever attacked you before about this feud?"

"No," he answered and then hesitated, realizing that her questions were some he should have asked himself before he'd taken off hell-bent for leather upon receiving Nanny Frye's letter. It *didn't* make sense—and yet, his brother may have been kidnapped over it. "I knew of the feud as family lore from both my grandfather and father. My father knew the present laird. They went to school together."

"They were friends?" she asked, as if startled by the information.

"What did the laird say?" he answered, curious to her response.

Miss Cameron didn't like having the questions turned upon herself. In the silence, Homer tried to drop his head and graze. Phillip tugged at his lead, a silent command for the disgruntled horse to be still. The movement gave her an opportunity to dodge his question. "He's hungry. We should let him rest for the night."

"Oh, no, Miss Cameron. You will not evade me, not after hounding me most of the night with your questions. What did the laird say? I'm assuming I was mentioned."

This time, she didn't dither. "Laird MacKenna didn't mention your father, but he did refer to you as his enemy. His first words to me were that we shared a common enemy—you."

"And he searched you out for that reason," Phillip said, stating a fact. Nor did he believe it could be coincidence that Laird MacKenna's interest in Miss Cameron would coincide with his receiving Nanny Frye's letter.

Phillip wanted to pull out the letter and study

it for new clues or hidden meanings but knew he must wait until he had a moment alone—

"So what did your father say about Laird MacKenna?" Miss Cameron pressed, interrupting his thoughts. "Did he consider them friends?"

"Not hardly," Phillip confessed with a snort. "When my father told me the story of the feud, he prefaced it by saying the MacKennas are a strange lot. At one time, they traveled in the same circles."

"Could something have happened then?"

"I wouldn't know," Phillip said, allowing his voice to echo the exasperation he was feeling. "Perhaps. Maybe. Certainly it is possible Father could have insulted the man. In fact, it would be probable. My father could be quite ruthless when he had a mind to be."

"Like his son?" she murmured.

Phillip narrowed his gaze at her. "No one has accused me of such to my face," he said, in a tone that had never failed to make any man freeze in fear.

It had no such effect on Miss Cameron.

She stood in the moonlight, her eyes shiny with intelligence, her back straight, and her head high. "Just because they don't say it to your face, Your Grace, doesn't mean it isn't said . . . or holds a ring of truth."

Damn, but he liked her courage!

In spite of himself, he had to smile. "Well done, Miss Cameron. Well done."

Now it was her turn to be surprised. Her brows came together. "I don't believe I've ever seen you smile before. Does that mean there is a truce between us?"

He let his smile widen before assuring her, "Absolutely not." Tugging Homer's lead, he began walking toward the hayrick.

Behind him, she said, "You'd best beware then, Colster. I am a fierce enemy."

Phillip almost laughed aloud at that statement. He turned, still walking, and said, "I hope so, Miss Cameron."

She didn't take offense. In fact, she gave a rueful smile and started following. "You're incorrigible. Perhaps I should believe the things they say about you."

"Your drivers and their friends are still back the other way. You could ask them," he said turning, the two of them falling into step together.

Miss Cameron gave a mock shiver of disgust. "No, I made my choice when I shot one of them. Better the devil you know." She said this last with such a cheerful attitude, Phillip did laugh. He couldn't help himself, and she grinned back at him as if she'd accomplished a miracle.

It bothered him a bit to be thought so sour.

Fortunately, they'd reached the hayrick, and he was happy to change the subject. "We are finally in luck. This looks good enough for the night." The hayrick was full of freshly mowed hay. He took off his greatcoat and spread it on hay. "Stay here while I scout out the area."

For once, she didn't argue but sank gratefully down onto his coat.

"And you, my friend Homer," Phillip said to the horse, who was excited to see so much fresh fodder, "you will graze over here." He led Homer over to a pasture and away from such a bounty of fodder. Removing his neckcloth, he used it to hobble the horse. Homer seemed content to give up his claim on the hay in return for a pasture of grass.

Phillip circled the area around the hayrick. Not far away was a line of trees and a running stream. He returned to tell Miss Cameron of his find. "I'll lead you to it, and you can have a moment alone," he offered delicately.

"You don't need to," she told him. "I can find it."

"I would feel better if you had an escort," he said.

"And I need a moment of privacy," she informed with a note of finality.

For a brief second, he thought of challenging her, but then realized exactly how tired she was. The braid she'd put in earlier was completely undone and, with her hair loose around her shoulders, she looked younger . . . but as determined as ever.

"You've done more today than an army of women," he conceded. "If you need me, call."

"I shall shout my lungs out."

He smiled at her terminology.

"Careful, Your Grace, or you shall make a habit of smiling," she chided.

"I'm always on my guard with you, Miss Cameron."

His words seemed to catch her a moment. He expected her to offer another protest. But then, without so much as a murmur, she left the hayrick.

He listened to ensure she was going in the right direction.

She was.

Phillip sat and was almost overwhelmed at how good it felt to finally relax. He couldn't wait to get these wet boots off. They felt molded to his feet.

Finally, he was able to have a moment of privacy for himself to review Nanny Frye's letter. He removed his jacket. There were rips in the seams at the sleeve. He pulled the letter out and tossed the jacket aside.

There wasn't enough moonlight this far into the hayrick to see the words, but Phillip knew them by heart. What he wanted to do was touch the letter, to feel it, hoping for some divine guidance as to its authenticity.

What if all this was a hoax? What if his brother *had* died?

The idea didn't ring true.

Whether it was false optimism or foolishness, deep inside, Phillip did believe the letter was true. Justin was alive.

But for what purpose would someone put into play such a treacherous scheme?

"Your turn." Miss Cameron's voice was the first he realized she'd returned. He'd not even heard a footfall. With a start, he quickly folded the letter and, because he'd thrown his coat aside and didn't want to make an issue of the letter, he slid it under his greatcoat beneath him on the hay.

She noticed his hasty movements. "I didn't mean to startle." Her gaze went to where his hand rested on the coat over the hidden letter.

"You didn't."

Miss Cameron moved over to the greatcoat and sat down. Immediately, Phillip rose, wanting to act as normal as possible. He placed his foot over the spot where the letter was hidden. "Felt good to take my jacket off."

She pulled her heavy honey blond hair over one shoulder and combed it with her fingers. "The stream is icy cold. It revived my spirits a bit."

"Good." He hesitated. She looked at him with askance. He realized she was waiting for him to settle down. He picked up his jacket. "Here, you can use this as a blanket."

Miss Cameron smiled her appreciation, her teeth white in the shadowy darkness, and he was struck by what a good smile she had. It was an honest smile, and the tension her sudden appearance had caused eased.

He was overreacting. He was being a complete fool. Since he'd first met Miss Cameron in the coach, she'd acted with courage and candor, and the least he could do was give her a little trust. "I'll be back," he told her. "See if you can get to sleep."

"Thank you," she said. He'd taken a few steps before her voice stopped him. "Your Grace?" He turned. Her gaze met his. "I've been thinking. You are right. I should return to London."

There. Proof that she wasn't in league with MacKenna. A surprising relief flooded through him. "I'll see to it in the morning. Now, sleep."

He left, his step lighter.

It didn't take him long to do what he had to do and during that time, he regained a bit of perspective. He was going to miss Miss Cameron. Most people never told him their true opinions. Charlotte Cameron couldn't seem to hold hers to herself.

He'd like to bed her.

The idea seemed to have materialized out of the thin air but once in his mind, it would not be shaken.

He wanted Miss Cameron. He wanted to bury himself deep within her. Just the thought of it made him as hard as an iron rod.

Phillip plunged his hands up to his elbows in the icy stream. The cold had no impact on his lust.

Dear God, what had come over him?

Elizabeth had been a dutiful wife, but she'd not liked the carnal side of marriage. Out of respect to her, Phillip had kept his needs contained. He had control over himself.

But Miss Cameron wasn't Elizabeth. She wasn't fragile. Indeed, if her response to his earlier kiss was any indication, she'd give as good as she got.

Phillip lowered his head to the icy stream at just the thought and splashed water on his face. He had to keep his wits about him.

He reminded himself that in spite of her advanced age, and willing kisses, Miss Cameron was quite obviously an innocent. The pull between them was strong, but not so much that he would compromise her virtue.

He couldn't bed her. He had to send her back to London. It was the right and honorable thing to do. Besides, if word escaped about their Scottish holiday together, she would truly be ruined, and all of her dreams of respectability would be lost because Phillip would not marry her. Not after the scandal of Miranda.

Admiring a Cameron and trusting one were two separate and distinct things. London would go whirling off its axis if the scandalmongers even had a hint that he and Charlotte had been traveling together, and he'd had enough of being the object of gossip for one lifetime. It would not happen again.

Besides, Miss Cameron might have many charms but she didn't have the requisite sense of class his duchess would need. Phillip had over-looked that trait once when he'd offered for Miranda and had paid a dear price. Never again would he join the ranks of those men foolish enough to compromise their public authority by chasing bits of muslin.

Still, that didn't mean he couldn't admire her. And, if he were a less principled man, he wouldn't hesitate to take complete advantage of their situation.

Of course, he'd first have to ensure there were no pistols or knitting needles close at hand.

This thought made him smile.

Charlotte. He even liked the sound of her name. It was like a whisper.

But she was not for him.

Finally certain he had his baser emotions in hand, Phillip walked back to the hayrick in good spirits and would have stayed that way save for the sight of Miss Charlotte Cameron standing by the door in the moonlight reading Nanny Frye's letter.

Chapter 5

*C*harlotte could not believe what she was read-ing. The moonlight had to be playing tricks on her. She strained her eyes as she reread the cramped writing two, then three times, her mind struggling to grasp the full import of the words.

Colster had a twin brother? An *older* one who everyone had thought had died but had been kid-napped by Laird MacKenna?

When she'd caught Colster reading this letter, and then scrambling to hide the fact of it from her, her curiosity could not be stopped.

Besides, he'd left the letter out . . . sort of. She'd not had to go digging around in his pock-ets for it.

And, reading it, she understood why he didn't want her to know of it. This brother would have been the duke. The *rightful* duke. The letter ex-plained why he was traipsing around Scotland by himself and why he was so tense, not that *he* needed an excuse.

A cloud crossed the moon, blocking all light— No, not a cloud. *Colster.*

Charlotte's throat went dry. She raised her gaze.

He pulled the letter from her fingers. She'd never seen him look so grim. "Curiosity is one of your failing virtues," he said.

"The writing was hard to read," she said, fear, and guilt, making her voice faint.

"But you read it," he said with certainty.

His voice was so quiet. He was angry. Very angry.

"You said we were enemies," she reminded him by way of a justification. "I caught you hiding it. I meant only to protect myself and my sisters . . . but I wish now I hadn't read it." She also wished her knees didn't shake so. His calmness was frightening. Still, she could not resist asking, "Is it true?"

He folded the letter. "I don't know."

"But you are on your way to see Laird MacKenna to find out."

"Yes."

"And that is why you were so violent when you realized I was riding in the laird's coach. You thought I was in league with him."

"Are you?" He'd moved inside the hayrick.

Charlotte turned, following him with her eyes. "No. I know nothing of this."

He picked up his jacket and tucked the letter into a pocket. His calmness unnerving.

"What are you going to do?" she couldn't stop herself from blurting out. "If that letter is true, you stand to lose everything."

"If that letter is true, I have a brother to protect and defend."

"Yes," she whispered, the true enormity of what he faced settling in. "I had nothing to do with this."

Colster tossed the jacket down. "I am certain you didn't. I didn't know at first . . . but I do now."

For the first time since he'd discovered her with the letter, Charlotte felt safe enough to release her breath in a sigh of relief. "And please, I won't say anything to anyone in London. You can trust me," she assured him, well aware that for the first time in her dealings with the duke, she had the upper hand.

He'd do anything to keep this information secret. Delicious possibilities poured into Charlotte's mind. Colster could see that Constance's name was on the list of all the important London hostesses. And with one word, he would return all the business her brother-in-law Alex's shipping firm had lost over the scandal.

Even better, he could do nothing to her personally now. Colster wasn't like Klem and his cousin. He was a man of honor.

She was as smug and happy as a cat who had the songbird in her mouth.

Some of what she thought must have shown on her face, because he said, "You aren't going to speak of this to anyone."

That depended on him, didn't it?

His face was in the shadows, but it wouldn't have made any difference. She was no longer intimidated by him.

"Of course not," Charlotte answered with a purr. "I'll keep mum to everyone in London."

"Oh, no, you aren't going to London."

This was just too satisfying. "I will go wherever I wish, Your Grace," she told him, proud to have finally outwitted her opponent. It was everything she could do to not dance a little jig. "You will have to trust me. You have no other choice."

Tension emanated from him. She couldn't see his expression, but she knew he didn't like this one bit—and that made her feel all the more powerful, something she'd rarely experienced in her life.

She braced herself, anticipating his worst.

Instead, he surprised by saying, "Well done, Miss Cameron. You've won the point."

"I've won the battle," she countered.

He stepped forward. She held her ground, uncertain whether she should run or not . . . until she saw he was smiling, his lips twisted in rueful respect. "Aye, perhaps the battle."

Charlotte was tempted to ask him to repeat those words. As it was, she couldn't help but happily smile right back to him. She'd done it. She'd won and victory was so sweet.

"You *can* trust me," she reiterated.

His smile flattened. "I pray it is so."

"I'm not that sort of person," she informed him.

"Are you saying I am?"

There was an edge of self-mockery in his tone. It pricked her conscience. She shouldn't feel any sympathy for him. "No, I'm saying I wouldn't blackmail you," she said, even though she would if *he* made it necessary.

His eyes, silvery in the moonlight, studied her a moment, his expression sober. "Thank you," he said at last. "But may I ask one favor of you?"

"What is it?"

"Would you help me get these boots off? The wet leather is about ready to drive me to madness, and I can't remove them myself."

The change of subject caught her off guard, and then made her laugh. "I know how you feel. I kicked off my shoes the first minute I could."

They were lined up beside the wall of the hayrick.

She held out her hand. "Here, let me have your heel. I used to do this for my father."

He sat back on the coat spread over the hay and raised his right foot, placing the heel in her offered palm. She tightened her grip. He pretended to wince. "You are a strong woman, Miss Cameron."

She nodded, relieved the unpleasantness of the letter was behind them. "It comes from years of chopping my own firewood, Your Grace."

"I daresay there are few earls' daughters who could make that claim," he answered, and she nodded her agreement. He really wasn't a bad sort. He just didn't like to be crossed . . . like any other man she'd ever met. She pulled on the boot.

It moved, not far, but it did move.

It was now a challenge.

Charlotte tugged again. This time the boot held fast. "Who made these? Hoby?" she asked him with a grunt, naming the most fashionable bootmaker in London. She yanked on the boot so hard she almost fell back on the ground. No wonder he wanted the boots off. She went back at it again.

Fighting the battle from his own end, with his own share of grunting, Colster repeated, "My bootmaker? No, Lobb."

Catching her breath, Charlotte said, "Lobb?

Isn't he out of fashion? I thought everyone of importance used Hoby."

His brows drew together. "You shouldn't believe everything you read in the newspapers. My father used Lobb—" He offered his boot to her again. She took it. "My grandfather used Lobb. *His* father used Lobb, and I—"

"Use Lobb," she said in unison, giving the boot a pull. It finally slid off. She took a step back from the exertion. In spite of being wet, the leather was still good and soft. She could see why he used Lobb. Setting the boot on the ground, she asked, "Will the next be as difficult?"

"No, this one is easier."

It wasn't.

But by the time they were done, she was laughing. She couldn't help herself. The hour was late, she was tired, and she'd spent a good portion of time being the Duke of Colster's lackey. She sat down on the far side of his greatcoat. He took off his stockings.

Her feet were bare, she'd removed her wet stockings when she'd taken off her shoes, but there was something, well, intimate about seeing *his* bare feet. They were strong, handsome feet. Long and masculine.

Heat crept up her neck at the yearnings his feet seemed to stir inside her. She reached for his coat, which he'd offered her as a blanket.

Colster was not for her. He was everything she'd ever dreamed of in a man—in spite of being such a formidable enemy—but no, he could not be hers.

After all, why would a duke marry an insignificant earl's granddaughter? Before coming to England, Charlotte wanted to dream such things were possible. However, now, after being around the *ton,* she knew she had a better chance of sprouting wings and flying than to ever become a duchess.

She settled in, wiggling into the hay, and tried to distract herself with its earthy, green scent.

He'd stretched out on the coat beside her, not really making a great effort to keep space between them.

Of course, she was so very conscious of him that even if he slept outside the hayrick, she'd be aware of every nuance and movement. She wondered if he was as aware of her?

She rolled on her other side, giving him her back.

He rolled, too—closer to her.

Charlotte could almost feel his breath against her shoulder. She debated moving farther away. It would move her off the coat and into the hay. For a long moment, she weighed her options, and in the end didn't move. He couldn't read minds. He didn't know what she was thinking.

And perhaps it wasn't prudent, and was certainly a bit silly, but she wanted to just lie still and pretend that a man like him could be hers. Was it so wrong to do so, just for this night?

Was it wrong to *like* having him this close?

Tomorrow she would be leaving for London, and they would, once again, be strangers. Just for tonight, she wanted to savor the camaraderie they'd discovered.

Colster wasn't asleep. She *knew* he was awake, just as she was aware of almost every little detail about him. She could even feel his mind was working.

"What are you going to do if the story in the letter is true?" she asked. "What if your brother is alive?"

"I'll bring him home."

"You won't worry about the gossip?" He'd been furious over Miranda's jilting.

"This is beyond the pettiness of gossip."

That was the right answer.

Charlotte folded her arms under her head. "If your brother was kidnapped at birth, I'd say this goes beyond retaliation for an ancient feud."

"I agree," he answered without reservation. "This is too evil to have survived centuries. Even if the letter is a hoax, what prompted it is something current. Something that happened recently."

She turned to look at him. "And you've never been to Scotland?"

"Not in my memory."

She waited a beat, and then whispered, "I know how you feel. I would fight demons for my sisters. I would give up everything for them."

"So I've learned," he answered dryly.

Their eyes met. It wasn't her imagination that she saw respect in his. Respect for her. It made her fluttery and tight inside.

Charlotte turned back on her side, knowing she'd best leave well enough alone. Colster was still dangerous to her, but in a completely different way than before. No man should have the power to make a woman feel the way he seemed to touch her.

She tried to focus on anything but him. She thought of Constance in boarding school not far from Edinburgh. Perhaps she should pay her a visit with the good news that they no longer had to worry about the Duke of Colster.

The diversion worked. Her eyelids began to get heavy. She closed them, thankful she didn't face the concerns Colster did about his brother—

He rolled closer.

Her drowsiness vanished. He was so near she could smell the spicy warm, masculine scent of his skin. If perfumers could capture that scent, she'd buy a dozen bottles. Perhaps even a hundred—

His arm came down over her waist. His relaxed hand rested close to her abdomen.

Charlotte couldn't breathe.

She should move.

She didn't *want* to move.

He must have fallen asleep and wasn't aware of what he was doing. It was natural that he turned toward her. He was probably being protective . . . or so she hoped—

His lips nudged her hair aside and kissed the sensitive skin of her neck below her earlobe.

Shock shot through her, mingling with the heat of desire centering in her pelvic region.

Charlotte knew she should edge away from him. It was the only thing she could do and keep her sanity. This man was dangerous. "I need to sleep—"

He cut her off with a kiss on her lips.

Charlotte knew she shouldn't let him do this. She should tell him to *cease* immediately—but she didn't want to.

They were alone in the dark. The air was sweet. His body warm and safe . . . and kissing him seemed the most natural thing in the world to do.

He raised his hand, placing fingertips against her cheek and turning her completely toward him. Just as it had been in the coach, she could only resist for the slightest moment before wanting to breathe him in.

His hand came back to her waist. The weight of it felt good, possessive. He nestled her hip against the flat of his abdomen and his legs. He was aroused. The length and hardness of him set her blood pounding. He wanted her.

She wanted him.

The first touch of his tongue against hers was startling. It brought her out of the moment. She shifted, pushing away. He returned his hand to her face, lightly holding her while he ventured further into the kiss and won her over completely.

Charlotte surrendered.

And why should she not? This was not London or any place of importance. There was no society, no rules, no responsibilities. All that there was, all that mattered, was the way his body fit with hers. He knew what they were about far better than herself. He was the teacher and she an apt and willing pupil.

His hand covered her breast. Her nipples tightened. He began placing small kisses along the line of her jaw, down her neck. His unshaven whiskers were rough, and exciting, against her skin. His fingers wound themselves in her hair, holding her fast.

He didn't need to worry. *She* wasn't going anywhere.

Charlotte slid her arms around his neck. She

kissed his temple, his hair, his nose. Her nose kiss made him smile. He lifted his head and looked down at her, his expression bemused. "You are so beautiful."

"So are you." The words had just popped out of her mouth in her excitement and eagerness, but she would not call them back. He was beautiful.

His teeth flashed white in the darkness. "Sweet, sweet Charlotte. You are a constant surprise."

Any resistance she might have had left melted. She liked being a source of surprise.

Certainly he amazed her—and when he brought his lips down for another kiss, she held nothing back. Dreams were made from moments like this.

This man was worthy of her. He wasn't like Thomas, narrow-minded and backward and expecting her to choose him over her family. No, Colster was the only man who'd ever challenged her as if she were an equal.

Miranda might not have been able to love him, but Charlotte knew with complete conviction she could.

He started undressing, pulling his shirt off over his head. They hadn't broken the kiss, and so for a moment they were both hidden in folds of white linen. It added humor to the anticipation of the moment, making her feel closer to him.

He ended the kiss and slid the shirt over his

head and down his arms. His muscles had the lean, well-defined lines of a natural athlete, and Charlotte swallowed to keep herself from purring aloud.

Colster smiled as if he knew what she was thinking. He returned to her side for another kiss. She placed her arms around his broad shoulders, wanting to hold him forever—but then his hand covered her *bare* breast.

She pulled away to glance down to where his hand rested on her, too shocked to pay attention to his lips seeking hers. Her sleeve was off one shoulder, and half her bodice was practically to her waist. Common sense reared its ugly head. "What are we doing—?"

He cut her off with hungry, demanding kisses, and she didn't care where his hands were. In fact, his fingertips lightly circling her nipple felt good. *Very* good.

All thoughts of protest left her brain. Constance, Miranda, Scotsmen, and feuds ceased to matter. She wasn't even Charlotte anymore. Her whole being centered on discovering the touch, taste, and scent of him.

When his mouth closed over her tight nipple, the pleasure was so intense she cried out. She curled her fingers in his hair and repeated his name as he introduced new and more enticing ways to please her. When he tugged at the other sleeve of her dress, the one still on her shoulder, she helped him take it off. She took it all off, kicking her skirts away to be gloriously naked beside him—and she felt no shame.

"Charlotte," he said as if delighted with her body and no praise had ever pleased her more.

She felt afire with her wanting of him. All skittishness had vanished. She'd been created to be with him.

He ran his hand up her legs with more purpose than he'd done in the coach. This time, she didn't flinch . . . and when she first felt his touch, she thought she would weep from the joy of it.

Charlotte knew what was going to happen between them. The tension between them was to the snapping point, and just as she did in every other facet of her life, she went after what she wanted now. Impatiently, she tugged at the band of his leather breeches. She'd given all. Now let him.

"You undo them," he ordered quietly.

Her fingers went right to his buttons. She twisted the first free, then the second. His skin was warm against the backs of her fingers. As she reached to unfasten the third, she brushed his erection.

It was the most incredible thing she'd ever touched. Different than what she'd imagined and yet exactly what she would have anticipated. She unbuttoned the remaining three buttons and pushed his breeches down so that she could feel all.

Colster rewarded her with a sigh of pleasure.

In her experience, men were hard, hairy creatures. She'd never imagined there could be anything about them this smooth. This soft . . . this sensitive. She ran a fingertip up its length in experimental wonder.

His reaction was immediate. With a low growl, he took her down to their bed of sweet hay, settling himself between her legs. "You are delightful," he whispered before claiming her with a kiss that sucked the very breath out of her body.

Charlotte was defenseless against such an onslaught. This was perfect. It was right. It was the way things *were meant to be*. From the moment he'd entered her coach, her body had ached to join his. She understood that now.

Colster combed her hair back with his fingers. Her breasts were flattened against his chest. Her legs cradled his hips. He kissed the line of her jaw, the underside of chin, encouraging her to arch back, lifting her hips slightly—and then he entered in one smooth, strong thrust.

The magic disappeared. Reality arrived in a sharp sear of pain.

She would have scrambled out from beneath him but he leaned his weight against hers, holding her in place.

"Gentle, gentle," he whispered. She didn't know if he spoke to her or was telling himself. "It's over. It won't hurt again."

The pain *was* ebbing, but the consciousness of reality stayed in place.

What had she done? A part of her wanted to weep. Another, the part of her still connected with him, wanted *more.*

Colster understood. "I'm sorry, Charlotte, but I can't let this end here. You'd hate me."

She hated him now. She'd hate him forever—

He began to move. Long, steady, careful thrusts.

Slowly, her body adjusted to accommodate him. What had seemed alien began to feel right as she stretched to accept all of what he offered.

And it was beginning to feel *good.*

She turned her head, searching for his kiss, needing his reassurance. He was right there, watching her, *caring* for her. This kiss was more personal than the ones they'd had before. Simpler and honest. After all, what was done was done . . . and she relaxed, releasing fully into making love to him.

Nor did Charlotte believe she was the only one affected. Colster seemed to lose himself. His kisses, too, were increasingly urgent. He reminded her of a starving man feasting on his first meal. He kissed her lips, her eyelids, her ears, and her neck. His thrusts went deeper and with more force.

He'd been right, the pain had been momentary. Charlotte's body began moving instinctively with his. She met each of his thrusts and found the rhythm they needed. In his arms, she imagined them dancers, and the music was the sound of their breathing and their own driving need.

She'd become wanton. This was the mystery of life, the need that humbled all of them. She grasped his arms, holding on for all she was worth.

This was brilliant. It was madness. It was divine—

Her senses hit a point sharper and more defined than the tip of a needle, and yet there was no pain. No, what hit her was pure, exquisite joy.

She gave a sharp cry. He held her tight as though he'd never let go. Deep muscles contracted. She'd couldn't move, could barely breathe.

At last, *she understood.* Finally, she knew why Adam would follow Eve, Paris would steal Helen, and her mother had left her family, homeland, and birthright for a man she had loved.

But Colster wasn't done.

No, he buried himself deep within her, holding her as if he'd never let her go—and she felt his seed release inside of her.

Charlotte was transfixed.

Here was the life force, the communion, the hand of God. It was the most amazing, critical moment of her existence. She was no longer flesh and blood but light and being. One with him.

This was the man she'd been waiting for all of these years. *Her* duke. And he was bolder and stronger and more handsome than she could have ever conjured from her imagination.

He stroked her hair, her waist. His heart was beating as rapidly as her own.

For a long moment, they held each other . . . until their bodies started to cool.

Colster lowered her to the coat, his body resting on hers. Charlotte smiled. His weight felt good. Her heart was so full of tender emotions she *knew* she'd never be sad or lonely again. She loved the feel of his weight upon her. She could spend her entire life this way.

Colster smoothed out her hair. It was then that she realized she'd had her eyes shut the whole time. She opened them and found him watching her. The tension that had always been so much a part of his personality was gone. He even looked younger.

Reverently, she reached up and pushed his hair back before laying her palm against the rough whiskers of his jaw. He was so perfect. Wonderfully perfect.

He turned his head and kissed the inside of her wrist. Those whiskers tickled. He eased the sensation by tracing a line on her skin with his tongue before looking back down at her.

What beautiful eyes he had. So honest and clear.

"Did you like that?" he asked.

"Yes," she whispered before repeating, "Yes, yes, *yes.*"

Her enthusiasm made him smile . . . but the expression in his eyes darkened. Immediately, she sensed something was wrong, and her doubts grew as he became more serious.

"What is it?" she asked.

He caught her hand.

Laced his fingers with hers.

For a long moment, he held her before saying in a world-weary voice, "You are not returning to London. Not without me."

Her heart leaped in her chest at the promise in his words. Dreams she'd not dared even to breathe aloud came to life. A duke. *Her* duke.

They'd become *one. Together.*

"Why?" she asked, both fearful and excited for the answer.

"Because, now," he said, his voice low in her ear, "we both have a secret we wouldn't want bandied about. Not unless you wish to be completely ruined."

His meaning struck her with the force of lightning.

She'd been deceived—and she'd been a willing victim.

Chapter 6

*A*s the full meaning of his words sank in, Charlotte drew back in horror—and Phillip *hated* himself.

Pride was what Charlotte Cameron valued. It was what had driven her to come to England and seek a future for her family through the time-honored system of making an advantageous marriage.

He had destroyed her worth on the marriage market. Without family connections or dowry, all she *could* offer a man was her purity, something he'd just ruthlessly taken. He'd stripped her of everything.

"It's your silence for mine. We are even." His conscience screamed at him.

"You did this on purpose?" she demanded. The set of her jaw tightened. She knew the answer, and yet she persisted as if wanting him to deny it.

"I did what I must," he answered, his voice cold.

Yes, he'd done what was necessary to protect his family and his name . . . and yet, theirs had been no ordinary coupling. It was almost as if the tables had been turned. He was as trapped as Charlotte.

For the first time in his life, he understood the full power of carnal pleasure. It had taken him unawares, *possessed* him, and it was all because of Charlotte. Her passion had matched his own. She'd awaken dormant desires, breached his fabled control.

She'd given without reservation—and, dear God, he'd taken. In fact, he was already stirring and ready to take again—

Phillip's thoughts broke off when he felt the upward movement of her leg. It was his only warning, and he moved just in time from having her knee kick his groin up to his throat. If she had made full contact, she would have turned him into a eunuch.

As it was, she'd kicked hard enough to double him over.

Pain forced him to release her. She came to her feet in one fluid, graceful movement. Tossing her hair over her shoulders, she stood silhouetted in the darkness against the doorway, hands on hips. "You deliberately seduced me. You *ruined* me."

"Ruined you?" he puffed out. "You've come damnably close to ruining me!"

Her response was to pick up his boots and throw them at him, one at a time, with all of her might. He warded them off with his hand.

Furiously, she whipped her dress up from the ground and put it on, fury making her movements clumsy. "I *trusted* you." Her voice sounded perilously close to tears. Her head came up through the neck hole.

"That's not true," he answered. "We haven't trusted each other for a moment."

"*You're right,*" she snapped. "But I did then. I let down my guard. God knows I wish I *hadn't.*"

With that last ringing indictment, she picked up her shoes and stockings and went storming out into the night, not bothering to take the time to lace up the back of her dress.

Phillip forced himself to stand. His thigh where she'd kicked him throbbed as he pulled on his breeches. Buttoning them enough to be decent, he went after her.

"Charlotte, stop," he ordered.

She kept going, marching with purpose toward Homer, who looked up in surprise to see them both out and about.

He caught up with her in the middle of the

field. Grabbing her arm, he swung her around to face him.

But Charlotte was not one to go quietly. She attempted to shake his hold free. When that didn't work, she doubled her fist and tried to strike him against the side of his face.

Phillip caught both her arms at the wrists, holding them behind her back and bringing her close to him. *"Stop this."*

"Let me go," she demanded, her tone as imperial as a princess.

"Not until I've had a moment to talk sense into you."

Her response was to bring the heel of her foot down hard on his bare foot. Once again, he released his hold. She took off running.

Anger propelled him forward. He caught her in three steps.

"I can see you don't want to be reasonable," he said. "We shall do this *un*reasonably." With those words he swung her up over his shoulder as if she were a sack of grain.

Charlotte was furious. "Stop manhandling me. Put me down. You are a dishonorable, disreputable *brute.*"

These were words that had never been applied to Phillip before. He'd always been the honorable one, the gallant—that is, except where Miss

Cameron was concerned. She had the uncanny ability to bring out the worst in him. She made him lose control. She made him vulnerable . . . and for that reason alone he must master her.

She struggled against his hold, but he would not let her go until he'd cooled down her temper. Then, perhaps, he could talk sense into her.

Reaching the stream, he waded into the cold water.

She went still. "What do you think you are doing?"

"You might want to remove your dress," he advised.

"I shall not."

"Very well."

Without pity, Phillip let her go, having the presence of mind to pull her dress up as she fell. She slipped right through it. He congratulated himself for saving the majority of it from getting wet.

Charlotte hit the water and came up gasping from the shock—and looking more lovely than any woman he'd ever seen. She was like a water kelpie, with her hair molded to her white skin, her breasts full, her nipples tight, and her eyes full of rage. "How *dare you*—" she started.

Phillip waited, knowing she had to have her say and that he well deserved it.

But she fooled him. She never finished what

invective she had in mind. Instead, her eyes filled with tears that she struggled to hold back and didn't succeed.

He took a step toward her, but she pushed him back with a hand to his chest. "Leave me alone, Colster. Just leave me alone."

Phillip didn't like her this way. He preferred Charlotte fighting and full of spirit. "You can't stay in the stream all night."

"I can't?" She struggled for a bit of her former bravado. "I will do whatever I wish," she said in a quiet, tight voice. "Besides, where else do I have to go?"

This was not what he wanted. He'd gone too far.

Phillip took the time to hang her dress on a limb of an overhanging tree before wading back to her. She turned from him, crossing her arms against her breasts. "Leave me be," she ordered.

He stopped. They stood less than ten inches from each other—and he realized the truth. "I can't."

A bit of her defiance returned. "That wasn't a suggestion, Colster. It was a command."

Hours earlier her high-handedness had rankled. Now, he was so relieved to see a return of her spirit, he grinned like a fool.

She caught sight of him. "What is the matter with you?" she complained. "You take me against my will—"

"*Against* your will?" he questioned, raising a doubtful eyebrow.

"It was *not* what I'd planned for this evening," she shot back.

"None of it has been what we planned for this evening. But upon my word, Charlotte," he said with brutal honesty, "I'd not have undone any of it."

He'd hoped his confession would soften her. He was wrong. "Of course not," she replied. "*You* got what you wanted."

He hated the bitterness in her voice. "No, I did what I must. And if you'd been me, you would have done the same. But that doesn't mean, Charlotte, that I wasn't as fully engaged as you were. The intensity between us was rare. It's not like this for everyone."

She glared at him through wet, spiky eyelashes as if suspecting that he toyed with her.

"Damn your pride, Charlotte," he said, and, placing a hand on each arm, he pulled her to him and kissed her. He'd not have her deny him. This was the only sensible thing to do, even if she'd probably bite off his nose for his effort.

Charlotte's body went rigid. She raised her arms as if preparing to use all her might to push him away.

Stubbornly, Phillip insisted.

There was a war of wills, and then her lips went warm and soft. He'd won.

Or had *she* won?

He couldn't tell. Because when, with a soft sigh, she wrapped her arms around his neck, Phillip lost the ability to think clearly.

He no longer felt the cold. It was if a spell had been cast over him. The moon, the water, and her nakedness heightened the enchantment. He could kiss Charlotte every minute of every day and never tire of it.

She broke the kiss. Leaning her head against his chest, she whispered, "I don't want this. I *shouldn't* want this."

"I know." He did. He ran his hands up and down her arms, warming her. "I won't let harm come to you," he promised.

"You already have."

"Charlotte—"

"What will become of my sisters?" she asked, cutting him off. She tried to turn away. He wouldn't let her go.

"Don't," he whispered. "Please don't. I'll see you through this."

"If I keep my silence."

He'd not deny it. "It's an even exchange. We each have a secret now."

The moonlight caught the doubt in her eyes as

she asked, "And how will you see me through this? Can you give me back what I've lost? What you have taken from me?"

"I didn't take anything that wasn't freely offered," he replied.

Her face paled.

He pulled her into his arms, hating to see her so frail, hating himself for being the cause. She trembled, but not from the cold. He tightened his hold. "Charlotte, I can arrange your marriage to a man of class and fortune. I have the power to make all your dreams a reality."

She attempted to pull away. "How do you know what dreams I have?" she dared to ask. "You don't even see *me*."

"*That* is not true." He slid his hand along her neck, his fingers in her hair. "I see you too well. Therein lies the problem," he confessed, before kissing her again.

This was not a hungry kiss as he'd given only moments before. His desire for her was still present and strong . . . but there was something else at work here, too. He wanted Charlotte to trust him. He wanted the walls down between them.

He wanted her.

The salt of her tears broke the kiss.

She looked away. "I don't usually cry. Not ever. There's no sense in it."

Placing a finger against her cheek, he forced

her to look at him. "It's a burden to always be strong," he answered. He knew.

"You don't seem to have a difficulty with it," she countered.

Phillip almost laughed at the assumption. "Look at me, Charlotte. I am out of my element. If that letter is true, the fate of my brother has stripped me of all trappings. They mean nothing if he isn't safe."

Some of the tension left Charlotte at this confidence. Family meant all to both of them. "Why did you come alone? Why didn't you bring an army?" she asked, the anger gone from her voice.

"I'm beginning to wonder that myself," he answered, wondering why he was being so bloody honest. Charlotte Cameron had the uncanny ability to see through him. She could use this against him . . . and yet he didn't believe she would.

Something lay between them. Something that had nothing to do with feuds, anger, or pride.

She attracted him with a force he'd never experienced for another woman. Not even Elizabeth.

Charlotte had slipped past his guard.

Tomorrow he'd worry.

Tonight, he wanted to make love to her again. He wanted to see if the fulfilling release he'd experienced in her arms was as powerful a second time as it had been the first. Perhaps not. Perhaps he would be free of her.

And if it was—? Phillip didn't want to think beyond the moment. He scooped the wet, naked woman up in his arms and started back to the hayrick.

"I can walk," she told him.

He silenced her with a kiss. He stood, holding her in his arms and kissing as if he'd steal her breath from her.

When at last the kiss ended, she didn't argue. Instead, her arms came up around his neck. He could feel her watch him as he carried her to the hayrick. He understood her doubts. They both had everything at stake—and it was this thought, as he walked toward the hayrick, that finally pierced his conscience. Lust and desire could not supplant honor. The cost would be too high.

Sober now, he entered the hayrick and lowered her to his greatcoat. He reached for her coat as a blanket. Charlotte's eyes were so huge they threatened to swallow her face.

"Don't worry," he told he quietly, torn between a desire to make love to her and an understanding that they had already gone too far. "I'm not going to take advantage of you. I've come to my senses. I'm not a complete bastard, Charl—"

His declaration was cut off as she rose, pulled him down to her, and kissed him with everything she was worth.

Any thought of being noble fled Phillip's mind. Instead, he kissed her back with all the passion of his being.

Their bodies melded together. He didn't even remove his breeches. It was all he could do to unbutton them. Her body, strong and resilient, met his thrust for thrust. He went hard and deep, finding his pleasure in hers.

What was more amazing, was that this time, his release was even more powerful than the last. He didn't bother to hold back. He couldn't.

It was as if he'd been destined for this woman. This was the way it was meant to be. He could no more have reined in his drive than he could have harnessed the moon.

Afterward, spent, Phillip held her in his arms, her coat covering them. For once, life made sense.

Her hair was still damp from the freshwater stream. Tired, sated, unspeakably content, he curled a lock of it around his finger.

Charlotte was the first to break the silence. "Is it always like that?" she asked, her voice lazy with sleepiness.

"It's never been like that," Phillip said honestly.

She lifted her head, her palm flat against his chest. "Truly?"

He smoothed her hair back before saying, "Making love to you is like touching the hand of God."

She laughed, pleased but not quite believing him. It didn't matter. Her long lashes brushed his skin as she closed her eyes.

Phillip buttoned his breeches, holding her close. He thought her asleep, but then she asked, "What *does* happen if your brother lives?"

He smiled. "Always curious," he accused.

"It's my besetting sin," she confessed.

Phillip chuckled, valuing the wit and friendship he was discovering in this woman, before confessing soberly, "I don't know what will happen. I only pray that whatever it is, I can make it right."

"You will. You're the duke."

But even dukes could be wrong.

"I believe," he said wearily, "that tomorrow we'll both return to the English garrison at Fort William. I can't do this alone. I shouldn't."

She stirred. Her eyes still closed, "If you find your brother, what of your right to the title?"

He hadn't thought that far. It was the one question he avoided, even in his own mind. "It's his by right," he whispered.

Against his chest, her lips curved into a smile. "It's the honorable thing to do," she murmured as if pleased. She fell asleep.

However, Phillip couldn't quiet his mind. He thought of a brother he'd never known, a history of Scottish intrigue . . . and a woman he wanted to trust.

It was a long time before he fell asleep.

Charlotte had never slept so well.

Cool air roused her. It tickled her nose, which she rubbed against warm flesh. Memories came rushing back. Colster. No wonder she felt so content.

She would have put her arms around him for a good morning hug, except his arm came over her first, but not in a lover's embrace.

It was a warning that something was wrong.

At the same moment, a strange, male voice said, "Good morning, Your Grace."

Charlotte opened her eyes and discovered a party of some eight rough-looking men crowded around them in the hayrick. They had beards and hair reaching down to their shoulders. They wore leather breeches and boots, swords and pistols. They could be robbers or rebels.

Their leader, a lean man approaching thirty with a hawkish nose, golden hair and beard, and green eyes so piercing they could have been shards of glass, stood over them holding the dress she and Colster had left hanging by the stream last night. "I can see the two of you enjoyed a romp in the hay." His deep voice held a rich, rolling brogue, every syllable Scottish.

Thankfully Charlotte had slept under her coat, and her modesty was still somewhat intact. Colster grabbed the dress out of the golden-haired man's hand. "Who are you?" he demanded with all the authority of a duke.

A gleam of derision appeared in the Scot's eyes. "Gordon Lachlan, kinsman to the MacKenna. He sent me to find you—" His gaze dropped to Charlotte. "—And Miss Cameron."

"You've found us," Colster said coldly. "We have no need of your assistance."

The corner of Mr. Lachlan's mouth curled into a smile. "I can see that, Your Grace," he said politely in his soft burr. "However, it is the wishes of my cousin that you return with us. As you have already learned, this is MacKenna country, and there is more than one here who carries a grudge against you. The laird fears for your safety."

The stern, stoic faces of the men behind Mr. Lachlan added an element of truth to his warning.

Charlotte knew Colster wanted to wish the man to the devil. However, when he spoke, his voice betrayed no emotion. "Give us a moment to dress," he said.

"As you wish, Your Grace," Mr. Lachlan said, his manner more mocking than respectful. With only the hint of a bow, he nodded for his men to join him outside.

Colster rolled to his feet. Seeing that Mr. Lachlan had moved his men a respectful twenty feet away, he offered Charlotte her dress, then held up his greatcoat to screen her from prying eyes. "Relax," he said. "Take your time. We don't dance to their tune."

"There are so many of them," she whispered.

He pulled on his own shirt and tucked it in his waistband before turning her around and tying her laces. His head close to hers, he said, "I want you to get away."

A shot of anxiety went through her. "What about you?" she asked.

"Don't worry about me." He reached for his jacket. Keeping his back toward the Scots, he pulled out his money purse and the letter, folding it around the leather bag. He slipped the package to her. "If the opportunity arises, I want you to run. Save yourself." He removed his signet ring from his finger and slid it on the thumb of her right hand, the only place it would fit. "Use this however you see fit."

"What of you?"

He pulled a piece of hay from her hair and tossed it aside before meeting her worried gaze. "I was meant to be here. That was decided the day I was born. I will settle this matter now." He picked up his stockings and boots and started to finish dressing.

The boot reminded her of helping him the night before and its aftermath. They shouldn't have lingered. They should have known the danger they were in and run while they'd had a chance.

Raising his voice, Colster said, "Lachlan, my lady's shoes and stockings are out in that field. Bring them to her."

None of the Scots liked being given an order. Lachlan frowned like the others, but turned to a tall, dark-haired, bearded man dressed in homespun. "Tavis, fetch the lady's shoes."

Tavis did as bid. He must have been accustomed to taking orders, for he didn't even so much as offer a parting scowl in Colster's direction.

Colster was on his feet now. He'd left the collar of his shirt open since the neckcloth had been used to hobble Homer. In spite of that, he still cut a dashing figure. He swung his greatcoat over one arm.

Charlotte had not moved from where he'd left her. "They could kill you," she warned, her every instinct saying this was true.

Colster boldly laughed away her fears. "They won't. Not yet, at least."

"I don't know that is true," she whispered. "Don't the Scots have a history of slitting throats?" Before she could say more, Lachlan's man Tavis arrived with her shoes and one stocking.

"This was all I could find," he said, his voice deep and musical with its soft accent. There was a kindness in this man that she sensed the others lacked.

"Thank you," she murmured, so upset she couldn't look at him.

"Charlotte," Colster said, when Tavis had joined his compatriots.

She shook her head. Her nerves were stretched thin. She had a bad feeling in her stomach.

Colster took her in his arms in front of everyone. "Look at me."

She raised her gaze, holding back tears.

He smiled at her and lightly ran his thumb across her lower lip. A lover's gesture. "Be brave."

It was what she'd needed to hear. She straightened her shoulders. "Laird MacKenna won't hurt you. I won't let him."

"Any authority you have over him will be greatly appreciated," he assured. "I'm not proud when it comes to my own neck. Now come. Let us show them our courage."

The stocking by itself was worthless, and the red garters she'd once been so proud of were lost in the hay. She slipped on her nearly ruined shoes, allowed Colster to take her hand in his own warm, reassuring one, and let him lead her outside.

The day was going to be warm. The skies were clear and blue. The air was filled with the gurgling sounds of the stream and birdsong. Nothing untoward could happen on such a beautiful day, or so Charlotte told herself.

Mr. Lachlan was already mounted on a handsome bay. He'd been speaking to a black-haired man of his height and age. They were quarreling but stopped when she and Colster walked out of the hayrick.

"Your Grace," Mr. Lachlan said, "my laird bid me to personally ride to him with the news of your capture. My cousin Bruce shall escort you."

Charlotte took an immediate dislike to Bruce. He was a handsome man but had cruel eyes.

"Bring that horse over here," Mr. Lachlan ordered, indicating Homer, who was snoozing in the sun. Again, it was Tavis who did the work.

"Don't tarry, Bruce," Mr. Lachlan warned his cousin. "The laird will be waiting." He put his heels to his horse and rode off.

Bruce watched him go. He looked to the others. "Gordon wants it all for himself, doesn't he?"

"He's doing as he was told," one answered in Mr. Lachlan's defense.

"I should have been in charge," Bruce muttered. "As it is, I'm being treated no better than Tavis."

Another man spoke up. "The laird treats both you and Gordon equal."

"But we are not, are we?" Bruce countered.

No one dared to answer him, and the response seemed to take his temper a notch higher. "I should have been in charge of this. I should have been in charge from the beginning. I know what needs to be done. Mount up," he ordered. He climbed into his own saddle before swinging his hard gaze toward Charlotte and Colster. "So you are the grand duke. You don't appear so mighty now."

Colster held his tongue.

Bruce turned to a rider with brown hair pulled back in a long queue, a broken nose, and a sweaty shirt. "Dougal, take the woman up with you."

Before Charlotte knew what was happening, Dougal grabbed her by the arm and heaved her up into the seat in front of him.

Colster moved forward to protest. "She rides with me." But before he could take a step further, his way was blocked as one of Bruce's men nudged his horse forward.

"You needn't worry about her, Maddox," Bruce said, speaking to Colster. "Especially since you won't be riding. Robbie," he said, addressing a barrel-chested horseman blocking Colster's path. "Do you have the rope?"

Before Charlotte realized what they were about, a running noose was thrown around Colster's shoulders. It fell to his feet. She cried out a warning but it was too late. Robbie pulled the rope tight around Colster's ankles and he fell to the ground with bone-jarring force.

Colster set to work to free himself, but it was too late.

"Take the Maddox to the laird, Robbie," Bruce said. "Take him *our* way."

With a glad whoop, Robbie set heels to horse and took off at a gallop, dragging Colster in a mad circle around the perimeter of the field.

Chapter 7

*N*o one knew better than Tavis what Bruce was capable of. After all, he'd stolen Tavis's wife.

However, dragging a man to his death without a hearing in front of the laird was not right.

It dishonored the MacKenna. It dishonored the clan.

Tavis glanced around at the others. Some appeared as uncomfortable as himself. Others grinned as if they thought it great sport. No one seemed ready to speak up against injustice.

And who was he to challenge those more favored—especially when this was his first, long-awaited opportunity to ride with the warriors?

Tavis had been raised an orphan. The laird himself had taken him in . . . but he'd always known he was an outsider, one who had desperately wanted to belong. Tavis wanted to prove his loyalty to the clan that had adopted him and for years he had secretly practiced at swordplay, honing his skills and waiting for a day like this to arrive.

"*Stop this*," Miss Cameron cried out. "You'll kill him."

No one listened.

Robbie spun his mount around and came charging back. The Maddox struggled bravely to free himself, but he was no match for a galloping horse. The only thing saving him right now was that the field had been freshly mowed. If they dragged the Maddox all the way back to Nathraichean, he'd be dead by the time they arrived.

If Tavis was wise, he'd mind his own business. Especially around Bruce.

But something he couldn't explain urged him forward. He seemed to have no choice but to step forward, leaving the coach horse and putting himself directly in Robbie's path.

Robbie realized the challenge. His face split into a grin, and he spurred the horse faster.

Behind Tavis, someone jested, "I put three guineas on the horse." His wager was met with hoots of laughter. They all resented Tavis's presence amongst them. They thought themselves better than he.

As a blacksmith, there were few horses in the

kirk that Tavis didn't know. The animals trusted him, especially when their masters, such as Robbie, were vicious. Tavis used that trust now and gave a low whistle.

All the horses lifted their ears. Even wild-eyed, Robbie's Dodger heard the whistle. But would he disobey his master?

The ground pulsed with the horse's hooves. Tavis refused to move, trusting the training he'd given the animal.

Dodger was almost upon Tavis when he decided to prove his namesake—he dodged to one side, so close Tavis could have touched the animal's sweaty skin.

And then the horse stopped abruptly and Robbie went flying over his head facedown into the field's soft earth.

Dodger looked at his fallen master, and then turned to Tavis, lowering his head. He knew there'd be hell to pay, but he had not betrayed the blacksmith.

The scorn and derision that had been directed at Tavis seconds before were now turned on Robbie.

Miss Cameron used the opportunity to escape Dougal. She scrambled out of his hold, hit the ground, and went running to help the Maddox. The man was either fortunate or had an extremely hard head. Other than his clothes being torn and dirty, he'd obviously not suffered any great hurt since he didn't waste any time in freeing himself of the rope.

However, Bruce was not pleased. He nudged his horse forward. The lines of his face were set in a hard frown. The laughter died immediately.

"Are you proud, Blacksmith, that you have shamed a man in front of his enemy?"

Tavis knew better than to answer. Bruce was a dangerous man. There wasn't a crofter in the kirk who didn't pray that the laird chose Gordon over Bruce as his heir. Unfortunately, the laird enjoyed playing the cousins against each other. He gave them challenges, asking them to prove who was the better man. Tavis could have answered the question for him—Gordon.

Robbie's growl of anger interrupted them and was the only warning Tavis received before the smaller man ran at him with a knife in his hand.

Tavis had the superior strength and agility. He ducked what would have been a death blow. The knife harmlessly sliced air. Tavis came up beneath Robbie and threw him to the ground. Before the man could collect his wits, Tavis pulled the short sword he favored from its scabbard at his waist and pointed the tip at Robbie's throat.

Seconds passed like hours as he waited for Robbie to admit defeat. He sensed the others' amazement. He knew he'd surprised them all, including Bruce. Regardless of what happened next, he had already won. The secret hours he'd spent teaching himself combat had paid off tenfold, and he was thankful the laird had let him ride out with the search party this day.

It was a pity Moira, the wife who had left him for another, wasn't here to see his victory.

The Maddox and Miss Cameron unintentionally broke the stalemate. One of the men shouted an alarm that the twosome had taken advantage of everyone's inattention and had start running for the shelter of the forest across the stream.

"Damn the lot of you," Bruce swore. "You are letting them get away. *Catch them.*"

Dougal made up for his earlier lapse by riding them down, reaching the woman first. He jumped from his horse. She cried out as he knocked her to the ground. He yanked her up by her shoulder, his knife at her throat.

The Maddox stopped. He held out his hands. "Let her go. It's me you want. Not her. Let her go, and I shall leave with you willingly." It was an offer Tavis would have made. A man didn't let a woman die for him.

Miss Cameron would have none of it. Even with a knife at her throat, she said, "Colster, don't trust these men."

Bruce rode up to them. "Quiet, woman."

She met his eye. "I am an honored guest of Laird MacKenna's—"

"Are you now?" Bruce interrupted. "Do you believe you will be so honored once he learns how we found you wrapped in your lover's arms?"

Miss Cameron's face flooded red, but she held her head high, defiance in her amazingly blue eyes. It was Bruce who looked away first.

"Tie him up, Robbie. Tavis, weren't you told to fetch that coach horse? Bring it over here." He indicated the stolen horse, the one Tavis called in his mind Ulysses. The laird didn't name all of his animals save his favorites, but Tavis believed each of God's creatures deserved a name. He'd chosen Ulysses because the tale was one of his favorites from those he'd learned from Father Nicholas.

Robbie angrily yanked back the Maddox's arms and tied his hands while Tavis brought the horse over.

The Maddox's hard gaze had never once wavered from Dougal holding a knife on the woman. He spoke to Bruce. "Release her. You have me. Leave her here."

"Your orders carry no weight here, Sassenach," Bruce said.

"She's *my* woman," the Maddox answered. "I'll kill the man who harms her."

The fierce certainty with which he spoke surprised Tavis. He'd been told the Maddox was a weak, pampered gentleman who had betrayed his proud Scottish roots for the foppish ways of the Sassenach.

This man wasn't weak. Nor would he be a wise one to cross.

Bruce dismissed the threat. "You are on our lands now, Maddox. *Our* rules." He looked over to Dougal. "Mount up and don't lose her this time. And you, Robbie." Robbie had remounted a very contrite Dodger. "Do you expect the Maddox to fly up onto the horse's back what with you tying his hands? Do you have any bloody brains? No wonder the blacksmith got the best of you."

"If you hadn't stopped me, Tavis's blood would be soaking into this field," Robbie vowed.

"I'm not so certain, cousin," Bruce answered. "You left yourself wide open. You got what you deserved. My *wife* is better with a knife."

Tavis hated when Bruce mentioned Moira in front of him. He hated having to pretend it was fine the laird had helped Moira divorce him so she could marry Bruce.

There'd been a time when Moira had loved him and had been proud to be a blacksmith's wife. That had been long before Bruce had noticed her and wooed her with gifts, money, and the possibility of being his lady if he was named laird.

Tavis had fought the divorce. He'd stood up to the laird, but in the end, the matter had been done without his consent. Money had been paid, church officials had winked, and the deed had been done. There'd been naught he could do to stop it. The laird had always favored Bruce. What he wanted, he usually received—that was until Gordon Lachlan had arrived in Nathraichean. And anyone who suspected Tavis was Gordon's man was exactly right.

Sooner or later, Tavis would have the opportunity to repay both Bruce and Moira—one for stealing his wife and the other for breaking her vows. But for now, he was still the bloody lackey.

"Help the prisoner on his horse," Bruce ordered Tavis.

Rebellion burning in his chest at being treated as a servant, Tavis laced his fingers to give the Englishman a leg up.

But the Maddox hesitated. "Thank you," the Sassenach said in a low voice intended for their ears alone. "I owe you my life."

The gratitude made Tavis angry. Saving the man's hide had not been his wisest decision. "Go to the devil," he told the Maddox, but the curse rang wrong in Tavis's ears. It didn't feel right.

Still, it had the desired effect on the Maddox. His gaze hardened before he let Tavis give him a lift up onto the horse.

Tavis handed the lead rope to Robbie, who began haranguing the Maddox that he'd best stay on. They'd not pick him up if he fell ". . . although the blacksmith might."

The others caught the jibe and laughed. Tavis ignored them.

The other men—Dougal, Peter, and Wills—gathered at the far side of the field, ready to leave. Robbie rode with his prisoner to join them. Bruce waited beside Tavis's horse Butter. She was an ill-tempered mare who was known for throwing the best foals and for throwing her riders. Tavis was certain it had been a joke amongst the men that he'd been given her to ride.

"You surprised me, Tavis," Bruce said. "I didn't know you were such a fighter."

Tavis mounted. Butter was anxious to join the other horses. She kicked out her impatience, but he easily maintained his seat. "We all do what we must in the service of the laird."

"Do you think he'll be pleased with what you did today?" Bruce asked, showing his crooked front teeth in a smile that didn't reach his eyes.

"MacKenna was keen to meet this Maddox," Tavis said. "He would not want him ripped to shreds."

"You may be right. Then, again, he may be concerned his blacksmith is taking on airs above his station."

"He chose me for this task," Tavis reminded him. "I'm here at his express order."

"And none of us can understand why." Bruce ensured he had the last word by kicking his horse forward. Setting off at a trot, he raised his hand, a signal they should all follow him.

Charlotte should not be here. She was not a player in this drama. The knowledge kept Phillip's back straight. He had a purpose and that was to protect her.

The man Dougal had tied her hands together so that even if she did escape, it would be difficult for her to run.

Phillip knew he was the reason MacKenna had invited her. What he couldn't understand was why? All of London knew that he and the Cameron girls were enemies—

He was stunned by the thought. Could that be MacKenna's purpose? Was she here as a witness to whatever MacKenna had planned? He glanced over to her.

She might be frightened out of her wits, but no fear showed in her face. Her pride wouldn't let it. He now knew her character well enough to understand that she wouldn't have let him in so close to her if she'd meant to betray him. That wasn't how Charlotte Cameron behaved.

Of course, that didn't mean she hadn't wanted

to wring his neck a time or two, and rightfully so.

Once they'd made it through this and returned to London, Phillip vowed he would make all amends possible—which included offering her his complete protection.

He'd also set her up as his mistress. She could have anything her heart desired. She'd never have to worry about her sisters again. He'd take care of all of them.

But first, he had to see the two of them through this situation.

Phillip studied each of the riders, searching for an ally. The man Tavis intrigued him. He was the outsider. The others didn't accept him, especially in the face of Bruce's open antagonism toward him.

He was about Phillip's height and a year maybe two older or younger. It was hard to pinpoint his exact age with that beard.

It had been Phillip's experience that, in every group, there was always one person who could be persuaded to do the right thing. Tavis had already demonstrated he had a conscience and the courage to act upon it. It was unfortunate he didn't have more power in this small group.

They were coming closer to the sea. The forest disappeared. Rolling moors, green from the recent rain, stretched out before them. The sky seemed to touch the earth here in a way Phillip had not noticed anyplace else in Britain, while gulls and terns rode the wind currents overhead, curious about the riders.

The road went up and over a knoll, bringing them to a windswept moor and his first sight of a medieval tower surrounded by a walled fortress sitting on a cliff overlooking the sea.

A chill of recognition went through Phillip. He'd seen this tower before. It had been a figure in his dreams, one he'd never understood. It now filled him with a sense of foreboding. Soon, he may learn the answers to not only Nanny Frye's letter, but also to disquieting questions he'd sensed in his own soul.

This section of Scotland was believed to be sparsely populated. Phillip could almost hear his peers laughing about nothing living up here but puffins, kittiwakes, and barking seals.

They were wrong.

A busy village of crofters' huts, daub buildings, and tents surrounded the perimeter of the fortress. He'd guess there may be as many as a thousand of them in the shadow of Nathraichean's tower. Sheep roamed freely across the moor along with goats, dogs, and children.

A shepherd noticed them and put out a cry, which set the dogs to barking. Men, women, and children came pouring from the direction of the makeshift village to watch their party ride by.

The sound of military drumming came from inside the fortress. A flag was raised above the tower, its colors a swath of green, red, and blue. The MacKenna colors.

Bruce signaled for his men to halt. "Here's a sight you will want to see," he bragged to Phillip.

At his words, the tower's gates slowly swung open, and Phillip watched in amazement as men streamed out of the fortress to take their position in regimental formation. They were a straggly lot, with long hair and beards, makeshift uniforms in the MacKenna colors and rifles at their shoulders. Their faces reflected the fierce pride of men with a cause.

They flowed through the gates like water, and just when Phillip thought there couldn't be more, they kept coming until a good two thousand strong stood before Nathraichean's walls. Here, in the most isolated reaches of Scotland, MacKenna had amassed an army, and there was no one in England the wiser.

This was what MacKenna had wanted him to see. Phillip knew that now all the way to his bones. Nanny Frye's letter had been a ruse, a contemptible trick to lure him up here.

As if confirming his worst suspicions, Bruce said, "Here are the men forced out by the Clearances and English policies, Maddox. Men who share your ancestry but whom you and yours have turned their backs on. The time of reckoning has arrived, and there is many a good Scot who is glad for it."

With those words, he put heels to horse and led the way toward the waiting crowd.

Phillip had no choice but to follow.

Chapter 8

C harlotte glanced over her shoulder to Colster. He watched the growing force of men with sharp concern in his eyes—and then his gaze switched to her. Responsibility sat heavy on his shoulders, and she knew he blamed himself for not sending her back earlier.

He shouldn't.

She wasn't afraid. After all, Colster had called her *his* woman. And he'd meant the words. He had declared himself in front of all these men.

The sense of wonder, of oneness she'd felt in his arms, had not been completely on her part. He'd shared it, too. On that knowledge alone, she would have ridden into the fires of hell.

Ever since her mother's violent murder, a fear of death had dogged her life. She'd longed for a safe place. She'd torn up her roots and dragged her sisters half a world away to find it.

Now, confronted by what had to be the most dangerous situation of her life, she was not afraid. She couldn't be—*she'd found love.*

Love was far, far different than what she'd imagined it.

Years ago, she'd thought she'd loved Thomas Grimshaw, but when he'd forced her to choose between her sisters or himself, she'd chosen her family.

Looking at Colster, she wasn't certain what her choice would be. Overnight, he'd come to be a part of her soul. Her destiny had always been to come to this place, to meet him, and to fall madly, irreparably in love with him.

At last, she understood why her mother had tossed aside family, heritage, and title to marry a penniless soldier. She'd chosen love. All those times when she'd claimed her children were her fortune, she hadn't been lying. She'd been content in her husband's arms . . . as content as Charlotte had been sleeping beside Colster in a hayrick.

Colster managed to push his horse close to hers. He dared to lean close to her, whispering, "Save yourself. Say I forced you, that I was a bloody brute."

There was no time for more. Dougal growled at him to get back while Robbie viciously yanked Homer's lead rope, pulling Colster away from her even as Bruce kicked his horse into a gallop. The rest of the party followed, and she was forced to hold on to Dougal or go tumbling off the horse in front of the solemn crowd of Scots gathered to watch her humiliation.

Save yourself.

Didn't Colster realize she couldn't? Her fate was intertwined with his. She'd proudly die at his side.

The crowd fell into step behind them. Small boys and dogs ran alongside. Charlotte could have sworn she caught a glimpse of Fergus, Klem, and their cousin Malcolm slinking amongst the crofters.

Bruce led them through the tower's gates into a huge courtyard teeming with people. Here, the atmosphere was that of a country fair, and one for the more genteel classes. Those who lived within Nathraichean walls dressed better than those outside, and here and there was a glint of jewels.

Many called out to the riders and shouted good-naturedly at Bruce and his men. More than a few called Tavis by name.

Three pipers with their bagpipes on their shoulders met them at the head of a street. They saluted Bruce, put their instruments to their lips, and turned smartly on their heels. They began leading the way toward the center of the castle keep while playing a sprightly military march. Charlotte had heard the bagpipes play only once before in her life, and that had been in an open field. Their music now bounced off the walls of the houses lining the narrow streets, magnifying the sound tenfold until it drowned out even the drummers who marched behind them and reverberated in the air.

It wasn't easy being the focus of so much gawking and rude stares. Charlotte could hear them talk about her. But who they truly saved their animosity for was Colster. One would have thought him the devil incarnate by the stares and crude gestures he received.

Colster carried himself well. Knowing his sharp mind as she did, Charlotte was certain he was busy thinking of how he would turn this to his own advantage—and he would. She had great faith in him.

And then Charlotte caught Tavis watching Colster. He was not like the others. His companions may belittle him, but Charlotte sensed he was no one's fool. He had his own mind and the courage to stand up for his sense of justice.

He would either be their enemy or their friend. If he was the former, he was the one person here who couldn't be bought.

The street ended at a village green large enough for training militia and performing maneuvers.

At the far side of the green was a three-story house made of limestone and detailed in the style of Palladian. The Duke of Marlborough, or Colster, would have been proud to own such a home.

A banner hung over the entrance. In colors of blue, green, and red was the depiction of a fist holding a sword while a stag leaped the blade.

As their party came to a halt, the pipers stopped playing, and the doors to the house opened.

Gordon Lachlan came out first, his expression somber, his hand on the hilt of his sword at his side. Charlotte realized he'd been tricked from the glory of this moment. He'd successfully led the search for Colster, but having found him, had been ordered to report directly to Laird MacKenna. She wondered if the laird had done this on purpose.

And then the laird himself came walking through the door, followed by several retainers.

In London, Laird MacKenna had been the epitome of an English gentleman.

Here, he dressed in gray kilt and leather leggings. His hair stuck up in all different angles as if he'd just risen from bed, and his face was ruddy from the salt air and the wind. He also appeared far older now than his square shoulders and straight back had led her to believe in Town and his salt-and-pepper hair was in need of a cut.

Bruce dismounted and fell upon one knee in front of the laird while hitting his chest with his first, a gesture of feudal servility.

Laird MacKenna didn't even pay attention. His gaze had gone straight to Colster. He took an unsteady step down the front stair. Gordon was right there to offer an arm for assistance, but Laird MacKenna waved him away. He studied Colster as if he were memorizing every detail about him.

"Amazing," he said at last in his soft, elegant burr. "You are the image of your father. I can't shake my amazement."

"You knew exactly what I looked like," Colster returned pointedly.

Laird MacKenna laughed. "Aye, I did. Our paths crossed in the House of Lords last month, Your Grace. You were too preoccupied with yourself to notice anyone beneath you. You reminded me then of your father. He was much the same way. He even refused to acknowledge those who trusted him for their livelihood. He was one of the first to sell," the laird said, raising his voice so that all gathered hear. "He was one of the first to betray heritage and country and send people from their homes."

Several heads in the crowd nodded. They'd come for justice, the sort they understood. Charlotte prayed Colster was careful.

He wasn't. He was a duke and accustomed to commanding the world. His response was to agree coolly, "My father was a bastard. What does that have to do with me?"

Laird MacKenna raised his hands in the air as if he were a prophet. "The sins of the father always visit the sons."

Colster's attention caught on one word of what he'd said. "Sons?" He leaned forward, his brows drawn sharply together. "Is the letter true?"

His response delighted Laird MacKenna. "The letter?" he repeated, lowering his arms. "I know nothing of a letter, Your Grace." The mockery in his voice belied his innocence.

Fury flared in Colster's eyes, and Charlotte feared he might lunge at Laird MacKenna, but at that moment, they were interrupted by the appearance of two women coming out of the house onto the step. One woman was Charlotte's age, with hair the blue-black of a crow's wing and skin so fair it looked like cream. She'd caught her hair in a net woven with pearls, and her dress was made of the finest purple velvet.

The other woman was much, much older. She was so petite she was no taller than the laird's shoulder. At one time, she'd been a spectacular beauty. Her hair piled regally on her head still held traces of the red-gold and her blue-green eyes radiated an intensity that age could never dull.

"He's here," the woman said with great satisfaction. "Has he asked after Nanny Frye?" she demanded, her fingers grasping the sleeve of Laird MacKenna's shirt—and Charlotte knew this must be Lady Rowena.

"He had just mentioned her, sister," Laird MacKenna answered.

Lady Rowena turned and her gaze unerringly singled out Colster. Her eyes grew alive with anger. *"She's dead."* She practically spit the words out at him. "The letter is years old. She thought I'd send it. I have. Yes, I have. Finally." She punctuated her words with a maniacal cackle of laughter that was unsettling.

Laird MacKenna spoke to the younger woman. "Moira, take my sister away."

Moira nodded to two female attendants who stood inside the door. They hurried out while she cooed to her mistress, "Come, my lady. It is time for our rest, and I've had something special prepared for your luncheon."

"Not the lamb. I don't like lamb," Lady Rowena complained.

"No, not lamb," Moira assured her.

"Go with Moira," Laird MacKenna gently urged his sister. "You need rest. We'll have the trial tonight. You want to be present for the trial."

"I *do*," Lady Rowena answered. "I've waited a long time for this."

"We both have," Laird MacKenna assured her.

Lady Rowena did not fuss as she was led away. Laird MacKenna watched her go before facing his people gathered before him. His expression was grave as he said in a carrying voice, "Your father did this. He drove her to where she is today."

"I know nothing of it," Colster answered, his voice not without compassion.

Laird MacKenna cut the air in an angry gesture. "It doesn't matter. Your trial is not about her but *them*." He swept an arm to encompass the crowd. "They've come from every corner of the Highlands. They've come to me searching for justice, and I've promised it to them."

"Or have you promised them insurrection?" Colster challenged. "You're encouraging them to rebel. You are urging them to certain death."

"What sort of life do they have left?" Laird MacKenna countered. "These people were loyal, proud Highlanders until the filthy landowners burned them out of their homes, homes their ancestors had built. And why? For the gold," he answered, rubbing his fingers together. "The lords of Scotland have forgotten the people. But I haven't!"

A shout of agreement went through the crowed, causing horses to startle and Charlotte to look around in amazement.

"I shall lead them back to their homes," Laird MacKenna boasted. "With my army, I shall set Scotland free of English traitors!"

The army of men behind them removed their swords and pounded them on the ground or hit shields with their fists, adding that noise to the swell of approval. "We'd die for you," one soldier called, and his words were quickly seconded.

Colster turned toward them. His hands were tied but he held his head high as he challenged, "I do not know what game MacKenna plays. However, he plays it with your lives. Once the Crown learns of your activities, it will be considered *treason*. Go, return to your families and your homes now while you have the opportunity. Do not choose war over peace."

"We don't have homes," a woman close to Colster shouted. "We have nothing."

Gordon Lachlan stepped forward. *"Save our pride."*

His statement was met by a thunderous agreement and Laird MacKenna's smiling approval.

Charlotte glanced at Bruce. If looks were daggers, Lachlan's heart would be cut out of his chest. The two men were rivals and Lachlan had just won this round. Good. She might not like Lachlan, but she despised Bruce as a bully. His type was the more dangerous.

Colster tried to speak up, "There is a way for change. It's in Parliament—"

Catcalls and hissing met his words.

He didn't give up. "—Think of your families and your children."

"We do," one man answered, speaking for the masses. "My mother died in the fire my landlord set to burn us out. 'Twas not right. She'd been born there. Her mother had been born there. She had more right to the land than the noble who gave the troops the order."

A chorus of agreement met his statement.

Laird MacKenna held up his hands. Immediately the crowd settled into order. "This shall be decided, later tonight." He looked to Colster. "Prepare yourself, Your Grace. A time of reckoning is at hand. Once, I promised your father it would be so. And I told him when it happened, I would win. My only regret is that he didn't live to see this moment." He nodded to two soldiers at the foot of the house steps. "Take him off that horse and bring him inside."

However, before the men could move, Bruce jumped to obey as if wishing to assert himself the way Lachlan had. He yanked Colster from Homer's back and shoved him forward.

"Careful," Laird MacKenna advised. "The duke is our guest until his trial this evening. We would not want him to believe we were barbarians, or *insurrectionists.*" He laughed at his own joke and turned a blind eye on the roughness with which Bruce pushed Colster up the steps toward the door.

However, once he'd come even with Laird MacKenna, Colster stopped. "Let her go," he said to the laird, referring to Charlotte. "She's not part of this."

Laird MacKenna's gaze flicked in Charlotte's direction. He took in her ruined shoes and clothing and her hair that was tumbled around her shoulders. Instead of admiration, his thin lips twisted into disdain. "We shall see," he answered.

It was all the response Colster was going to receive before Bruce cuffed him in the back of the head and pushed him through the door, where the soldiers waited to help.

"And what of me?" Charlotte boldly asked. "Am I to receive the same hospitality?"

Laird MacKenna came down the steps and walked to the horse she rode behind Dougal. The animal pranced a step until Dougal tugged on the rein, a command for him to stand still.

"I'm disappointed in you, Miss Cameron," Laird MacKenna said. "I'd taken a liking to you. I'd thought we shared a common enemy. I believed you incorruptible."

"I am."

His eyes lit with secret amusement. "I can see that."

Charlotte ignored the hot color flooding her cheeks. She would not be ashamed, not for loving Colster. "Was this the reason you invited me?" she demanded. "Did you expect me to be a witness to the game you played with the duke?"

"At first." The humor left his expression. "Actually, I had a thought of making you my lady. I arranged an introduction because of the stories I'd heard, but I came to admire you."

"We obviously barely knew each other if you believe I would be a party to such as this," Charlotte answered.

He frowned as if taken aback that anyone would dare to speak to him this way. She braced herself, fearing the worst—but then he began clapping. "*Brava*, Miss Cameron. Spoken with the spirit of a Colonial." He turned to his people. "She's from America," he said in his genteel, rolling accent. "She's been raised in the wilderness amongst savages, and yet her people defied the king *and won*. We can, too!" he said, curling his hand into a mighty fist. "We *will* win because we have a cause, and our cause is just!"

His claim was met with a roar from the crowd. These people were desperate. Charlotte could see by the pinched look in many faces and the raggedness of their clothing that these people would do as he wished because they had no other choice.

Laird MacKenna turned back to her. "Help Miss Cameron down, Dougal, and be gentle about it."

Dougal slid to the ground. He put his hands up to help her down. Charlotte didn't move. "I assume I am *not* a prisoner," she said loudly.

The laird had been conferring a moment with Bruce, but his attention was on her. He smiled regretfully. "I wish I could honor your request, Miss Cameron. You are a fascinating woman, but from what Bruce is telling me, I'd best not let you have free rein of my castle."

"I'm a prisoner, then," she insisted, raising her voice so all could hear and perhaps realize what a tyrant he was. Perhaps they would come to their senses. She'd met men like him, men who saw raw territory as an opportunity to build their own private kingdoms.

Laird MacKenna laughed and confirmed her suspicions by saying, "I enjoy your show of spirit, lass, but here, I am king. There's none that will gainsay me. My word is law. So you'd best tuck away your pretty defiance and behave. I hold your life in my hands."

With those ominous words, he turned back to give Bruce an order.

Charlotte swallowed. She should keep quiet.

Her eyes met Gordon Lachlan's. He lifted an eyebrow as if to tell her to behave.

She couldn't. "Will *I* be on trial?" she demanded quietly of Laird MacKenna. If something happened to her, who would see to Constance's welfare? Or be there for Miranda if she should need Charlotte?

Laird MacKenna's patience was wearing thin. "No, Miss Cameron," he assured her, "I don't need a trial to handle you."

"I shall not be a willing captive."

"Good." He turned to Dougal. "Tavis can help the woman down. You go with Bruce, and I'll see the two of you in an hour in the hall."

Charlotte had little choice but to let the blacksmith help her from the horse. He was kind enough to untie her hands. The crowd around them was dispersing. She felt their curiosity, but they didn't ask questions. Laird MacKenna was right. These people trusted him to lead them. If he slit her throat, there would be none to argue.

The dark-haired beauty named Moira came out on the step. She caught Laird MacKenna's attention. "Lady Rowena is taking her nap."

"Good," the laird answered. "I want her in her best mood for the trial this evening." He nodded to Charlotte. "Escort Miss Cameron upstairs. You know which room to take her to. Tavis, accompany them."

The blacksmith motioned Charlotte toward the proud beauty. Charlotte's legs felt wobbly from the ride, but she was relieved she carried herself well.

Laird MacKenna was quickly being swamped by petitioners seeking his attention. However, as they passed Laird MacKenna, he said to Tavis, "I want you here this evening. You shall stand beside me."

"I?" Tavis asked obviously surprised.

"Bruce told me what happened in the glen. You did right. I wanted him alive."

Charlotte was pleased, and relieved, that Laird MacKenna's intent was not to kill Colster. Perhaps they would have this "trial" Laird MacKenna kept talking about, money would be paid, and she and Colster would be free to return to London.

She prayed that was true.

Inside, the house was cool plaster walls and marble floors. It could have been any house in England and served as a testament that Laird MacKenna was no pauper. He couldn't have made the money for such a house with sheep, not and feed as many mouths as were waiting outside his gates.

But there was something else Charlotte noticed. She felt a stiffness between Moira and Tavis.

As they were preparing to go up the stairs, Bruce came in the door looking as if he wanted to hit something. "Where are you going?" he demanded of Moira.

"I'm doing the laird's bidding," she answered.

Bruce's scowl deepened, his gaze hardening on Tavis. "I'll be finished in a moment, *husband*," Moira said, and started up the stairs. Charlotte's mind went alive with questions. Moira had chosen that last word deliberately, but for whose benefit? Hers?

Charlotte followed her up the stairs with Tavis bringing up the rear. Bruce had no choice but to stomp down a hallway.

They walked until they came to a door at the end of the hall on the first floor. Moira opened the door, nodding for Charlotte to step forward.

Charlotte didn't know what she had anticipated, but it certainly wasn't to find herself in a lovely bedroom decorated in soft greens and blues. A fresh breeze from the open windows carried a hint of salt and the call of the birds nesting on the rocks below the cliff. A huge four-poster bed with carved railings dominated the middle of the room. There was no fire in the stone fireplace.

"This is the Sea Room," Moira said. "I hope you find it comfortable. The coachmen brought your bags, and you will find we've unpacked for you. Your clothing is in the wardrobe." Even Charlotte's brushes had been lined up on the dressing table before the mirror.

Moira walked over to the windows. "These overlook the sea. Come, take a peek."

Charlotte did as ordered and peered out. The side of the house was a straight drop down the cliff to rocks and angry waves below.

"You can try to escape this way," Moira said politely. "But not one has done so and lived."

"Do you entertain many prisoners?" Charlotte couldn't resist asking.

"From time to time," Moira answered evenly. "The laird is not without enemies."

"And what does that say about him?" Charlotte suggested, unable to keep the hint of sarcasm from her voice.

"Every man has enemies," Moira answered. "But Nathraichean shall never be overcome. Her walls are too strong."

She didn't wait for Charlotte's response but walked toward the door, where Tavis respectfully waited in the hall. "You are a prisoner, Miss Cameron, but we don't want you to be uncomfortable. I shall send a tray of food up and drink. Is there anything else you would like?"

"Well, if I can't have freedom," Charlotte answered, matching her tone to Moira's practical one, "then I'd like a bath with rose-scented soap."

The Scotswoman frowned. "You are pushing your boundaries, Miss Cameron."

"You don't have soap up here?" Charlotte asked sweetly.

"We have soap," Moira said, the pretense of hospitality leaving her eyes and voice. "A maid will be up with tub water—and your smelly soap."

"I would like to see His Grace, the Duke of Colster," Charlotte said, deciding to ask for everything.

"Don't try my patience, Miss Cameron," Moira advised, and shut the door. A key turned in the lock.

There was something about Moira Charlotte just didn't like. For that reason alone, she crossed over and tested the door anyway.

It was locked.

But sometimes doors could be unlocked.

Charlotte bent to inspect the keyhole. She couldn't see anything because the key was still in place.

A second later, she learned why. Tavis and Moira were having a conversation. "Tavis, what is going on between you and the laird?" Moira asked, her voice low as if not wishing to be overheard.

"You lost your right to ask questions a year ago when you left me," he answered insolently.

"Oh don't be stubborn. Something is going on, something *you* don't understand."

"Do you?"

"I'm trying to."

"For your husband's sake or your own? I'm sorry, Moira, I've crossed your husband once today, and it was one time too many. If you have plotting to do, you must do it yourself."

"I do this for him," she lashed back. "He's not like you. He's ambitious."

"As are you."

"Yes," she agreed. "Yes, yes, yes. And I don't trust Gordon. Don't make a mistake, Tavis, and throw your lot in with him just because you are angry with me. 'Twould be foolish."

"I shall remember that."

He must have turned to walk away because Moira said, "Wait."

There was a pause. Charlotte had to strain to hear her next words. ". . . I still love you."

To Charlotte's ears, the admission sounded contrived.

"I can see how you do," he replied, his voice tight. Charlotte was relieved he wasn't gullible.

"You never asked me to stay, Tavis. You were the one who never asked. *I* put the question to you."

"I never asked, Moira, because I knew the answer. You didn't want me. You chose Bruce. Are you happy? He's a hard man. I warned you, but you didn't believe me."

Instead of answering, she asked again, "What does the laird want with you?"

Tavis made an impatient sound. "You heard, Moira. I saw you linger to get an earful. He wants me there this evening, and as he does with most things, he offered no explanation."

"He didn't ask for Bruce. It's made Bruce angry—"

"Bruce is always angry. 'Tis your bed you made, Moira, and you are welcome to it." He walked off, and Moira slammed Charlotte's door with her fist in frustration.

Charlotte hurried to the other side of her room, lest Moira enter and she be caught eavesdropping. She called out, "Enter?" as if she'd just heard the sound.

There was no answer.

Fifteen minutes later, there was another knock on the door. Without waiting for her response, the key turned. Dougal entered carrying a huge metal tub. Several servants followed him, carrying buckets of water, linen towels, and a soap that smelled of the spring flowers. Another maid carried a tray of food.

Charlotte decided to push the limits of her captivity. "I think after my bath, I shall go for a walk."

"You shall not," Dougal said. "I'll be outside the door. You are not to go anywhere until the laird sends for you."

She made an "oh" with her lips and sat down to wait by the window while they finished preparing her bath. Beyond these walls were blue skies and freedom. She'd heard trappers talk about being held captive by Indians. They'd all said the same thing—one had to be ready to run at a moment's notice.

Charlotte would make certain she was.

Dougal and the servants left. Charlotte lifted the covers over the plates. Roast mutton stared back at her. She wondered how she could store some of this for when they could escape—

Colster's voice said, "Charlotte?"

For a moment, she thought she'd imagined the sound. Then she heard him again. *"Charlotte."*

His voice came from inside the room, but she was alone. Leery now, she looked around.

"Over *here*, Charlotte." He sounded more determined, and she realized his voice came from the cold hearth. She ran over to it.

Chapter 9

"Colster?"

Phillip could not contain his relief at hearing Charlotte's voice. He'd gambled that she was close. He'd been standing by the fireplace, leaning against the mantel, trying to think of a way out of this room when he'd overheard talking.

His room was next to hers. Their fireplaces shared the same flue. If this had been a true medieval age house, the walls, even at the back of the fireplace, would have been too thick for sound to travel. But this was a modern building and the workmen cut corners as they had on anything he'd ever had built.

He'd waited for silence, and then waited what seemed an interminable amount of time before daring to speak.

"I'm in the room next to yours," he said in a

low voice, uncertain how far sound would carry along the chimney pipeline.

"I feared they'd thrown you in a dungeon," she said.

Phillip glanced around at his room with its furnishings fit for a wealthy landowner. "I would rather they had. There doesn't seem a way out unless I can fly. What of you?"

"I'm the same."

"But you've not been harmed?"

He held his breath until she said, "No."

It was the answer he wanted to hear. Not knowing how much time either of them had until someone came or an alarm went up, he immediately said what was most important, "Charlotte, I want you to escape. I'll try and create a diversion, something that will take their attention off of you. When that happens, run. Don't look back. Don't worry about me."

Without a moment's hesitation, she said, "I will absolutely do no such thing. We are in this together, Duke. Perhaps *I* shall create the diversion, then *you* should run."

Duke. Her irreverence made him smile. There wasn't another woman on this earth with her spirit.

Or another one that he trusted.

He had no close friends. No one he could

confide in that he knew wouldn't gossip or turn the information against him . . . until now.

They had started off enemies, but he realized they were cut of the same cloth. Charlotte understood honor. She had pride and was protective of those in her care. These were qualities he understood, that he admired.

He settled down as close as he could against the chimney wall that separated their two rooms. He wished he could reach through stone and mortar to touch her. To feel the softness of her skin and smell her hair and kiss that impudent mouth. "Please, Charlotte," he said. "I must know that you are safe."

Again there was a pause. At last, she said, "If I can escape, I will, but you must promise the same thing."

"I won't leave without you." The words came to his lips without debate. The loneliness of his life threaded through him. "I can't," he admitted. "I rather like having you around."

There was a beat of silence, and then she said quietly, "I rather like you, too."

A warm feeling spread through him, one he didn't recognize at first. *She liked him.* And *she*, of all people, had every reason not to.

He thought of the night before, of making love to her. She should hate him.

She didn't.

"Charlotte, the letter is a fake." There, he'd said it. "It was a trick to get me up here."

"I feared it so," she answered. "How do you feel about . . ." She let her voice trail off as if not wanting to mention his brother.

"I feel like a bloody fool," he said bluntly. And he felt disappointed.

"Is that all?" she pressed. "I'd be angry, too, but I'd also have such deep regret over not discovering someone I'd missed all my life."

Her words ripped open his heart.

Tears burned in his eyes, tears he forced back. "It's nothing," he said, his voice tight. "You can't miss what you've never had."

"That's true for some people . . . but not you. He was your twin. There had to be some connection between you, even from birth. You shared the same womb."

"He died, Charlotte. At birth. He was never truly ever born."

"I don't believe that, and I don't think you do either. If you did, you would never have traveled all this way, Colster."

"Then I was played a fool."

"You are not a fool for wanting to believe. A fool is the one who cares only for himself. That's not you, Your Grace. It never has been you."

The truth of her words sank into him. The tension built by anger and despair evaporated.

"Laird MacKenna is a fool, a cheat, and a liar," Charlotte finished. "And I shall tell him such the next time I see him."

Her crisp condemnation startled a laugh out of him. Dear God, he loved this woman. She made him grin like any lovesick fool—

Phillip broke off the thought, his mind, the rational part, the *ducal* part sounding an alarm as loud as a hundred fire bells.

He was falling in love.

The thought was so startling, he sat upright and bumped his head on the top of the chimney. With a soft oath, he practically crawled out of the hearth and scrambled to his feet.

He was falling in *love*? His brain choked on the thought.

Miss Cameron—Charlotte, was the *worst* person for him to—

Phillip shook his head hard as if he could shake the idea out of his brains. He'd never wanted to be in—

He broke off, unable to repeat that one word.

Love.

It had never been part of his vocabulary. Not really.

He'd thought he'd loved Elizabeth. Theirs had

been the usual courtship and marriage. But his feelings were nothing in comparison to the sense of connection he had with Charlotte.

Phillip backed away from the hearth. He hit the wall and couldn't go farther.

He'd not known Charlotte more than a day . . . and yet she'd quickly become like his right arm. She was loyal, brave, and consistent.

It had to be the sex.

It had been too potent between them, too tumultuous. He doubled his hands into fists, reminding himself once again how often it had been suggested by those who dared to approach the subject to him that it was unnatural for a man to endure prolonged celibacy. Foolishly, he had denied their claim. And now he was paying the price.

What he felt for Charlotte wasn't love. It was *lust*.

Yes, that made perfect sense.

Lust *and* love—

Phillip raised his hands to his head, wanting to pound these errant, irrational thoughts out of it.

God, the wags in London would be tickled pink to see him now—*lusting* after her the way he was . . . *and* loving her.

A breeze came through the window, carrying the freshness of clean, salt air. Phillip turned and stared at the water outside beyond his reach.

There was not a soul in sight. Not even a bird in the sky.

But he wasn't alone.

His world had expanded to include Charlotte. Beautiful, spirited Charlotte, who was the exact opposite of Elizabeth. With Charlotte, sex hadn't been about lust. It had been a joining, a melding of two souls. For so long, he'd thought of himself alone—and now he wasn't. He'd been one, and now he was two.

The only problem, aside from the irritation of gossips, something he'd have to weather no matter whom he married, was that Charlotte was not the sort of woman a man of his rank and class took to wife. She didn't have the lineage to be a duchess. Her family was bad *ton*. They'd even proved it when Miranda jilted him.

The best he could offer Charlotte would be his protection. He'd gladly keep her and love her for all the days of his life.

He just didn't know how she would feel about the idea, but he had an inkling. To even mention such a suggestion would hurt her pride. She would see it as lowering her station.

On the other hand, he could argue with her that being a duke's mistress was far more important than being any other man's wife—

Phillip broke off the thought with a frown. It might be true, but Charlotte would never believe such claptrap He'd have to bring her around to the idea slowly. He'd wait until the best possible moment to make his offer.

And he had to make her love him. To want to be with him in spite of the slight of never being his wife. He had a responsibility to his title. But he couldn't give her up either.

"*Colster,*" her voice said from the fireplace.

He turned from the window and looked at the cold hearth.

"Are you still there?" she whispered.

Phillip walked over to the fireplace, feeling as if the floor tilted right and left. Love was different than he'd imagined. It should have simplified life. It didn't. He now had more worries than ever before.

"I'm here," he said.

"Is something wrong?"

"What makes you think that?"

"Your voice sounds funny."

She was far too astute. A man had to have his wits around his Charlotte. "I've been thinking," he said truthfully.

"About the trial? What is this over, Colster?"

"I don't know. No one has told me anything."

"Colster, I have a request of you." She sounded as if she'd moved closer to the wall separating their two rooms.

He knelt. "What is it?"

"If anything happens to me, please, you must look after my sister Constance."

Constance would be the youngest. He barely remembered meeting her. "Is she in London?"

"No, I sent her to a Madame Lavaliere's boarding school here in Scotland. It's in Ollie's Mill, a village close to Edinburgh."

"Why did you send her all the way up here? We have schools in England."

"Yes, but none would take us. They all feared incurring the Duke of Colster's wrath."

Phillip felt the barb in her voice. "They should have known better. The Duke of Colster isn't that sort of man."

Silence was her response.

"I'm not," he insisted. "I can't help it if people want to believe I am. Why did you send her to school anyway?" he asked, deciding a change of subject would be wiser.

"She needed polish. Mother had drilled us girls on social graces. It had been a game we'd played with her. However, Constance was too young when she died to remember the lessons. If she is going to marry a man of title, she needs some polish."

"What if she doesn't want to change who she is?" he dared to ask.

"She must," Charlotte answered. "I want her to be happy. This is the best for her."

"Are you happy?"

"Surprisingly, yes. Especially right now."

He settled closer to the wall, wanting to ask her what she meant. Wondering if it had anything to do with him.

But their conversation was interrupted by the sound of someone at the door. The key scraped in the lock. Phillip jumped to his feet and faced the door as it opened.

MacKenna walked in.

The proud set of the man's head reminded Phillip of his own father. It was arrogance, he realized, a failing of which he himself was guilty.

The laird looked around the room. "I hope you find your accommodations satisfactory, Your Grace?"

"I'm not accustomed to being a prisoner anywhere," Phillip counted.

MacKenna smiled. "The guard outside your door overheard someone talking." When Phillip didn't answer, he added, "Sound carries in this house. Have you discovered that?"

"I regret to say I haven't had the opportunity," Phillip answered, hoping Charlotte could overhear them and would know to keep silent.

At his silence, MacKenna's head seemed to shrink down in his shoulders. His lips twisted into a mirthless smile. "I've had to wait a long time for this meeting."

"You could have set an appointment with my secretary Freedman. It would have been simpler."

"But less rewarding."

"What reward do you seek?" Phillip asked.

The older man shook his head. "One I fear you would never understand. I look forward to this evening. It has been a long time for my clan. 'Out of the ashes we shall rise victorious,' " he quoted.

"I'm not familiar with the quote."

"It's no quote but a prophecy. It was made by my ancestor as he stood on the gallows and was hanged for treason. A Maddox should have been hanging beside him."

"We had the good sense to leave."

"Or turn traitor."

Phillip dropped all pretense of civility. "What do you want? You are an intelligent man. I can't believe you would bring me up here for some ancient feud. Whatever your reasons or purpose, this is personal."

A gleam of appreciation appeared in MacKenna's beady black eyes. "You're right. My only regret is that your father isn't here to see the price he must pay."

Phillip leaped on the clue. "So this was a matter between you and my father?"

"You will find out at your trial."

"My trial for what?" Phillip demanded.

"For being the son of such an arrogant man as

William Maddox," the laird replied, every word singed with hate. "You are being tried because he's gone from me now but that doesn't mean my revenge won't be just as sweet. After all, you are cut in his image."

"But what do you gain?" Phillip wondered. "What purpose is there? I am not my father."

"No, but you'll do. You'll break the curse my sister has lived under ever since the moment she laid eyes on the man."

"The curse of what?" Phillip pressed.

"Of what your father did to her," MacKenna barked out. He stared as if he could see the words in the air. When he focused on Phillip, he appeared a man possessed.

"Your father ruined her. He used her in the coarsest way and tossed her aside. She was so young and beautiful back then but he broke her." His brogue thickened with each word. "We were schoolmates, and he ridiculed me about his conquest in front of my mates. You see, she'd fallen in love with him. She tumbled into his arms like a silly milkmaid. I warned her to avoid him, but he sought her out."

MacKenna trembled he was so angry. "He used her, Colster, in the worst manner possible— and she allowed it. She thought she loved him. And he was a *duke*. What woman doesn't want to marry a duke?"

Phillip couldn't say anything. His father had been a distant figure in his life. Phillip had always thought it was because of his mother's death . . . now, he had a flash of insight that, perhaps, that had been his father's nature. The only meaningful conversations they'd had dealt with the responsibilities of the title.

"He got her with child," MacKenna said. The flat statement seemed to age him a score of years. "He ruined her."

A child? Phillip braced himself, hesitant, uncertain, as he asked, "What happened then?"

"She lost a bit of her mind. She turned to a witch to help her lose the babe. The spell or potion worked, but left Rowena unable to have children and robbed her of what little sanity she had left." His shoulders sagged as if he carried a great burden. "She had been such a sweet, naïve creature, and your father robbed her of that."

"And is that what I'm on trial for this evening?"

"We'll say it is the feud, but you and I will know different. We'll know the truth."

"The truth?" Phillip challenged. "How can you talk to me about the truth after that trick of a letter you sent?"

MacKenna raised one brow. "Trick?"

"Nanny Frye's letter."

" 'Twas not a trick. It's the truth."

Phillip reeled back.

MacKenna grinned.

"I told you my sister lost her mind a bit. With the help of that same witch, she pretended to be a midwife. They put your mother in labor, and my sister took your brother."

The floor seemed to disappear beneath Phillip's feet. The world, as he knew it, had gone mad.

"I can see you were afraid to believe the letter," MacKenna said, his gaze narrowing shrewdly. "I'd be worried, too, if I knew I stood to lose a dukedom. And what can you do about it, man?" He laughed, obviously enjoying himself. "My sister may be a bit touched in the head, but she exacted a fitting revenge—"

Phillip cut him off by flying the few feet between them and wrapping his hands around the older man's neck. "The letter is true?" he demanded, not only wanting to hear MacKenna's confession again but also wanting to choke the life out of the man. "She *did* steal my brother?"

MacKenna clawed at Phillip's hands, trying to pull them away. Phillip wasn't about to let him go. The two of them staggered around the room, the older man desperate to escape, before strong hands pulled Phillip off of MacKenna.

The guard had overheard. Phillip didn't recognize his guard, but Dougal, the one who had been charged with Charlotte, was with him. Phillip hoped that Charlotte realized here was a chance to escape and struck out to keep the guards as occupied as possible.

He was outnumbered. They quickly subdued him, throwing him none too gently facedown on the floor.

MacKenna gasped for breath, rubbing his throat with his hands. "Get out," he ordered his guards.

The men didn't move immediately, obviously confused by the order.

"Get out, I say," MacKenna repeated and had enough strength shove one toward the door. Dougal and his compatriot left. "Shut the door," MacKenna ordered. They complied.

Once alone, Phillip waited for the laird's next move.

"It was never meant for your mother to die," the laird said. "She was an innocent."

This was not what Phillip had anticipated. He studied MacKenna a moment, and then said, "You knew."

"Well. I was in love with her." All softness left his face. "But she wanted your father. She wanted the *duke*."

"And jilted you," Phillip surmised.

MacKenna held up a hand in protest. "Jilted? No. Only you have had the honor of being jilted,

Your Grace. Your mother didn't even see me. I could dance with her, and she'd not remember my name. I was a Scottish nobody." He smiled, the expression humorless. "That will change. Soon all of Scotland and England will know my name. I shall be known as the Protector. As the one who freed Scotland from the greed of the lords. My name will go down in history." His eyes glowed with a fevered brightness. He did see himself as heroic, and if Phillip didn't stop him, hundreds, maybe thousands would die.

Phillip rose to his feet, convinced MacKenna was mad. "My mother won't know. She died of grief over what she thought was my brother's death."

The laird's eyes saddened. "She did. I told Rowena it was wrong . . . and she said that if your father had been a better man, he would have been there for your births. He would have protected you. She was right."

"My father was an important man who was often called upon to convey the king's business overseas."

"When his wife entered the birthing room to give him an heir, his place was outside her door. He would have recognized Rowena if he'd been there. You can't hold him blameless."

There was truth in his words. Phillip focused on what was important. "Where is my brother?"

"Do you mean where is the *true* Duke of Colster?" MacKenna laughed. "He's where I want him."

Phillip struggled with the urge to throttle the Scotsman again. "I want to meet him."

"You will. Soon enough. But first, we'll have our trial." MacKenna moved toward the door.

"A trial over what?"

"Over your crimes, Your Grace. Over the wrongs that have been done to my people."

"And I'm to answer for all of England?"

MacKenna nodded. "If you are found guilty." He opened the door. "Rest, Your Grace. You will need your strength and your courage."

"Send Miss Cameron away," Phillip said before the laird could leave. "She is not a part of this."

The laird laughed, the sound bitter. "No, she wasn't. If I have ever misjudged anyone, I have misjudged her."

"Why is she even here?" Phillip asked, wanting the answer.

"I liked her. I fancied her. I wanted her here for my moment of triumph. Women have a habit of making fools out of us men, don't they, Your Grace?" On those words, he left the room. The guard shut the door and locked it.

A terrible coldness settled over Phillip. MacKenna was no more right in his head than his sister. If the story in the letter was true, what sort of fate had his brother suffered all these years?

He walked over to the fireplace and knelt. "Charlotte?"

"Yes."

"Did you hear what was said?"

"Very little," she confessed. "Was that MacKenna? What did he say?"

He told her a quick synopsis of what had transpired.

There was a long, thoughtful pause before she said, "Colster, be careful."

"Wiser advice has never been given," he answered, and heard her laugh.

It helped to have her here. Already, he had confided more in her than in any other person in the world. The realization made him think about his father.

When exactly had he become as cold and distant as his sire? Or was it the title that did that? The weight of responsibilities and of expectations?

"What are you thinking?" she asked through the stone.

That it was a relief to finally have someone to confide in, someone to trust. There was strength in Charlotte. True womanly power.

But he'd not tell her such. He already felt vulnerable enough, and that wasn't going to free them of this dilemma. No, he needed to think, and to be ready to act when the time came. He wasn't beaten yet, and MacKenna was about to discover that Phillip could be a formidable opponent.

"My brother is alive," he answered.

"The letter wasn't a fake."

"No."

"What shall we do?"

He liked the way she said the word "we."

"I want you to get some rest," he advised. "I don't know what is planned, but we'd both best have our wits about us."

"And what of you?"

"I have much to do. MacKenna will find me no easy target for his mock trial. I'll defend myself and win. Better yet, I shall find my brother."

"I pray that you do," she answered.

So did he.

Chapter 10

$\mathcal{T}$avis's cottage was attached to his black-smith's forge. Inside, Father Nicholas, a renegade French priest who had escaped the Terror of his homeland decades before, drowsed near the hearth, where a small fire warmed his bones.

Like so many others, Father Nicholas had come to Nathraichean because he had nowhere else to go. No one knew where he'd come from, and he rarely discussed his history.

At one time, he'd counseled Lady Rowena; but she'd turned on him as she did all who served her, with the exception of Moira. Tavis had come upon the priest shivering in his sleep on the ground outside Nathraichean's walls. Everyone else was afraid to take the old man in lest they anger Lady Rowena, but Tavis had felt he had nothing to lose. Moira had left him, and the cottage was too empty and silent without her.

And while age may have clouded the priest's eyesight, it had not touched his mind. He came awake the moment Tavis closed the cottage door. Lifting his head, he asked in French-accented English with just a hint of a brogue, "What is the news? Why did the laird send for you this morning?"

Rubbing a tired hand over his face, Tavis answered, "He had me ride on the search party he sent out for the Maddox. I'm hungry. I've got bread and cheese. Do you want anything?"

"I'm fine," the priest started to answer, and then stopped. "A glass of wine would not be so bad?"

Tavis snorted with friendly disdain. The priest had already uncorked the bottle, and it sat on the table beside two cups. He poured a measure into one cup before turning to the cupboard, where he would slice bread.

Father Nicholas left his chair by the hearth and crossed to the table. He carefully moved his fingers across the wood until his hand found his cup. "Did you find the Maddox?"

"We did. He was in Darry Boden's hayrick with a woman." Tavis poured himself a measure of whiskey that Ragnor MacKenna had given him in exchange for some smithy work. It wasn't the best, but it would do.

"A woman?"

"Aye." Tavis sat down heavily in the chair across the table from the priest's. His cottage was not large but neat and tidy. It had belonged to Moira's father, Angus, the blacksmith the laird had apprenticed Tavis to years ago.

"The laird had invited the lass to be a guest," Tavis said, "but she ran off with the Maddox instead. Guess she fancied a duke. They are all the same," he concluded. "They'd sell a man's soul for money." After all, that was why Moira had left.

She'd wanted to be a fine lady with pearls for her hair, and Bruce could give her those things. The love she and Tavis had once shared had meant nothing.

He drained his glass and would have reached for another but stayed his hand. He'd been drinking too much lately. "Moira wanted to talk to me today."

The priest set down his glass. "For what reason? What has it been—close to a year since she has spoken to you?"

"Eighteen months since she walked out my door . . . but who is counting?" he added with wry self-derision.

Father Nicholas smiled his understanding, but Tavis stood, suddenly on edge. It was as if someone ran the tip of a knife down the back of his neck. This niggling sense that something was not quite right had been with him all day. He shifted his weight, taking an anxious step right before turning left. He'd had this feeling once before— the day Moira had left.

However, this time, it was much stronger.

"What is it, my son?" Father Nicholas asked. "Sit down. Relax. You've worked hard this day."

Tavis noticed his leather apron tossed over a chair by the hearth. He'd been on his way out the door to his forge when the messenger had arrived with the news the laird wished his presence.

He hated that apron and all it represented. His soul longed to be free of the forge and fire.

"I had a taste of something today," he confessed. "Of something I've wanted for a long time. I liked riding with them, Father. I liked being one of the warriors——even if they made me ride Butter and do all the grunt work."

It had felt as if he should have been one of their number all his life.

"Of course, I may have botched my chance to ever do it again."

"What happened?" Father Nicholas asked.

"I confronted Bruce." Tavis told him the story. "Being dragged all the way to Nathraichean would have killed the man. Of course, Bruce is angry. I humiliated him."

"Are you sorry?"

"No," Tavis answered stoutly. "The man took my wife. The laird bought my divorce. He paid for it with his own coin because he favors that worthless sow Bruce. But matters will be different in the future. I shall not be so gullible." He clenched and released his fists at his side. "Not now that you have taught me to read—"

"You were a very apt pupil," Father Nicholas demurred. "It was an easy matter. I was surprised how quick your mind is."

"Why? Because I am nothing but a smithy. I learned quickly. I've always learned quickly, but I've naught had the chance. And now, perhaps, I can win Moira back. Perhaps now, she will see that I'm every lick as good as that bastard Bruce."

"*Mon fils*, she betrayed you."

Tavis's chest tightened. "She was lured away with pretty things. If she wasn't so pretty herself, Bruce would never have looked at her."

The priest shook his head. "You forgive too easily. Bruce could not have persuaded her if she had not been willing."

"I'll win her back." Tavis looked around at his cottage's humble furnishings. It all appeared so poor now when, in truth, there had been a time when he'd thought himself the richest of men—because he'd had Moira. They'd known each other since childhood. He'd always loved her.

Father Nicholas leaned forward. "Do not be blind."

"I know they were lovers," Tavis answered, waving him away as if he could make any protests disappear. "But that was Bruce's fault. Moira is too sweet to understand such evil."

"No, she just cuckolded you."

The words were damning in their truth. They ripped Tavis's breath from his body. "No one has dared speak to me thus—"

"I say what is whispered behind your back," Father Nicholas said calmly. "Sometimes a man needs to hear it."

Tavis's response was to bring his fist down on the table in a rare show of temper. The tabletop caved in; the wine bottle went flying.

For a second, Tavis stared at the damaged table. He never gave free rein to his anger. Orphans learned to keep their feelings close.

The priest was unimpressed. "So you have a temper, *mon fils*. No one questions that. We question your wisdom—"

"Temper?" Tavis shook his head. "I have a *rage* inside of me, Father. There are times since the laird and Bruce took Moira away from me that I could have torn down this whole fortress with my bare hands. They had no right to take a man's wife. Not *my* wife. She was all I had."

"She left willingly."

Truth made his words cruel.

Tavis didn't stay to hear more. He picked up his leather apron. "I've got work to do." He slammed his way out of the cottage.

Work waited for him at the forge. He stoked the fire. The flames leaped to life. He envied them their freedom.

Angrily, he picked up the tongs and used them to shove a bent plow blade into the fire. He'd pound that blade into submission. He'd mold it back into something useful.

He just wished he could do the same for himself.

The blade reminded him of the time Lady Rowena had attacked him with the garden hoe.

He'd been a lad of no more than six and already living under Angus's roof. He'd been sent on an errand but had met some boys who wanted him to play a hiding game with them. The temptation to join them had been powerful. He'd been anxious to set aside the errand and searched for a good hiding spot. He found it in the laird's garden—and that was his first memory of Lady Rowena.

She'd been the one to ensure he knew he was an outsider.

Lady Rowena wasn't a true lady. The title was a pet name from her childhood. They said she'd insisted on keeping it. As she'd grown more troubled in life, the courtesy title seemed to give her comfort.

The child Tavis hadn't known any of this. He'd seen her from afar, of course, on holy and fair days, but he was stunned by her beauty upon seeing her so close.

She had golden hair and eyes that mirrored both the sky and the sea, a blue-green the likes of which he'd never seen. She wandered amongst the flowers and the shrubs designed for her pleasure and stepped close to where he hid beneath some bushes close to a hole in the garden wall. She was singing, the sound high-pitched and nonsensical but Tavis had liked it—until he made a sound.

She caught him spying on her. Her beautiful eyes had gone wide and wild. She'd started pulling at her hair and calling him names. He'd been too frightened to run, certain he would be in trouble no matter what he did. But he took off as fast as he could when she picked up a garden hoe. She swung it at him, calling him the "Devil child."

Her aim was true, and she'd hit him on the temple, but Tavis had kept running. It wasn't the blood from the cut on his face that had scared him as much as the expression on hers.

He'd avoided her after that. She'd calmed down some over the years but then, few saw her, and when they did, it was like today, only for a wee bit, and she didn't seem to recognize him.

However, Tavis had learned an important lesson that day. He didn't stray from his errands ever again, and he kept quiet. Nathraichean was the only home he'd known. There was no place else for him, especially if what Lady Rowena had said was true and he was the Devil's child.

He pulled the plow out of the fire and carried it with the tongs to the anvil.

The Devil's child.

The reason he had let the laird arrange a divorce was because he'd been afraid to leave.

Now, he wished he had. He wished he'd taken Moira, kicking and screaming if need be, away from here. Having her for a wife had been the only good thing that had ever happened to him.

And he hated knowing Father Nicholas and the rest of the clan were right. He hated knowing that she had *willingly* left him.

"Hey!" The boy's shout startled Tavis from his dark thoughts.

He turned and was so surprised to see Ian Munro standing there, he almost dropped his hammer.

"I didn't mean to startle you, Tavis," Ian apologized. "I thought you saw me approach, but you didn't say anything."

"I was woolgathering," Tavis admitted. He

liked Ian. The lad was all of thirteen, skinny as a pole, with a pinched face and a thatch of red hair on his head. He was also the man of his family. They'd once lived on Sutherland land. The *Duke* of Sutherland, a man who spent most of his time in London . . . just like the Maddox . . . and had tossed aside his responsibilities as chieftain of his clan in return for profit. He was one of the strongest supporters of the Clearances and probably never lost a wink of sleep while families lost their homes.

Ian's father had died trying to protect the family's home after the troops had set fire to it. The lad's mother was not faring well. She was heavy with child, her sixth, and Tavis had overheard gossip that she might not last through this pregnancy. "What is it, Ian?"

The boy held a sickle with a twisted blade and a broken point in his hand. It was dull with rust so had been out in the elements for some time. "I found this. Someone threw it aside. Can you fix it, Tavis?"

Tavis examined the tool. He understood what a good find this was for the boy. Those burned out by the Clearances escaped with little more than the clothes on their backs. With a sickle, Ian could help cut hay and earn food for his family.

Of course, there was a reason this one had

been tossed aside. To fix it would mean creating a new one.

Tavis looked at the boy, and said, "You know I can. It will be better than new when I'm done."

His expression determined, Ian said, "I can pay you when I get work."

Tavis shook his head. "Pay me? For this little bit? Why, I'd feel a scoundrel for taking money for doing nothing more than pounding the rust off and doing a bit of straightening."

Ian's face relaxed at his good fortune. "Will it take long? I can help the others on the morrow if I have my own tool."

"I'll have it done in an hour."

The boy was so happy he would have jumped up and down—except he wasn't a boy. Not any longer. He was a man. Careful to contain his enthusiasm, he said, "I'd been to the other smithies, and they said they'd have to make new."

"You should have come to me first," Tavis told him. "That's why I'm the best."

"You are," Ian agreed. "I feared you'd be too much for me. Thank you, Tavis. Thank you very much."

"Go on with you. I'll see you in an hour."

Ian ran off, but when he thought he'd gone around the corner and Tavis couldn't see him, he jumped in the air, punching it with one fist.

And Tavis felt like a hero.

Father Nicholas had come out of the cottage and now came up behind. "You can't keep giving your work away for free." This was an old argument between them.

"I thought you all had taken a vow of poverty," Tavis answered.

"Yes, but *you* haven't. And I prefer a full belly." Father Nicholas laughed at his own humor and sat in a chair beside the forge. "Are you still angry with me?" he asked.

"'Tis not you I'm angry at," Tavis said, putting the plow blade aside and setting to work on the sickle, "but myself." A new thought struck him. "The laird is going to make the Maddox stand trial this night."

Father Nicholas frowned. He didn't like these "trials" the laird liked to hold. He said they had nothing to do with a court of law. They were more for MacKenna's ego. Usually the clan gathered to listen while the laird lectured. The evening would end with the defendant being lashed.

Many enjoyed these events. Tavis and the priest did not. "He wishes me to stand by his side this evening," Tavis said.

"Why would he do that?" the priest asked, as surprised as Tavis had been by the request.

"To irritate Bruce, I imagine. Ever since Gordon has arrived, Bruce cannot be certain he will be laird."

But the priest wasn't interested in the struggle between Gordon and Bruce. Instead, he surprised Tavis by asking, "What did you think of the Maddox? As a man?"

The picture of the Sassenach's stubborn pride rose in Tavis's mind. Something about him made Tavis uncomfortable.

"Well?" Father Nicholas prompted.

"I didn't like him." He pulled the sickle blade from the fire and began pounding the hot metal, an effective way to end that topic of conversation.

A moment later, knowing he was being ignored, the priest rose from his chair and went inside.

"Would your brother look exactly like you if he were your twin?" Charlotte asked from her side of the wall.

Darkness was only an hour or two away.

She'd let Phillip work but now, she wanted these moments to talk to him. And he was willing as well.

"I don't know," Phillip answered. "Some twins don't look anything alike. And the MacKenna clan seems to have an aversion for the razor."

She smiled in agreement, then asked seriously, "But isn't there some sort of connection between twins? If he was physically close, wouldn't you feel drawn toward him?"

"Like a magnetized rod?"

"Or brothers."

Colster was silent a moment. "I don't know . . . and I feel like an idiot for having to admit it. I've always been confident of what I should do in any circumstance, until now. Charlotte, if Justin and I ever meet, he would have every right to hate me. *Justin.* He probably doesn't even know his Christian name, let alone he was born a duke. Who knows what MacKenna may have done to him?"

"None of this was your fault. *Or* his."

"And yet *we've* paid a price. That is, if it is true. This could be another of MacKenna's tricks."

"You have to believe it isn't, Your Grace," she answered.

"I *want* to believe it isn't," he confessed. "I want him to be alive." He paused, and then added, "And stop calling me 'Your Grace.' There's been too much between us, Charlotte. Besides, if Justin is alive, then I must become accustomed to not hearing 'Your Grace.'"

"Can you?" The idea was intriguing. Most men held on to what they possessed.

"I *will.*"

She heard the steel in his voice. It made her smile because *that* was the man she knew . . . although her opinion of him had changed drastically over the last two days. He was far more companionable and honest than she'd ever imagined he would be. He was as mortal as the next, perhaps more so because of the weight of the title. He was not allowed to make errors. Not with everyone watching his every move.

"Phillip," he said.

"What?" she asked, mystified.

"My name is Phillip. Say it. Let me hear it from your lips."

His voice had dropped to a more intimate tone. Heat rushed to her cheeks and belly as she whispered, "Phillip."

"Phillip and Charlotte," he said from the other side of his wall.

Phillip and Charlotte.

If she had paper and pen, she'd write it down, wanting to see the names in physical form.

"Charlotte, are you there?"

She placed a hand on her belly, warning herself not to be giddy. "Yes, I am . . . *Phillip.*" She liked the name.

"I need for you to know, I'm sorry—" His voice broke off. She leaned closer to the stone.

"Phillip?"

He didn't answer, but then she overheard male voices, too far away to be distinct.

They'd come for him.

She stood, wanting to stop them from taking him. Her door remained closed. She waited. Minutes passed. No one came. It was as if everyone in the world had disappeared and left her alone.

But MacKenna wouldn't do that. Sooner or later, he would come for her. She'd crossed him, and she felt she knew enough of his character to believe such a slight would not go unpunished.

The hour was growing late. The sky was turning soft shades of pinks and purple.

If the laird of Nathraichean thought she would be a docile captive, he was wrong. She wasn't going to shirk or beg. She was the Duke of Colster's woman. Charlotte and Phillip.

Charlotte had on a serviceable day dress. It had seemed a sensible thing to wear considering the circumstances. However, her mind had changed.

She crossed to the dressing screen where her meager wardrobe was hanging and reached for a soft blue India muslin trimmed in gilt spangles. She had satin slippers to match. Her plan had been to wear this ensemble to impress Laird MacKenna.

Now, she would wear it to prove she wasn't afraid of him.

For once, her hair cooperated, and she styled it high on her head with a sapphire blue ribbon woven through it. When she was done, the mirror over the washbasin showed she looked her best. A calmness settled over her. A sense of purpose, of destiny. She sat on the edge of the bed and waited to be summoned—and then remembered

Nanny Frye's letter and Phillip's coin purse in the hidden pocket of her skirts. They were both still there.

There was no pocket in the blue muslin. Charlotte searched through her belongings until she find the small purse designed for evening. It had a long, golden silk cord. She poured the coins out of Phillip's purse into her own. He had four guineas, more than enough to take them where they needed to go at the moment. She folded them in Nanny Frye's letter, and then put the purse around her neck, tucking it beneath her gown for safety. It made a strange necklace, but she doubted if anyone would notice.

At last, she was prepared to wait.

Shortly after sunset, a knock sounded on the door. "Yes?" she answered.

The door opened, and Gordon Lachlan entered, flanked by two guards. His sharp gaze flicked over her evening finery and his brows lifted in surprise. There was a note of respect in his crisp, musical brogue as he said, "Miss Cameron, are you ready to go downstairs?"

"I am, sir."

"Then, please come this way."

Charlotte stood and moved forward. She feared for herself; she feared for Colster. But she was ready to do battle.

Chapter 11

*T*he laird enjoyed ceremony. It was a testimony to his growing power and stature amongst the Scots, and he used it well, or so Tavis thought.

For this evening, Laird MacKenna had ordered a platform built beneath a silk canopy of green and gold. What seemed to be a thousand torches lit the night. They were all around the marching green, which could hold five hundred spectators or more.

It was crowded to capacity tonight. No one wanted to miss what the laird kept referring to as the "trial" of not only one of the despised Maddox . . . but of an English noble with Scottish roots. A noble who was like the other greedy bastards who had burned them out of their homes.

These were people who valued the old ways when the chieftain of the clan, be he duke or laird, took care of them. Times when they all had known they'd have roofs over their heads because they lived in the same cottages their fathers and their fathers' fathers had lived.

The Clearances had changed all that. Lives had been destroyed, and there was fear they would never recover. These people had come to Laird MacKenna because they wanted justice—and tonight, they may receive it . . . or some measure of it. For that reason alone, they wore MacKenna colors.

Tavis understood their anger. He hated feeling powerless and, like them, would have done anything he could to have his old life back. Of course, he never would have questioned his lot in life if the laird had not made him divorce Moira. There was anger in him. He felt betrayed.

And it gave him great pleasure to be standing on the platform beneath the silk canopy when Bruce moved to take his place.

"What are you doing here, Tavis? Go stand with the crowd."

Before Tavis could answer, Gordon came up behind them, and in his quiet voice said, "The laird wants him here."

Bruce turned, irritated as always to have Gordon interfere. Both were forceful leaders. Both were tested every day by the laird. Both wanted to succeed him.

If Bruce was named heir, Tavis *would* leave.

He'd not think twice. He had his trade, and he had his pride.

But he wanted to take Moira with him.

Bruce's piggy eyes narrowed. "You've come into favor lately with the laird," he observed to Tavis. "But I have no doubt you won't disappoint him . . . just like you did your wife."

Tavis took a step forward, ready to wipe the ground with the man, but Gordon stepped between them. He placed a warning hand on Tavis's arm. "Ignore him," he advised.

"It's bloody hard when the man sleeps with your wife," Tavis answered.

"She's not yours," Gordon said. "Not any longer." He pulled Tavis away from Bruce, taking him off the platform to a quiet corner. "I can imagine how you feel. However, the laird has confided in me that he has plans for you. Our cause is growing, Tavis. Every day, more and more men come to our banner. I've talked to the laird. He's pleased with your sword training—"

"He knows?"

"It isn't easy to hide a big hulk like you doing anything, let alone working with weapons. Aye, he and I have both seen you practicing before dawn. You have a natural gift. He is pleased. He wanted me to tell you that."

The laird had seen him? He'd sent Gordon to tell him?

"I want to become one of the warriors, Gordon," Tavis said, daring to voice aloud his deepest dream.

Gordon didn't laugh. Instead, Tavis read approval in the man's eye. "Good. I expect you to ride beside me when we take on the English and reclaim our land. We are going to chase them out, Tavis. Every one of those who betrayed their own kind. They shall pay." He held out his hand, an invitation for Tavis to join in not as a crofter but as an equal.

Tavis clasped Gordon's hand firmly in his own. "I'm your man."

"I know," Gordon answered, "and proud I am to have you, Tavis."

The laird climbed on the platform just then. The two men broke apart and turned in respect. The laird nodded to them as if he knew what they'd been discussing. It made Tavis feel important.

The MacKenna walked to the front of the platform. The crowd had quieted at his first appearance, but when he raised his hand in greeting, they gave a great shout. He signaled Dougal and Wills, who escorted Miss Cameron, the Maddox's woman, onto the platform. Tavis and Gordon had to step back to make room for her. Bruce was on the MacKenna's other side.

Miss Cameron was a lovely woman, and a fitting mate for any warrior. Her spirit told Tavis that the Maddox was not some cosseted noble. She had not gone off into a fit of hysterics when captured and even now appeared as regal as a queen.

For the briefest moment, their gazes met, and she stopped so abruptly Dougal almost bumped into her. Her eyes widened in disbelief. She took a step toward Tavis, her lips mouthing a name.

Dougal, thinking she may be attempting an escape, blocked her way with his arm. She frowned at the arm, and then looked up at the guard as if surprised to find him there, before turning back to Tavis.

The laird saw all of this. "Tavis, step back," he ordered, moving forward to take Miss Cameron's arm. "Come," he ordered.

She stared at Tavis, and then shook her head as if dismissing something from her own mind.

"I believe our blacksmith is frightening Miss Cameron," the laird said to everyone gathered close enough to hear. They laughed.

Her brows came together, and she lowered her head.

The door to the main house opened again, and Tavis dismissed Miss Cameron from his mind as Moira and two maids led Lady Rowena out of the house.

Lady Rowena had never married—nor seemed as if she wished to. Everyone knew that she'd suffered an "unfortunate tragedy" in her youth, but no one, to Tavis's knowledge, knew what her misfortune had been. Over the years, her mind had deteriorated. One day her wits could be sharp, her memory intact, and in the next, she would not even remember her brother's name.

It made no matter. The laird was devoted to his sister. Now, he directed her to a chair beside his.

Tavis waited for Moira to notice him. She was unusually lovely tonight in a gown of green trimmed in lace. The wind caught tendrils of her hair, which was held back in a gold-and-jeweled band.

Her first action was to smile at her new husband—but then she caught sight of Tavis standing beside Gordon. The corners of her mouth tightened in disapproval.

The solemn wail of a piper cut the air, calling those gathered to attention. The crowd quieted.

The doors to the house opened again, and Tavis turned with everyone else. He expected to see the Maddox led out. Instead, John Rae, one of the laird's closest confidants, stepped out onto the step holding high with both hands the weapon known as the Sword of the MacKenna.

Torchlight caught the sword's golden scabbard as Rae walked past the platform to take a place on the ground in front of the laird. Tavis, like everyone else, was in awe of this weapon. He'd held it once, years ago when it had been bought to his late father-in-law Angus for repair. It was perfectly balanced, a piece of craftsmanship like no other.

This had led MacKenna men into battle since time remembered. Few had ever seen it, but every lad from the age of three and up knew of its handle covered in scarlet leather and hilt set with rubies.

Solemnly, Rae bowed to the laird, who nodded in return before raising his hand, a signal for the drummers to start.

Again, the doors to the house opened. Two of the McKenna's strongest men marched out, with the Maddox between them. He carried himself well. Like Tavis, he was a tall man although not as muscular. He wore the shirt, breeches, and boots he'd been captured wearing. A beard shadowed his jaw, but his head was high, the set of his shoulders straight. In spite of his hands being tied together in front, he appeared every inch a duke.

As the piper joined the drummers, the crowd erupted into hoots and challenges of the sort any good Scot would use against an enemy as the Maddox was marched to the front of the platform and a position to the right of John Rae. The duke took it all in stride. He surveyed them coolly, showing no fear.

"You know, Tavis, he looks enough like you to be your brother," Gordon whispered as if surprised.

Tavis frowned. He saw no resemblance.

And then he felt Miss Cameron staring at him. He turned and frowned his displeasure, but she didn't look away. Instead, her eyes slid back to the duke . . . and he knew she was drawing comparisons. Was that the reason she'd acted so surprised earlier?

Every fiber of his being rejected any comparison between himself and the dreaded enemy of the clan.

Laird MacKenna lifted his hand, and the music stopped, the last note of the bagpipes drifting around them.

In a ringing voice, he said, "Phillip Maddox, Duke of Colster, you have been charged with crimes against Scotland. You have betrayed your heritage and your country. You have stolen the lands of honest folk and burned their houses. How say you?"

"Not guilty," the Maddox answered, his voice calm and sure.

In answer, the crowd hooted their opinions.

Tavis had to admire the duke. The laird enjoyed holding these "courts." Many a man had broken down crying at this moment, afraid for his own life and with good reason. In Nathraichean, Laird

MacKenna was the law. He held more power than the king, and no one would gainsay him. Few in Britain cared about the comings and goings of this distant part of Scotland.

Of course, if they had, the laird could not have built his army. He was often fond of saying that someday, all of Britain would know the name MacKenna—and Tavis believed it would be so.

But the Duke of Colster was not like the laird's usually frightened victims. With a spirit that was admirable, he said, "In fact, I *welcome* a trial. The time has come for us to speak as men about the problems our great country. If you have a complaint, you don't take the law into your own hands. You carry it to London. You carry to the king."

"The king won't hear us!" a man shouted from the crowd. "He only listens to his lords."

"The MacKenna is *our* king," another threw out, and his words were quickly seconded.

"Then try and be damned," the Maddox answered. "But know that the eyes of God are watching here. That Justice exacts a price on those who are cowardly."

His was the sort of bravado the Scots liked, and Tavis noticed it had no small impact. Many yelled what they thought should be done with the duke, but others were impressed.

"And try me, too," Miss Cameron declared

suddenly. She shoved Dougal aside to say to the people, "His Grace is innocent of all those charges, and you all know it."

The duke turned to her, shaking his head. "Charlotte, no—"

"*Yes*," she answered, cutting him off. "I can't stand to watch this mockery of a trial without speaking out."

Laird MacKenna stood. "Silence, Miss Cameron, or I shall have you carried away, forcibly if I must."

The duke immediately seized the moment to be contrary. "She has the right to be heard," he said. "Or do you censure that, too?" He turned to the crowd. "You've put yourselves in the hands of a tyrant. He's preparing for a very foolish and costly war. Do you not see that? Do you not fear for your children and their futures?"

The laird, too, addressed the crowd. "You came to me because there was no one else. 'Those who have great power have an obligation to see to the welfare of the less fortunate,'" he quoted. "Do you know those words, Your Grace."

The duke frowned. "Those are my words."

"Yes, you gave a speech I had the privilege of hearing. When I returned to Nathraichean, over five hundred of these people had arrived at my gates. They'd lost their homes, their livelihoods, and their dignity—all while *you* were making a pretty speech. Tell us, Your Grace, you are one of those in power. Have you seen to the welfare of those less fortunate?"

Soberly, the duke said, "My estates are well taken care of—"

"That is not enough," the laird said. "You've had opportunity to address the Scottish question, haven't you, Your Grace? It has been brought up in the House of Lords. What was your response?"

For a moment there was silence, and then the duke answered, "I don't recall."

"Of course not," the laird said, his disdain clear. He turned to his audience. "I spoke. I took our cause to the House of Commons. Only five men cared enough to attend and hear what I had to say. After all, who was it but some 'farmer'? That's what they called me, clansmen. I was introduced as a farmer from the north, and the five in attendance fell asleep. I spoke of children with no food in their bellies, and *they*"—he swept a hand to include the duke—"slept."

The laird paused to ensure everyone was with him. He was a dramatic speaker and not a soul moved as he looked down, and asked, "Your Grace, Duke of Colster, have you ever been so hungry that your stomach is cramped from it?"

The duke didn't answer. There was no purpose to it.

But he appeared surprised when the laird

continued, "When only last week, you were challenged by one of your peers to end the Clearances, what was your response, Your Grace?"

The lines of the duke's face tightened as if he were surprised by how specific the laird was in his charges. In a quieter voice, he said, "I said that Parliament must not tell individual landowners what they can and cannot do with their property." He faced the crowd, unafraid to plead his case to them. "What belongs to a man is rightfully his. If Parliament can take what they wish when they wish it, then all property rights are no longer sacred."

The silence from the people as they listened was deafening. They shared the laird's opinion. They were the ones who had been betrayed when the old way gave over to the new.

Laird MacKenna turned and looked at his sister and smiled. She sat with her hands folded in her lap, her expression one of concentration. He turned back to his people. Quietly he asked, "What do we say to those who believe their power gives them right?"

The crowd burst out in angry cries.

"Is he guilty?" the laird asked.

"Yes," the people roared back.

One man shouted, "Let us send a message to London they can't sleep through this time."

The laird raised his hands. "Then let me pass sentence—"

The Maddox whirled around forward, his eyes bright with anger. "You can't pass sentence on such flimsy nonsense," he charged before being roughly pushed back by his guard. "This is no courtroom. No meaningful evidence has been given against me."

"You are right, Your Grace," Laird MacKenna answered. "At last, you understand. Here, the king's rules hold no importance. It's *my* will that is obeyed."

"To say such is *treason*," the duke shot back, "and decries the rule of law and God."

At that moment, Lady Rowena stood from her chair and came to stand beside her brother. *"Yes,"* she said, "the judgment should be from God. *Judicium Dei.*"

The Maddox didn't understand immediately but those of Clan MacKenna did. They gave out a shout of approval and began chanting, *"Judicium Dei."*

The laird let them go on a moment before stopping them. "Do you understand what my sister has called for, Your Grace?"

"Judicium Dei?" the Maddox repeated, still confused. "The judgment of God. The medieval term is *Wager of Battel*?"

"Very good," the laird answered. "Your education in the law serves you well. Do you understand what it is?"

"A fight to the death," the Maddox said.

"Aye, where God decides the victor. Let Him who is Almighty pass His judgment through a fight between two warriors—your clan and ours—to the death."

There wasn't anyone hearing his sentence who wasn't amazed. Even John Rae appeared surprised to learn the reason he had carried out the sword.

"This is barbaric," the duke protested. "I have no desire to fight anyone. Especially with broadswords."

"A duel is always the way to settle a matter between gentlemen," the laird answered.

"This is not a duel," the duke answered. "What you want is an execution."

The laird didn't deny his words. Instead, he smiled and said, "Prepare to defend yourself, Your Grace. Untie him, Ian, and offer him your sword," he instructed one of the duke's guards.

"No," Miss Cameron cried, but she was quickly shoved aside by Dougal, and no one paid attention to her after that. The crowd was too busy spreading the word amongst themselves of what was about to happen. People began pushing for a good view of the action.

Lady Rowena placed her hand in the crook of her brother's arm, silent tears running down her face. He patted it. "I promised you justice. I said one day, he would pay. Choose your champion, Sister." Only those on the platform could hear what he'd said.

"This isn't justice, MacKenna, but a vendetta," the duke accused, shouting to be heard over the excited babble of the crowd. "It has nothing to do with people's homes or starving children."

"On the contrary, Your Grace, it has a great deal more than you can imagine to do with those matters," the laird answered. "John, bring the Sword of the MacKenna forward. My sister is to choose who shall fight for our clan's honor."

The crowd went quiet, waiting to see whom she would choose. Tavis didn't understand any of this. The laird was a student of medieval architecture and customs, Nathraichean's design was a testimony to that, but he had never invoked *Judicium Dei* before—although he'd long had a fascination with it.

Tavis had the niggling thought that the Duke of Colster's accusations could be true.

While John held the scabbard, Lady Rowena drew the sword out. It made no sound as it slid from its golden sheath. She raised it high so that sharp, wicked blade could catch the torchlight.

Any man claiming to love Scotland could not help but be affected by the sight of the lady and the sword.

She looked around.

Bruce stepped forward. "I shall fight."

"And I," Gordon quickly offered.

The other warriors straightened, ready to defend their clan and Scotland.

But Lady Rowena refused to consider them. Instead, she moved with stately grace along the front of the platform. She turned, and her gaze landed on Tavis, standing not far from her on the dais.

She approached him with the sword. "You, Tavis. Will you be my champion?"

Tavis was stunned. She smiled. Her eyes were clear and her brow unworried. "I need a warrior," she said. "You are the only one who will do."

He dropped his gaze to the sword hilt she offered, aware that all watched. This was the moment of his dreams—however, the duke was right. The laird didn't want a fight, he wanted an execution . . . and Tavis didn't know if he had the skill or the nerve to kill another. Not in this manner.

The crowd had started shouting his name, over and over, growing louder with each repetition.

Tavis looked around, stunned to be, at last, the center of so much attention.

And then he saw Moira standing not far beyond Lady Rowena. Even *she* repeated his name.

He took the sword.

Chapter 12

The blacksmith? They wanted him to fight the blacksmith?

This didn't make sense to Phillip.

He shook his head. Like any gentleman, he had trained with swords. He'd even played around with broadswords, although he had no desire to do battle with them.

But expecting him to fight the blacksmith was ridiculous. Phillip would kill the man, and he'd not have that on his conscience—especially since the blacksmith had saved his life. He ignored the sword his guard, Ian, held out to him, more worried about what was happening to Charlotte than his own life.

"I'll not fight," he shouted. "This is mockery of justice. It's barbaric."

"Barbaric?" MacKenna questioned. He looked around at his people. "This is how *they* think of

us. There is no justice to them, save for *their* justice." To Phillip he said, "This is our custom for solving disputes. Our way, Englishman. You fight, or you die."

His words whipped the people into a frenzy. "Fight or die," the crowd shouted, and Phillip realized he had no choice. Tavis stepped off the platform, the man's earlier reluctance having disappeared. He whipped the air with his weapon, and the Sword of the MacKenna seemed to sing.

Ian shoved the blade of his sword into the ground at Phillip's feet and backed away to join the others forming a ring around the two would-be combatants.

Phillip looked to Lady Rowena on the platform. Her eyes were bright, her fingers curled like claws as if she were a hawk ready to pounce on her prey and appearing more animated by the second. It was as if she'd waited for this moment. Plotted for it. He curled his fingers into his palms, refusing to touch the weapon—

"Take up the sword," Tavis ordered, his own strain over the situation etching his voice. "Pick it up."

Phillip shook his head. "I won't kill an innocent man."

"Strike him down," MacKenna ordered.

Tavis raised his sword and pressed the tip

under Phillip's chin. In one smooth movement, he could slice Phillip's throat open.

Charlotte's voice cut through the air. She'd managed to free herself and was running to the edge of the platform. "No, Tavis, *don't*. He is your brother! Do not kill him—"

Laird MacKenna whirled and savagely backhanded her across the face. She went flying across the stage to land on her side on the ground. She didn't move.

Phillip would not fight for himself—but he would fight for Charlotte.

He'd murder MacKenna with his bare hands. "Get out of my way," he ordered the damn blacksmith.

"Fight," the man said.

Phillip's temper snapped. "Fool." Raising his voice, he announced, "I'll fight, and when I'm done, I'm coming for you, MacKenna. I'll send your black heart to hell." No one struck his woman.

In one fluid movement, he wrapped his hand around the hilt of his sword and brought it up to cleave Tavis in two.

But the blacksmith was lighter on his feet than one would have thought. His shirt was ripped clean open, and the crowd gasped but Phillip could barely see or hear anything in the haze of his temper. He had to get to Charlotte.

* * *

Tavis knew his advantages. He was about the same height as the Maddox but far stronger. Even as the point of the Sassenach's weapon sliced his shirt, he brought his own up with a twist of his wrist, almost flipping the Maddox's sword from his hand.

A flicker of disbelief appeared in his opponent's eye. Tavis used that momentary surprise to attack. His blade should have run his opponent through. It didn't.

The Maddox seemed to anticipate his move and leaned to the left. Tavis's sword harmlessly stabbed air, bypassing the other's body by a hairbreadth.

The thrust also brought Tavis in close to the fight, and the duke used it to his advantage. A warning flickered through Tavis a beat before the Maddox buried his fist in his gut.

This duke was no soft nobleman.

And he was stronger than he appeared.

His fist would have doubled over a lesser man than Tavis. But it wasn't the fist Tavis had to watch out for but the elbow to the chin.

A flash of lightning went through his brain. He stumbled back, but the punches cleared his mind. He understood this sort of fighting. Their duel would be no genteel meeting but a battle of bruisers, and let the best man win.

However, the Maddox didn't want to stay and fight. He started toward the platform, turning his back completely upon Tavis.

Certain he was going after the laird, Tavis reached out and grabbed a handful of the Maddox's shirt. The man turned, bringing his sword down toward Tavis.

Steel met steel. Once, twice, three times the air rang with the clash of metal. The duke's blows reverberated with enough force to make Tavis's arm ache. Tavis answered back in kind.

Whoever said the English were weak were wrong.

Then again, Tavis fought well, too. He managed to stay between the duke and the laird so that Maddox had no choice but to fight.

The tactic made the duke angry. He wanted Tavis out of the way, something that Tavis not only sensed, but seemed to experience. It was as if he could feel his opponent's frustration.

If the Maddox feinted left, Tavis had already anticipated the move. If he went to thrust, Tavis knew to step back.

And the same could be said in return. Time and again the duke responded to Tavis's attack almost before Tavis made the move himself.

At one point in the fight, Tavis thought he had him. He found an opening and swung hard. His opponent surprised him by dropping to the ground and somersaulting like an acrobat at the fair back onto his feet.

The crowd gasped in approval. Some even clapped.

Tavis was stunned.

He'd *known* that was what the Maddox was going to do. In his mind's eye, he had imagined it and even felt his own body tense in preparation.

Something was not right. There was a force here he couldn't understand. It was in the velvet of the night air and the dancing flames of the torches.

Gone was any pretense of the art of swordplay. They hacked away at each other, each blow stronger than the last. The minutes dragged on. Both dripped with sweat, and their breathing grew labored with the exertion. They no longer were aware of anything other than themselves. The crowd, even the laird, no longer held importance.

Up and down along the parade ground they battled. Tavis's arm was numb with exhaustion, and still they fought. This was not like any of the other contests Tavis had witnessed—this was a brawl for survival. By the time this contest was over, only one would be a victor. The other would be dead.

And then Tavis felt himself trip. The crowd had not backed away quickly enough, and he'd stumbled over someone's big foot.

It was a stupid mistake. His feet tumbled over each other. He lost his balance. His guard came down—and the Maddox shoved him to the ground. The Sword of the MacKenna went flying from his fingers.

Tavis reached out, wanting it back. His hand grasped its hilt as he turned to face the Maddox who stood over him with his sword raised, ready to be dropped in a death blow.

Beneath Tavis was cool spring grass. Above him the heavens and the stars that held answers to questions he'd long asked.

In the end, it was not such a bad night to die.

The moment Tavis went down and Phillip raised his sword was electrifying. It was as if the world had come to stop—but not for Charlotte.

She'd regained her senses. Like the others, she'd watched the battle between the two men with a fascinated intensity.

However, this moment broke through the haze in her head. These men weren't two strangers. They were *brothers*.

She'd noticed the resemblance, although it was more than the beard that distinguished the two men in looks. No, Phillip and Justin were not identical twins, but there was a very strong connection nonetheless. It had been the glance that Justin/Tavis had given to her in passing, a look so completely Phillip, it had caught her by surprise.

And now, Phillip was about to kill his brother. His sword was raised, and yet he did not move, his expression uncertain.

Perhaps he'd realized . . . ?

Charlotte started toward the front of the platform just as Justin's fingers found the hilt of the Sword of the MacKenna. He raised the weapon. Phillip was wide open to a mortal blow. She drew up short, certain she would witness his death.

And yet, neither moved. The two men stared at each other in apparent surprise. It was as if they *knew*.

Lady Rowena went frantic. She screamed, *"Kill him."*

Neither swordsman moved.

She turned to Laird MacKenna, who appeared as fascinated with the battle as everyone else. "Make them die, brother," she demanded. "Make them kill each other."

And Charlotte had her proof. Her imagination had not played her false. She raced down the platform steps and placed herself between the men, shielding Justin with her own body.

Every muscle about Phillip was tense. Sweat covered his brow. The same was true for his twin. "Please, Phillip, no," she said quietly. "He's your brother. Your *brother*."

Phillip frowned at her as if having trouble comprehending her words.

Justin went to push her away, but she'd have none of it. "You don't understand, do you?" she said to him. "You have no idea, but look at Colster. Truly look at his face. It's *your* face."

"We look nothing alike—" Both Justin and Phillip started at the same time. They stopped, wary.

"See? You've felt it, haven't you?" Charlotte said, talking rapidly now, needing to convince them. "You *are* brothers. I know it sounds fantastic, but it is true," she answered. "You were stolen by Lady Rowena at birth, Tavis. The two of you are twins. Can't you see it?"

"Twins?" Justin shook his head. "You are moon-crazed. We don't look a thing alike." He moved away from her, coming to his feet.

She wasn't about to give up. Rising with him, she said, "You have the same hair color, the same eyes, the same nose—and the stubborn nature."

Those overhearing her started laughing. A few jeers were called. Someone said, "Get on with the fight."

For his part, Phillip appeared as wary as Justin was. Charlotte turned to him. "You must see it."

He glanced at his brother, his doubt plain. But then he looked to Laird MacKenna. "Is it true?"

His voice sounded as confused as Tavis felt. "Is the blacksmith my brother Justin Maddox?"

"Justin?" the blacksmith repeated. *"I'm no bloody Maddox."* He raised the Sword of the MacKenna and swung it wide.

Phillip pushed Charlotte down to the ground, saving her, before he rushed Justin. He grabbed the wrist of his brother's sword arm. "Listen to me. I know this is the wrong way to hear this news, but you are being used. We are *both* being used to pay for what our father did to Lady Rowena. It's not about Scotland or the clan or even ancient feuds. It's about *revenge,* do you hear?"

Justin tried not to listen. He pressed his sword down, trying to force Phillip to step back.

Phillip wouldn't give up. "Our mother died giving birth to us," he said. "Lady Rowena pretended to be a midwife. She tricked everyone and stole you. She told Mother her baby was born dead."

"No," Tavis shouted, using all his strength to shove Phillip aside.

The duke quickly recovered his footing. He faced his brother, offering himself. "No one anticipated twins. I was born later after Lady Rowena left with you. After your death, I was too well guarded for her to get close to me. She took you, Justin. She stole you from your rightful family, from your heritage."

"I'm no Maddox," Tavis protested, but it was weaker than before.

"You are more than a Maddox," Phillip answered calmly. *"You* are the *rightful* Duke of Colster."

Silence had descended over all who watched the scene between the brothers. Charlotte looked over to Laird MacKenna, who stood with his arm around his sister's shoulders. Her madness now was clear for anyone to see. Her eyes burned like coals and her lips were twisted in gleeful satisfaction. "Tell him," Charlotte ordered. "It's time. You've received your pound of flesh."

"Have I?" the laird answered.

Justin turned too, his expression disbelieving. "It is true?"

"That you are a blacksmith?" Laird MacKenna answered. "A rough-hewn, dumb in all things that have to do with being a gentleman, oaf. Oh, yes, that's true. That you can't read or write your own name? That's also true. That you are the true Duke of Colster?" His grin widened. "Only if Colster doesn't kill you first. If he does, who is the wiser—"

"I'll not kill him," Phillip jumped in. "He's my brother."

Justin turned to him. His voice full of confused rage, he demanded, "How do you know this?"

"I received a letter last week," Phillip answered.

"It was the deathbed confession of my childhood nurse, who had helped Lady Rowena steal you. I don't know how long they've had this letter. Or why they have finally decided to make their evil plan known. Miss Cameron is holding it for me. You can read all for yourself."

"He *can't* read," the laird announced. "Can you see him with your sophisticated London crowd?" The thought made him smirk. "Or dining with the king as you do? By the by, it's a pity you don't know your Gaelic or you'd have realized the relationship earlier. Tavis means 'twin.'" He smiled at his own jest.

That was it, the confirmation.

Justin appeared as if he'd been struck by a thunderbolt.

Charlotte's heart broke as he stepped back, away from everyone. He turned, seeing people watching him as if he were some oddity, the Sword of the MacKenna slack in his hand. "My entire life has been a lie?" he asked. "How many of you have known?" His gaze landed on an elderly man in a priest's cassock. "Did you know, Father Nicholas?"

The priest shrank back but Phillip stepped forward. "He signed Nanny Frye's letter."

It is a terrible thing to witness a man realizing he has been betrayed.

"I tried to make it up to you, *mon fils*," the priest said, a hint of French accenting his brogue.

Justin moved away from him, stopping as he reached Phillip's side. "What else happened?" he asked in a hoarse voice as if knowing there had to be more to this tragedy.

"Our mother died grieving over her firstborn son," Phillip answered. "She caught a fever and was buried beside the casket we thought contained you."

"I placed a dead dog in it," Lady Rowena said proudly. "No one checked. I sealed the casket myself even while the babe was being delivered to my brother."

"Why?" Justin asked, his question echoing one Charlotte knew had been Phillip's.

"It was justice that claimed her life," Lady Rowena declared. *"Judicium Dei.* The judgment of God."

Justin looked down at the silver sword he still held in his hand. "I swore loyalty to this. I'd waited for the day I could serve you proudly," he said to the laird. "And you were laughing at me the whole time. You took my wife, the only thing I had of value because you knew this day would come."

"I did," the laird answered without hesitation.

Phillip stepped up to him. "You are not alone," he said in a low voice that only Charlotte could hear. "I'm here now. No one will ever separate us again."

Instead of answering, Justin looked over to Gordon. "Did you know?"

"I knew nothing."

"Then beware my tale," Justin warned him. "This man"—he nodded to the laird—"raised me. He believes he knows me. He's wrong. You've made an enemy, laird."

Bruce interjected himself. "We are quaking in our boots, blacksmith," he said smugly.

In answer, Justin raised his voice, speaking to all. "I can read," he said. "The laird is wrong in believing I'm a stupid oaf. Perhaps that is the gift Father Nicholas gave me. And now, in my hand I hold the Sword of the MacKenna."

With a sweep of his arm, he used the Sword of the MacKenna to knock down the poles holding the silken canopy in place. The fabric came down over the heads of those on the dais. Lady Rowena started screaming as if she'd been attacked by banshees.

"*Run*," Justin ordered, and went racing around the platform. Neither Phillip nor Charlotte had to be told twice.

Chapter 13

*L*ady Rowena's hysterical screaming sounded as if someone were being murdered and the confusion of the moment allowed Phillip, Charlotte, and Justin the opportunity to escape.

Several men jumped in their paths to stop them, but both Justin and Phillip were good with fists and a sword. Justin jumped a hedge and went running across a garden. Phillip waited for Charlotte, sweeping her up in his arms and placing her on the other side. "Keep running," he ordered, even as someone grabbed his shirt.

He dispatched his pursuer with a jab in the nose. The man dropped, and Phillip jumped over the hedge to where Charlotte waited. "I said run," he told her.

"I am. Now," she answered, as he took her hand, and they followed Justin.

He knew his way well. There was no light save

moonlight. He led them to a garden wall and stopped. Phillip had been expecting a gate.

"What now?" he demanded.

"We climb." Justin lifted himself onto the wall, easily scaling its seven feet. On top, he bent over and offered a hand.

"You're next," Phillip said to Charlotte, who took Justin's hand and was easily lifted to the top. Phillip climbed the wall himself. The rim was a foot wide and overlooked roiling sea and jagged rocks.

"Come," Justin ordered, and started running along the wall without any apparent fear of losing his balance.

Charlotte stood frozen in indecision, a hand holding her long skirts, which could trip her. "I can't," she whispered. She looked to Phillip. "I'll fall. It's dark."

Phillip didn't hesitate. He swung her up in his arms, juggling both woman and sword. She started to panic. "What are you doing?"

"Carrying you. You can't do this with your skirts."

"And you can see where you are going better with me in your arms?"

Phillip grinned at her. He stood at a precipice on top of the world. One misstep could mean death and yet, he had no fear. "With you in my arms, I can do anything."

It was the truth.

The boredom and futility that had dogged him in London was gone. He'd rather be fully alive with an army of mad Scots on his tail than experience ever again that listless sense of being alone.

"*Come on,*" Justin urged them in a hoarse whisper. He waited for them at end of the wall. Phillip didn't weigh the outcome but began moving toward his brother. Each time he set his foot down, he expected it to be his last, but miraculously he didn't falter.

He handed Charlotte over to Justin, who lowered her to the ground without incident. They stood on the landing of a stairway in front of a small loft door. Justin opened the door. "This way."

All was pitch-black inside the room, but the air was filled with the smell of hay and horses. "Where are we?" Phillip asked.

"The hayloft. It runs down the center of the barn above the stalls. The laird designed it himself. He likes his hay stored high. It lasts longer that way. Be careful, there are drop holes over each stall to feed the horses. You don't want to fall through one."

He gave his warning just as Phillip was finding out for himself. His feet gave out from under him. He dropped his sword in surprise. Charlotte gave a cry just as he broke his fall by grabbing the edge of the loft floor. For a moment he hung there, his feet dangling in the air . . . his sword hit the ground. The horse in the stall startled and began dancing. His warning nicker was answered by another on down the line.

Justin squatted down at the edge of the opening. "I told you to watch yourself."

"I'm not a quick learner."

His brother snorted his agreement. "Well," he said with resolution, "we all have used that way sooner or later. Go on, let yourself fall the rest of the way—wait, which stall is it?" He leaned over. The horse grumbled and Justin made a concerned noise.

Phillip's arms were starting to ache. "What is it?"

"That's Cyclops's stall. A mean one. He'll crush you with his hooves."

"Are you kidding?" Phillip demanded, his arms ready to fall off.

"Yes," Justin said, a trace of humor in his voice. He gave Phillip a shove and Phillip fell, his landing softened by a pile of hay bedding.

The horse in the stall, a black shadow in the darkness, moved out of his way and whinnied an alarm but did not attack.

"Catch her," Justin said a beat before he dropped Charlotte into Phillip's arms.

"What about you?" Phillip asked his brother.

"I'm going to use the ladder," Justin's droll voice answered.

"Very funny," Phillip said.

His brother laughed. But he wasn't joking. The sound of his footsteps moved away from them.

"Here's the door," Charlotte said. She had been investigating, running her fingers lightly over the wood walls. "I've got the latch." She opened it, and the horse was the first to run out, knocking Charlotte back into Phillip's arms.

He tightened his hold for a moment, but then his toe hit his sword. "Finally, good fortune," he muttered, picking the weapon up.

Justin appeared beside them, another moving shadow. "I've bridles in my hand. Can you ride, Miss Cameron?" he asked.

"I will," she said. "I'll do anything to get out of here alive."

"Good, lass. Let's see if we can tack up some of these horses. I want the one you let escape. Her name is Butter. She's a demon but the best mare in the barn."

"Why not take another horse?" Phillip suggested.

"Because she throws beautiful foals, and she's the least the laird owes me—"

His voice broke off just as they all noticed a crack of light by the barn's main door. The men raised their swords. The door creaked as it opened.

A small figure holding a candle slipped inside and closed the door before turning and discovering he was in danger of being run through. Their visitor was a boy who almost dropped his candle at the sight. "Tavis?"

Justin recognized the lad. "Ian, what are you doing here?"

"I thought I could help. They are coming this way for you, Tavis. They knew you would be heading here."

"Thank you for the warning, Ian. Now go before anyone spies you here."

"I want to help."

"No," Justin said with more force. "Your mother needs you. I thank you for the warning, now take care of yourself."

The lad didn't argue but started to turn away. Charlotte stopped him. "Please, may I have your candle?"

Ian offered it to her. "Thank you," she said. "Now go. Tavis is correct. Don't let anyone know you helped us."

The boy turned, but before he left, Justin said, "You are a brave, brave lad, Ian. I'm proud to know you."

"I'm proud to know you, Tavis," he answered, and left.

Charlotte faced the men. "We need to create a diversion. It's an Indian trick. I say we set the barn on fire."

Justin's jaw dropped. "You want to set my barn on fire?" he asked incredulously.

"Yes," Charlotte said without remorse.

Phillip could have kissed her. Was there another woman in this world with Charlotte's ingenuity? "She's right. It's the only way we will escape."

"But the horses—" Justin protested.

"We ride them out," Phillip said. "Once the fire starts, they will stampede."

"This sounds like a good way to get our necks broken," Justin answered.

"It is," Phillip said, clapping him on the back and aping his earlier cheerfulness when he'd fallen through the hayloft. "But it is the only plan we have." He opened the nearest stall, set aside his sword, and started putting the bridle Justin had given him over the horse's head. It was Homer. The animal nickered a greeting. "Charlotte, it is Homer. He's coming with us."

Justin had stuck the Sword of the MacKenna in his belt while he bridled Butter. Charlotte busied herself by walking up the aisle and opening stall doors. Horses stuck their noses out, uncertain whether to leave or not. This was not their routine and they were leery.

"I don't want one of the horses hurt," Justin insisted.

"They won't be. And the barn should do well, too, if MacKenna and his men set to work and put the fire out," Phillip said. He had started moving hay and straw out into the aisle. "We'll start the fire here. It will take longer to spread on the dirt floor—"

"No, we can't do this," his brother objected.

"Justin, we have no choice," Phillip said, only to have his brother grab his arm and whirl him around.

"Stop calling me Justin. I hate the name."

"And this is all madness," Phillip agreed. He looked into his brother's angry face. "I know it seems insane, but right now, we don't have time to sort it out. It's either this or the three of us end up hanging. Now let's go."

Justin didn't argue. He bridled a bay and lifted Charlotte onto its back. She sat astride and reminded Phillip of a warrior princess. He was so proud of her. He gave her hand a squeeze. There was no time for anything else.

She handed him the candle. He took up his reins and hurried his horse and the candle to the front of the barn. Minutes were like seconds. MacKenna's men would be upon them at any time. Justin hustled the horses out of their stalls, directing them toward the door. "Go," he ordered.

Phillip started to open the door. "No," Charlotte said. "Start the fire first. We need them panicked, and we'll ride out with them."

"That's madness," Justin objected, even as Phillip was already heading to the back of the barn.

"Get ready," he said, and tossed the candle into the pile of dry hay. It burst into flame. Heavy smoke filled the air. Now the horses were alarmed. They shoved against each other as they rushed to the door that Justin threw open.

The animals charged out of the barn. Charlotte's and Justin's horses ran with them. Phillip had barely mounted Homer before he was on his way following the others—and almost running over MacKenna's men in his flight.

They were only a hand's width away from him.

Phillip didn't know if they had just arrived or if the stampeding horses had scared them back. He did know he'd been seen.

A shout went up for him to stop. A shot was fired. Phillip heard it whistle through the air. It struck the horse in front of his. The animal screamed and stumbled. Homer almost toppled but regained his footing and charged ahead, wanting to leave behind confusion at the barn.

It was at that moment the Scots realized the barn was on fire.

Charlotte had been right. The diversion worked. A cry went up, and MacKenna's men had to contain the fire lest it get out of control and spread through the whole fortress.

The horses charged down the streets. Justin broke away, bringing Charlotte's bay with him. Phillip saw them in time and followed.

They raced through the streets. Phillip had no idea where they were going and wondered how they would make it through the heavily guarded front gates.

Justin took them down a side street. It was dark here and quiet. Justin stopped at the fortress wall and dismounted. Puzzled, Phillip followed suit, helping Charlotte down. Justin led them to a group of hedges. He pushed them aside to reveal a door-size hole.

"Does MacKenna know this is here?" Phillip wondered.

"No," Justin answered. "He taxes every sheep and sack of wool that comes in and out of Nathraichean. We had to devise some way to save a few pennies. I doubt if even Bruce or Gordon knows of it. Go along. You first, Maddox. I'll bring up the rear."

Homer started to balk about going through the doorway. Phillip wooed him with soft words, and the animal relaxed.

On the other side were the moors along the cliff. No alarm was sounded. There weren't even patrols scouring the countryside for them.

For all intents and purposes, they were free.

Charlotte had trouble getting her bay to go through the door. Justin prodded from his end, and the horse obeyed. Phillip helped her remount and climbed back on Homer.

Justin closed the door behind him. He stabbed the Sword of the MacKenna in the ground and grabbed Butter's mane, preparing to mount when the door opened again.

Both men turned, ready to do battle, but it wasn't the laird's men who stepped out into the moonlight but Bruce's dark-haired wife, the one who attended Lady Rowena.

Justin paused. "Moira?"

"Tavis, you can't leave," she said, coming toward him. "I don't want you to."

His brother shook his head as if he couldn't believe his ears. Phillip readied his sword.

Justin held up his hand. "It's all right. She's my wife."

"Your wife?" Phillip had not imagined his brother married. He should have. It made sense . . . and he'd also heard the touch of eager vulnerability in Justin's voice. "If she is coming with us, let's go," he warned. "We don't have time to waste."

"Is that why you are here, Moira? You want to leave with me?" Justin asked, reaching out for her.

She caught his hands. "Tavis, I don't know. You are in so much danger. Please, give me the Sword of the MacKenna. Let me see if I can persuade the laird to forgive you."

"Forgive?" Phillip repeated. "It's MacKenna who should be asking forgiveness. He stole Justin's birthright."

But she ignored him. Instead, she said, "You can't be the duke, Tavis. Your place is here at Nathraichean. Give me the sword, and I will do everything in my power to protect you."

To Phillip's amazement, Justin appeared to waver. This woman knew his brother better than he did, and it galled him. But he was not going to give up Justin without a fight. "If you love him, come with us."

"She loves another," Justin said, his voice heavy.

"I don't really love Bruce," she claimed. "You gave me up, too. You could have wooed me back. The laird told me it was what you wished."

"Moira, I begged you to stay. Have you forgotten? I was given little choice," Justin said bitterly.

Phillip could literally feel Justin's pull toward this woman. He *sensed* their history. For a flicker of a moment, he understood her power over Justin.

She cooed to him now, her voice more seductive than a siren's call. "I know, I should have listened. I have been so unhappy without you. Come with me. Let us return together." She placed her hand on the hilt of the Sword of the MacKenna.

Justin started to speak, but Phillip wouldn't let him. "No," he said. "You must come with us." He nudged Homer toward his brother but was stopped by the sound of voices from the other side of the wall. "They are coming," he warned. "Justin, get on your horse."

"Come with me, Moira," Justin said. "I love you—"

His words were interrupted by Charlotte's warning, *"She has a knife."*

Phillip turned in time to see Moira stab Justin in the shoulder. It would have been his heart save for Charlotte's warning.

Moira pulled the Sword of the MacKenna out of the ground. She gripped it with both hands and raised it to attack Justin again.

A savage anger came over Phillip. He kicked Homer forward and grabbed Moira by one arm, giving her whole body a shake. The sword dropped. Phillip lifted her up. She kicked out at him. But at that moment, two men started out the secret door. Phillip bodily flung her at them. She screamed as her weight knocked them down.

Meanwhile, Charlotte was ordering Justin not to attempt to pull out the knife. "Leave it in. It will stave off the bleeding."

"How do you know?" he demanded.

"She knows," Phillip assured him. "Let's go. Charlotte, ride on, ride on. Justin come."

His brother picked up the Sword of the MacKenna. "This is mine." He leaped onto Butter and together the twins chased after Charlotte. Within minutes, they'd left Nathraichean behind.

Justin took the lead. They galloped their horses for a good hour. There was no sound of a chase being given. Phillip could only surmise that by scattering the horses and burning the barn, they had prevented the Scots from following.

On Justin led them. He rode as if the hounds of hell were tearing at their heels. Finally, Phillip knew they had to stop, or else they'd ruin their mounts. Reaching the shelter of trees beside a stream, he reined Homer in. Charlotte's followed.

Butter moved on a ways before stopping, and Justin leaned forward, practically falling to the ground, and that's when Phillip realized how badly his brother may have been wounded. He hurried to help him only to have Justin shove him away.

"Leave me alone," he ordered, staggering to keep his balance.

"Let me pull the knife out," Charlotte said. She'd slid off of her own horse. She began ripping the hem of her petticoat to make bandages. "It needs to be removed."

Justin dropped heavily onto a log to sit. His face over his beard was pale in the night, and Phillip realized it wasn't the wound that pained him . . . but its source. He'd wanted to believe Moira would go with him and was ashamed to be duped by her again.

Charlotte gave Phillip a nod, a silent instruction for him to leave them alone. Phillip didn't have to be told twice. Justin's resentment of him was clear. He made himself useful by collecting the lathered and spent horses and cooling them down by walking the perimeter of their little haven.

He could hear Charlotte's soft words and Justin's grunt of pain as the knife was pulled out. "Is he going to be all right?" he called.

"I believe so," Charlotte said. "The wound is clean, and if I can get the bleeding to stop, it should heal quickly. Here, remove your shirt."

At last, good news.

Phillip set the horses grazing. He used the reins to hobble them and noted with a wry smile that he was becoming quite adept at being his own groomsman.

He heard a footstep behind him and turned,

expecting to see Charlotte. He was surprised by his brother.

Justin stopped. In the moonlight, his home-spun shirt was dark where the blood had stained it.

"Is Charlotte as good at tying a bandage as she is everything else?" Phillip asked, wanting to keep the tone light between them.

Justin would have none of it. "They will come after us."

"I'm not afraid of MacKenna or any of his men," Phillip said. "Not now. We are well out of the reach of his petty fiefdom, and I know we both plan on staying ahead of him. I say we head to Edinburgh and turn him in to the garrison there."

"Turn him in?"

"We have no choice, Justin. He's built an army. He plans insurrection—"

His brother cut him off by punching him right in the jaw with a doubled fist.

Phillip stumbled back.

"Don't call me that bleeding name anymore. I'm not Justin. My name is Tavis, and *I'm not your brother*."

But instead of anger, Phillip felt pain—his brother's pain. He was keenly aware of the turmoil inside Justin.

Wives' tales and superstitions about twins

flashed through Phillip's brain. He grabbed his brother's arm to prevent him from charging off, well aware he might be repaid with another hard right to the jaw. "What was my wife's name?"

"What?" Justin asked, irritated.

"I'm thinking of my wife's name. Tell me what it is." Phillip focused on the word *Elizabeth*.

Justin looked beyond him to where Charlotte stood, and then back to Phillip. "You are balmy."

"What is her name?" Phillip insisted.

"I don't know, and I don't give a damn."

Now Phillip had a strong urge to punch his brother. "Don't believe me," he shot back. "However, let me assure you, you are as obstinate as our father was. Stubborn beyond reason as well you should be because whether you like it or not, you are Justin Robert Maddox born at Darnal Abbey in 1775. You were the firstborn of William Maddox, fifth Duke of Colster. Your mother was Rosemary who died shortly after giving birth to the two of us, believing you were dead. Your grave is beside hers in the family plot at the Abbey and every month on the first, flowers are placed there at my order and have been for ten years or more."

"You don't understand, do you, duke?" Justin said with some of Charlotte's irreverence. "I don't give a damn. I don't have what I want. I don't have Moira. She was the only decent thing that had ever happened to me. And she's gone. That bitch that attacked me is not the woman I once loved. They've changed her. *And I want her back.*"

"It's not in your hands," Phillip said soberly. "You can't change the minds of others."

"Aye. Others. I'm always living to please others."

Phillip hated the derision in his voice. Charlotte approached, she held in her hand Nanny's Frye's letter. He took it from her gratefully. "Then live to please yourself. But before you refuse any of what I'm offering you, read this. You have been robbed, but only if you let yourself be abused in this manner."

Justin didn't make one move toward the letter. "You and your letter. I believe it all sounds like bollocks."

"I didn't travel all this way and put my life in danger for bollocks," Phillip answered.

"I don't know why you're here," Justin flashed back. "But I was *better off* when I'd never laid eyes on you."

"Better off?" Phillip's temper snapped. "*They were using you.* They sought to destroy us."

"Us?" Justin snorted his thoughts. "It's *me* everyone wants to destroy. *Me* that has had to carry the brunt of things. *Me* who has paid."

"That's not true—" Phillip started.

"Of course it's not true, not to you, who has been living your fat and easy life—"

Phillip hit him. It was a reaction, a way to make him stop spouting anger, of saying things that twisted Phillip's insides into knots.

Justin's head snapped back from the force of the blow, and Phillip came to his senses. What the devil had he just done? He'd never struck out in anger. He was the diplomat, the negotiator.

His brother raised the back of his hand to his lip. It was bleeding. He looked at Phillip with undisguised disgust. "You would have thought we had enough beating up on each other for one night." He shook his head. "Well, *I've* had enough. I hope our paths never cross again." He turned and began walking toward his horse.

Shaken, Phillip took a step after him. "You can't leave."

"I'm not staying around." Justin tried to un-hobble his horse with one hand, a difficult task at best.

His attitude didn't make sense to Phillip. Why was he so angry? "You're walking away from a dukedom."

"So you say." Justin straightened, his task only half-accomplished. "Or perhaps I've decided the price of being your brother is too bloody high. Lass," he said to Charlotte, "hand me that sword."

Her eyes were wide in her pale face as she handed him the Sword of the MacKenna. "Where are you going?"

"I'm returning the sword. It belongs to them. To my clan," he answered.

"If you return to Nathraichean, they'll kill you," Phillip said.

"We'll just have to bloody see, won't we?" Justin answered. He used the sword to slice off the other end of the rein still tied to the horse.

Awkwardly, he climbed on Butter's back, grabbed her mane, and rode off into the night.

Chapter 14

Stunned not only by the violence between the two brothers but also the outcome, Charlotte stared in disbelief after Tavis—

Justin, she amended. His name was Justin. If she was confused, she could only imagine how he must be feeling.

Phillip whirled to face her, his eyes glints of moonlit anger. "The bloody fool."

"It's been a hard day," she said. "His whole life, everything he's believed about himself, has suddenly turned out to be a fabrication."

"Do you think it has been any easier for me?" But Phillip didn't wait for her answer. Instead, he took a step after Justin as if he would chase him—then stopped, his body rigid with tension.

"He's nothing more than a dumb beast anyway," he muttered, speaking more to himself than to her. "He can't be the duke." He turned to

Charlotte. "Can you imagine him in a meeting with the king's counselors?" He gave a bitter laugh. "He'd embarrass us all."

Charlotte heard beyond the angry words. She heard the disappointment. The guilt. She wanted to do nothing more than to wrap her arms around both him and Justin and pull them close—and yet, she couldn't. She was the outsider.

Instead, she crossed her arms against her chest, holding herself tight . . . and finding herself unable to not at least offer a comment. "It's not your decision, Phillip. It's his."

"Yes, it is," he agreed, stepping back, his hands forming hard fists. "And he made it, didn't he? He's going to get himself killed." He shook his head. "I *am* the duke. He could never be me. He runs at the first challenge. And what is back there for him? A wife who would kill him for her own gain—?"

"They are divorced," Charlotte corrected.

"What?" Phillip barked as if deliberately not comprehending.

"I said they were divorced. She's not his wife. Not any longer."

Phillip pressed the heels of his hands to his temples. "Divorced? How do you know this?"

"I overheard her talking to him earlier today. I don't believe it was by his choice."

"The Duke of Colster *can't* be divorced. It's unacceptable. No one divorces."

"Your brother Justin is," she replied, losing all patience with him. "Moira left him for Bruce. From what I understood, Laird MacKenna literally handed Moira to his favorite. Justin didn't want them to separate."

"Does it matter?" he asked derisively. "Look at him. He's taken off at a tear. The next time we see him, his head will be on a pike."

Charlotte's own temper started to swell. "Yes, it matters. It matters to him. And if you are thinking to belittle me into not speaking, or want me to stand here like some mute minion while you rant, *you* have the wrong woman, *Your Grace*."

He swung his gaze around to her. She braced herself, certain that once his mouth opened, his words would be razor-sharp.

Instead, in a complete about-face, the tension left his shoulders. "You're right," he admitted. He looked back in the direction his brother had left and stood there for a long moment in silence.

Charlotte took a step toward him. "You want him back in your life."

Phillip drew a deep breath and released it before saying, "Of course I do. I'll forever be the duke if he doesn't return."

"Isn't that what you want?" she asked, uncertain of the answer.

"Yes. No." He drew a shaky breath and released. "What happens to me if he takes it?" He
paused, and said, "What happens to me if he
doesn't?"

His stark honesty humbled her. "You are a
good duke, Colster."

He mocked her with a snorted opinion. "Are you
coaxing me out of my black mood? A second ago, I
was arrogant." He sounded tired, disappointed.

She took a step toward him. "You are *always* arrogant, Colster, duke or no. You are also honest,
loyal, and really quite wonderful for leaving
everything you had behind to come find your
brother."

"He doesn't see it that way."

Charlotte nodded agreement. "Please, listen to
someone who has suffered siblings for years—
they rarely do what you wish they would. They
do what they *must*." She placed her arms around
him, letting her body say what she dared not
speak aloud—*I am here, let me comfort you, let me
love you.*

"I've made it worse," he whispered. "I thought
to save him, and, instead, I've made it worse."

"I thought the same with Miranda. But once I
let her free to make her own choices, she found
her happiness."

Suddenly, he wrapped his arms around her
and held tight as if he dared not let her go.

A sense of rightness filled her. In his arms was where she wanted to be, where she *needed* to be. She craved his touch, his warmth, his very being.

Tears came to her eyes. She struggled to hold them back, but Phillip felt her slightest movement. He leaned back.

She feared looking at him. Feared him knowing what was in her deepest heart. Feared being so vulnerable. But Phillip knew. "Thank you," he whispered. "Thank you for knowing me better than I know myself . . . and still liking me."

She more than liked him. She loved him with a fierceness that grew with each passing moment.

He leaned his head close to hers. "And you're right. I must let him go. I need to take care of you, and I need to inform the proper authorities that MacKenna has built an army."

He wanted to take care of her.

Phillip stepped back, lacing his fingers with hers. No gesture could have commanded her attention more. She could feel the energy radiate through his fingers and into hers. "Are you all right to ride?"

"I'm tired," she admitted, "but I know we must keep moving."

His teeth flashed in his smile of approval. "That's my darling," he said. "Come. The horses are rested enough. Let's put as much distance as possible between Nathraichean and ourselves."

He didn't have to make the suggestion twice although she was weary of riding. Her bottom was numb and yet, what choice did she have?

Phillip knew what she was thinking. As he gave her a leg up onto the bay's back, he said, "You've been so good, Charlotte, over these past days. Just a bit more, and then you'll never have to get on the back of a horse again."

"Promise?"

He laughed. "Promise." He mounted Homer, and they set off in the opposite direction Justin had taken. Fifteen minutes later, they came upon a good road running southeast. Phillip decided to travel east. "They won't be expecting that," he assured her. "We can go south later, after we are certain we are far away enough to lose them."

Charlotte didn't argue. She was too tired to waste energy on words.

The road began following the winding curve of a rushing stream. The sound of running water was a potent lullaby, and dawn was only the matter of a few hours away.

Charlotte had just yawned for the seventh time when they rounded a curve and came upon a bridge over the stream. On the other side was a nestled group of cottages around the rambling building of a small inn. A sign hung over one of the doors. Phillip dismounted and started for the door.

"Perhaps we should keep going," Charlotte said. "There can't possibly be anyone awake."

"I'll wake someone. We can't continue traveling, not without sleep. Do you have my coin purse?"

She pulled the embroidered purse from its hiding place and removed the silk cord from her neck before handing it to him.

Phillip pounded on the door. He had to do it a third time before someone finally came. The door opened a crack and a man in a nightcap stuck his head out. "Yes?" the sleepy innkeeper inquired.

"We need rooms for the night," Phillip answered.

"The night's almost over," came the response.

"I know," Phillip said.

"I only have one room."

" 'Tis all we need," Phillip said, and he named a price he'd pay for the room that was enough to make the innkeeper throw aside caution and open his doors.

She should protest, her common sense told her, while another part of her was perfectly amenable to the arrangement. After all they'd been through, sharing a room with him was the least of her worries. And, the truth be known, she wanted to lie beside him. Even just for one night.

The innkeeper lit a candle and led them up the stairs to the first room at the top. Charlotte was so tired all she could do was put one foot in front of the other. "What are your names?" innkeeper asked.

"Smith," Phillip said. "Mr. and Mrs. Smith."

He didn't look to Charlotte for permission, nor did she challenge him. It was easier this way.

The room they were shown was built under the eaves of the roof. A narrow bed took up most of the floor space, and there was one window, shuttered closed against the night air.

The innkeeper lit a stub of a candle on the room's only other piece of furniture, a bedside table.

"The privy is outside in the back," the innkeeper said. "I don't do pans. We passed the back door on the way up the stairs. There's a rain barrel next to it for washing." With those words, he and Phillip's money were gone.

Phillip looked around, and said, "Well, it's serviceable."

Charlotte nodded, and crossed her arms, very aware that they were alone. *Mr. and Mrs.*

Phillip was completely at ease. He nodded to the bed with its sagging mattress and chuckled. "The mattress has seen better days, but if it had been fluffed goose down a mile high, I couldn't be more happy to see it. I have to see to the horses. Do you wish to go outside now for the privy accommodations?" He acted as if the two of them alone was the most natural thing in the world.

Mr. and Mrs.

But it wasn't. Charlotte knew that . . . and, standing in this room with him, knew she was accepting it.

This was a complete reversal in her life, a defiance of her moral code. She'd been the guardian for her sisters. Especially in later years when their father's drinking had made him incapable of protecting them. Her life's mission had been to regain the heritage her mother had tossed aside for love. Charlotte had been the one to remind her sisters that they were ladies, granddaughters of an earl. They had a birthright, and they weren't going to compromise it by giving their virginity to any frontiersman or hapless soldier. They were going to marry dukes.

And here, she'd given hers up for a duke.

Mr. and Mrs.

Charlotte forced herself to set aside pretenses. There would be a price for her actions. She did have the power to end this now.

At her continued silence, he offered, "If you don't want to come out now while I take care of the horses, I'll come back and take you downstairs later."

He smiled, and her heart skipped. Any protest died. It was as if he cast a spell around her. He was her dreams come to life. He was so hand-some, even in shirtsleeves and several days' growth of beard shadowing his jaw. Few men were as masculine as Phillip—and was it so wrong to live the dream . . . or to want to believe there was *more* between them?

"I'll go down now," she murmured.

"Come along then." He held open the door.

She practically ran out of the room.

Phillip knew Charlotte was tense. He thought he knew why. He picked up the candle stub and fol-lowed her.

In the few days they'd been together, she had challenged, defied, and tested him in a way no other in his life had, male or female. Only she had the courage to speak up to him when others would be silent . . . with the notable exception of his brother.

But now, she hurried down the dark stairs as if being followed by the devil—and, in a way, he was. She had a moral code. He'd taken her inno-cence and sooner or later, they'd have to discuss the future.

He didn't know if he relished that conversation any more than she would.

The night air felt good. He offered her the can-dle. "You keep this. I shall see to the horses."

She didn't speak but took the candle from his

hands. Their fingers brushed, and she pulled away as if she'd been burned by hot wax. He didn't think she had.

It was he who frightened her. His presence that had turned her skittish.

Once again, Phillip hobbled the horses and turned them loose to graze in the back of the inn. There was water in the stream and plenty of grass. They would be fine.

He was only gone five minutes, but when he returned to the back door, Charlotte was gone. She'd left the candle for him by pushing it into some soft earth.

She'd not waited.

In a way, that may be just as well. Perhaps he and Charlotte should keep their distance.

He snuffed out the candle, pressing the hot, soft wax between his fingers, aware of a deep-seated disappointment and a sense of relief. What could he offer Charlotte?

In truth, right now, he was a duke who might not be a duke if his brother claimed the title. He was a man who had just had everything he'd believed about himself shaken. The world was no longer black-and-white. The old code, the one he'd lived by, that everyone he knew of means and substance valued might not accept his brother . . . or himself.

The only thing he'd thought he'd had was Charlotte, but she'd gone on ahead.

The room was pitch-black when he opened the door. He opened the shuttered window, letting in moonlight and a breeze that eased the staleness.

Charlotte slept on the far side of the bed, hugging the edge. Her hair spread out over the counterpane. With her upturned nose and sweep of dark lashes, she looked like an angel.

She'd not undressed or slipped under the covers. He didn't know if this was due to exhaustion or if she was keeping all barriers up between them. He suspected it was a little of both—and the latter made him angry.

He wasn't some ogre who jumped on unsuspecting women. Well, he had used her to his advantage, but Charlotte hadn't been unwilling. Certainly she knew she could trust him now . . . didn't she?

As if to prove his trustworthiness, Phillip gently removed her shoes. She didn't wake.

He undressed, managing to pull off his boots himself. He left on his breeches and climbed under the covers. There. That should please her.

Folding his arms under his head, he lay on his back and tried to think of anything but the woman by his side. He resisted the urge to touch her hair or gather her close. He would not offer her protection, not if she didn't want it—

She turned to him, her hand moving up to rest on his chest. Her palm flattened over his heart.

Phillip didn't move. He didn't dare breathe. His body went hard with a force that was staggering. He wanted her this close to him. In fact, he needed her—but not, he realized, just for act of sex. He wanted her closeness, her warmth. Her trust.

And now, here she was, snuggling close to him as open and guileless as a child, her body curved to accommodate his.

God must be laughing—

Her lips brushed his neck.

Phillip held himself still, thinking he was imagining this, praying he wasn't.

She traced her soft kiss with her tongue.

He rolled her up onto his chest. Her eyes opened and met his. Her hair created a curtain around them.

"Do you know what you are doing?" he asked. "I'm not stone, Charlotte. I don't want to be."

"I'm not either."

"And yet?" he prompted. "Speak to me, love. What is it you fear?"

The tension in her body fled. Her eyes softened. "You called me 'love.' Do you mean it, Phillip?"

He didn't hesitate. At this moment, she and this bed were the center of his world. "With all my heart."

Her lips came down on his, kissing him deeply.

Phillip didn't resist. He kissed back. Theirs was a passion that had to be obeyed. He surrendered to it now. Whatever the future held was unimportant at this moment. Nothing mattered save the feel, taste, and texture of this woman in his arms.

He threw back the covers and began kissing the tender skin right below her chin. She sighed with pleasure, the sound music to his ear. He ran his hand down over the curve of her waist, turning her toward him and giving himself the access he needed to unlace her dress.

She stroked his side, running her hand up over his shoulder and around his neck. She slid her tongue across the line of his bottom lip, the sensation of it went straight to his groin. Phillip tossed aside seduction in favor of pure unbridled lust. He had to have Charlotte and soon.

He pulled at her bodice, not caring if he tore her dress or not. He wanted to touch her breasts, to hold their weight and taste them. She was perfectly formed for him. A goddess.

"Beautiful woman," he whispered. "Warm, willing woman."

She smiled, her fingers unbuttoning his breeches, her hand finding the length of him and closing around him.

All the blood left Phillip's brain. He couldn't think, let alone reason when she held him like this and yet, he'd not have her release him for any amount of gold.

Phillip slid her dress up over her head and tossed it to the floor. She wore nothing but her garters and stockings and looked delicious. He kissed her shoulder, her breasts, her stomach, causing her to release her hold. He didn't want them to go too fast. He wanted this to last.

She squirmed as his whiskers tickled her belly and giggled when he nibbled soft, soft skin— before dipping lower and kissing her intimately.

Charlotte sucked in her breath in shocked surprise. She started to pull away even as her legs parted for him.

Phillip placed his hands on her hips, insisting that she let him, that she trust him.

Elizabeth would never have let him attempt such a thing. She might have shut her bedroom door to him altogether.

But this was Charlotte. There were no doors between them, or boundaries.

Charlotte whispered his name, sounding a bit panicky and yet amazed. He smiled. If ever there was a way to bind a woman to a man, it was this one. Her pleasure gave him his. The sheets pulled as she curled her fingers in them. Her breathing grew rapid, more urgent. He could feel the tension coiling inside her. Taste the building pressure. She twisted as if seeking a moment's respite. He wouldn't let her escape. She whimpered, the sound ending on a moan. His name became her plea, a prayer begging him to help her seek release. It drove Phillip, maddening him with a desire to see her fulfilled.

And then she gave a sharp gasp. Her hips raised, and he could feel deep muscles contract. He knew where she was—and that he'd been the one to bring her there.

Without hesitation, he rose and thrust himself deep, marveling at her heat, at the blessed tightness. Was there ever a woman as magical as Charlotte?

His release was immediate and even more intense than hers. More intense than any he'd ever had before. Her heat fused them, joining him to her forever—

The moment was broken when the man in the room next to theirs pounded on the wall. "Would you keep it quiet in there?" a thick Scot's accent said.

Phillip frowned, brought back to the here and now by the man's rude interruption. He barely recognized his surroundings, had to think a moment to realize where he was. It was as if he had journeyed to the heavens and back. The world had changed. It looked the same, but it wasn't.

No, his life would never be the same.

He looked down at Charlotte, and she appeared

equally startled. A thin coat of sweat covered both of them, and he still held her hips in his hands.

An instant's panic flashed through him. She was vitally precious to him. What right had he to be here with her now? Charlotte had wanted a duke. She wanted marriage. Considering the current state of affairs, he didn't know if he could offer her either.

And then she smiled, and he couldn't help but shove doubts aside. They didn't matter. Not right now.

He grinned back, resting himself on top of her, the two of them hugging as if they could climb into each other.

"I don't want to leave this place," Charlotte whispered. "Or this moment."

"I don't either." He'd never so fully meant a statement.

She pulled back and studied him a moment, her expression serious. "Don't dwell on it," he ordered. "We'll sort it out in the morning, but don't spoil this moment."

"Can we sort it out?" she wondered.

He knew what she asked . . . and couldn't answer. What sort of commitment could he, a man so uncertain of his own future, make?

"We will," he vowed.

This time, when he kissed her, she responded.

Sweet, sweet Charlotte.

There was nothing else for him to do but make love to her again.

Charlotte lay awake long after Phillip fell asleep. His body was curled around hers, his hand tucked between her breasts, his other arm cradling her head.

His whiskers were still prickly, and her skin burned from where they'd rubbed her in some embarrassing places.

She'd never felt so completely content or as unsettled.

She was in love.

A void in her life had been discovered and filled beyond all expectations. Dear Lord how it had been filled. His warmth seeped into her. She snuggled toward him, needing to be as close to him as possible. His legs were entwined with hers, her foot resting on the top of his.

And she knew that this intense need, this desire was dangerous. In a short amount of time, Phillip Maddox had consumed her life with his. Effortlessly, she had compromised her every principle. He had only to touch her, and she'd fall into his arms.

The first signs of dawn began to lighten the sky

to shades of purple and pink. The rooster crowed repeatedly, and she wondered if he wasn't trying to give her a warning.

If Miranda or Constance had let a man do what she'd let Phillip do to her, she would have been ashamed of them. However, she felt no shame. She craved more.

Covering his hand with hers, she confessed, "I care for you far more than I should."

His answer was to shift his weight, enveloping her even more with his body as if he'd never let her go, and she prayed he wouldn't.

Charlotte woke, surprised she had fallen asleep.

She wasn't certain exactly what woke her. At first, she thought it was the sun streaming in through the window, its light so bright her eyes didn't want to open. Sounds of life came from the outside—voices of travelers setting off on their way and bidding farewell to the innkeeper, the clop and stamping of horses' hooves as they set off on their way, the barking of a dog—

Someone was in the room.

Charlotte made the realization the same time Phillip did. He sat upright, throwing a protective arm over her body. "What the devil!"

Justin sat on the edge of their bed, one leg crossed over another, the Sword of the MacKenna resting on his thighs. He sliced an apple with the dirk his divorced wife had used to attempt to kill him. He smiled, his teeth white in his beard. "Morning, brother."

Chapter 15

*U*namused, Phillip said, "Go away."

Justin popped a large slice of the apple in his mouth before saying, "I thought you would be happier to see me."

Phillip ran a hand over his face. Charlotte had dived beneath the sheets. She was mortified. He could feel the heat of her embarrassment. "And I thought you didn't want anything to do with me."

"Would you really give me the dukedom?" Justin said, cramming another piece of apple in his mouth.

"We can discuss this later. Go downstairs and wait. As you can see your *uninvited* presence is not welcome."

"Oh yes, I've heard all about the two of you," Justin said, giving no indication of preparing to leave. "Apparently, you kept half the inn up last night with your caterwauling. The guest next door was demanding his money back."

That was it. Phillip rose from the bed naked, marched the two steps to the door, and threw it open. "Out."

Justin leaned back against the footboard, resting his weight on one arm—the very image of a gentleman of leisure. "Well now," he said to Charlotte, a half smile playing on his lips. "We may be twins but here is one *big* difference between us." He pinched the air, his thumb and forefinger no more than an inch apart. "My brother's pecker is a puny thing compared to my bonny—"

His boast was cut short when Phillip grabbed him by the ear and gave it a savage twist. Justin yelped but that didn't stop Phillip. He led his brother by the ear to the door and shoved him out. "Downstairs," he barked before shutting the door in Justin's face.

"What a bloody pest," he muttered to himself, and then turned to see Charlotte in the bed, her hair mussed, her lips still swollen from his kisses of last night. Thoughts of his brother vanished.

"You are beautiful." The compliment just tumbled out of his mouth. He took a step toward her but was stopped as Justin pounded on the door with all his force.

"Don't keep me cooling my heels downstairs," he ordered. "I'm not a patient man."

Phillip answered by pounding the door back.

His brother burst out laughing, and then there was the blessed sound of his footsteps clumping down the stairs.

"Everyone heard us?" Charlotte said, alarmed.

"He's just saying that," Phillip assured her. How good it was to wake up with a woman. He liked seeing her all rosy and pink and well loved in the morning. "It's all part of his crudeness." He climbed into the bed, ready, willing, and very, very able to take Charlotte in his arms.

She thwarted him by sliding out the other side of the mattress, pulling the sheet with her as she went and wrapping it around her nakedness. "We were loud," she whispered, mortified. "A man did yell at us through the wall."

"That man was jealous," Phillip said. He grabbed a piece of the sheet, winding it around his hand to bring her close enough to sit back on the bed.

Charlotte resisted, tugged at her sheet, keeping her breast covered. When she blushed, she turned red from her toes to her hairline. "You should go downstairs. Your brother is waiting."

"Let him wait," Phillip murmured, giving the sheet one hard yank and winning it from her.

With a small gasp of feminine alarm she reached for her dress, which was still on the floor where he had tossed it the night before. Phillip looped his arms around her waist, pulling her down to the bed beside him.

He threw a leg over hers, using it to weigh her in place while he stroked the soft skin of her waist. No woman had ever been so lovely to him. He kissed her neck. "You are the only breakfast I need."

This time, she didn't fight.

Her lips curved into a smile. "I'm not."

"You are," he promised, his voice low. "I want you every single morning and perhaps for lunch and dinner, too."

She laughed, raising a hand to cover her mouth as if embarrassed.

"Don't," he said, taking her hand and holding it between them. "Don't ever be shy around me, Charlotte. You need never fear me, or keep secrets, or hesitate in saying what you think and need. I'd do nothing to harm you. Ever." He pressed her palm around his arousal.

Her lashes swept down over eyes darkened by anticipation. "But you want to gobble me up," she protested. Her fingers caressed him.

"And other things," he agreed, slipping his finger inside her. Her muscles contracted. "Amazing," he whispered. "You are amazing."

She blushed, and he was charmed. He kissed her shoulder. "And if I could find a silk the color of your hair or the red rose of your nipples," he continued, "I'd swath it over every window and chair I own." He kissed her breast.

Her legs bent, an invitation . . . and yet she took his face in her hands, forcing him to meet her eyes.

"What?" he asked, turning his head to kiss the inside of her arm.

"Please, Phillip, I need a moment to talk to you."

Phillip didn't want to talk. However, he gave her his attention, knowing he must before he could move on to immeasurably more interesting matters than conversation.

Her eyes look troubled. "What is it?" he asked.

She hesitated, taking a moment to wet her lips as if nervous. "I could care for you," she confessed, her voice low as if fearing being overheard.

"I know," he answered. "I want you to care for me." He nuzzled her neck and shoulder. Her breast was only inches from his mouth. Considering the matter resolved, he started to lower his head but she pulled him back up.

Her fingers curled in his hair. She made him look at her. "What will happen? Perhaps, we shouldn't be this involved."

He didn't pretend to mistake her meaning. "It's too late. We're both involved."

"Are you?" she asked, her voice anxious.

Phillip settled himself on top of her, letting her feel the power of his arousal. "I'd protect you with my life, my Charlotte. Do you understand? Name your price."

Her expressive eyes studied him a moment. "Marriage."

He heard the word as if from a distance. Her heat distracted him. In truth, at this moment, he would have agreed to anything. Later he would sort it out. Later, he could explain that as much as he loved her—and *he did*. He knew that to the depths of his bones. This was more than mere lust. Charlotte was a piece of his soul. She alone defied, challenged, and irritated him in ways no one else ever had, and he adored her for it. She was the voice of reason, his conscience, his partner. But as much as he loved her—he could never marry her.

He had responsibilities to his family's estate, to the titles—not just the ducal one but the numerous others that had been gained over the generations.

That didn't mean that he wouldn't love, honor, and support her. There wasn't anything he wouldn't do for Charlotte. But he'd learned a lesson in the aftermath of her sister Miranda's jilting. A nobleman paid a price for going outside his own class.

"Marriage," he murmured, clearheaded enough not to commit to a direction. Instead, he punctuated the word with a deep, soul-drinking kiss.

He knew what Charlotte liked in her kisses. He knew she wouldn't resist. She didn't. With a soft sigh of contentment, her body melded with his. He slid inside her, and conversation was forgotten.

Charlotte fell back to sleep.

Phillip raised from the bed carefully, not wanting to disturb her. She slept as if exhausted, and he needed a moment to speak to his brother alone.

It had been over an hour since he'd sent Justin downstairs. He dressed in shirt, breeches, and boots and took the backstairs leading to the outside. The cold rain barrel water felt good. He washed the best he could. His whiskers irritated him. He rubbed his jaw with his hand and went in search of the innkeeper, whom he found in the taproom cleaning the tables.

Justin was there, too. He sat with his arms crossed, his chair tilted back against a wall. "Did you have fun?" he asked Phillip, his eyes alight with anger at being made to cool his heels.

"It took a while to get dressed," Phillip answered without apology, thinking to himself he needed to school his twin in manners—although he would not do it with the innkeeper present.

"I imagine," Justin said with a doubtful snort, one the innkeeper echoed.

Phillip was going to have to do more than "school" his brother. He may need to beat him.

Giving Justin his back, Phillip said to the innkeeper, "I need a razor and shaving soap. Do you have any?"

"I can get that for you," he answered. "It will cost you."

"Whatever. I need it now. And," he said, catching the man before he left the room, "I'll also pay for your guest who made a complaint this morning. He sounds like a mean one. I'll not have you inconvenienced on my account."

The innkeeper raised his eyebrows to his hairline, a new sense of respect easing into his attitude for Phillip. This time, when he started to leave the room, he gave a short bow.

Phillip turned to his brother, who said, "You didn't ask how much the man would charge you."

"I have the amount to cover a razor," Phillip answered and decided he wanted an ale for breakfast. He felt good, better than he had in ages. He went behind the bar and helped himself to tankard and ale from the barrel. "Do you want one?"

"Aye."

"Have you had anything to eat?"

Justin's gaze narrowed. "No."

Phillip carried the two tankards to the table just as the innkeeper returned with a well-used, but sharp, razor and a cake of soap. "What do you have to break our fast?" Phillip asked him.

"Depends on what you want—my lord," the innkeeper added the title with caution. Phillip didn't correct. Let the education of Justin begin. "I have some sausages."

"And bread?" Phillip wondered.

"Aye, the wife baked it fresh yesterday."

"Good," Phillip said. "We'll take that and some cheese."

"No, *we* won't," Justin said. He brought his chair down to the floor. "I don't like cheese, and I can order for myself."

Phillip had never heard of anyone not liking cheese. It was one of his favorite foods. However, he didn't want to start a quarrel with this diffi-cult, surly, ill-mannered fellow who just hap-pened to be related to him. "Order, then," he said, and took a chair opposite Justin's at the table.

"I'll take bread and a sausage," his brother said. He lifted his tankard and drained it down in one smooth gulp. "And another ale." There was an unmistakable challenge in his voice. Per-haps he thought to school Phillip . . . ?

He wouldn't.

Phillip drained his own tankard, proud to take less time than Justin. He set the tankard down. "I'll have another, too."

The innkeeper looked between the two men as if confused by the undeclared contest between them, and then understanding dawned. "Are the two of you brothers?"

Phillip could have said yes. He didn't. He waited to see what Justin would say—and that was nothing. His brother hunkered down as if trying to ignore Phillip's presence.

Silence stretched a long moment with neither Phillip nor Justin speaking. The innkeeper made an annoyed sound. "You've already helped yourself to the ale. You can do it again. I'll be back with your sausages and cheese."

When they were alone, Justin snorted, and said in his rolling brogue, "Funny how you didn't speak up and answer the man's question. I thought you insisted in being in charge of the world."

"Me? I was waiting for you." Phillip lifted his tankard, and then remembered it was empty. He set it back down. The brew had been a bit flat to his taste, much like his reunion with Justin. His brother was turning out to be the most obstinate, annoying man ever. He didn't even like cheese. "Everyone likes cheese."

"*I don't,*" Justin answered, rising to get more ale. He didn't bother to take Phillip's tankard.

"Perhaps," Phillip suggested, "you would have been happier if I'd left you with MacKenna."

Justin ignored him until he returned to the table. He tilted back in his chair again, his gaze shifting away to a far corner of the room.

Phillip was tempted to tell him he was being a complete horse's arse. However, he reminded himself that *he* was a diplomat. He'd negotiated with hordes of irritatingly rude people. He should be able to manage a one brother.

"So what brought you back?" Phillip asked. He rose from the table with his tankard. He stared across the room toward the bar.

"The money."

Of course. Phillip stopped dead in his tracks. Outrage flowed through every vein in his body. He'd risked his life for this man, a man who was turning out to be alarmingly common.

"I am the oldest," Justin said, "and that makes me a duke." And then, to add emphasis to his words, he belched, the sound carrying in the stillness between them. His gaze met Phillip's. Almost gleefully, he said, "Having second thoughts yet?"

His belligerency tested Phillip's calm veneer. "Perhaps you'd prefer staying in Scotland."

"It's too late," Justin said. "You've convinced me. I want what you have. Perhaps even take a gander at Miss Cameron since she seems fond of dukes."

That was it.

Phillip calmly walked over to the table, set down his tankard, and grabbed his brother by the throat, shoving the table and chairs that were empty aside in the process.

But Justin wasn't in the mood to take being throttled. He kicked chair out of the way so that he could get free, and then threw his fists at Phillip. In a blink, the two of them were battling it out across the taproom.

Charlotte heard a crash and the grunts of exertion. She knew what was happening. She'd witnessed far too many fights on the frontier not to know the sounds.

The twins were at each other again.

She'd napped a few minutes after Phillip had left but had realized she'd rather be with him. Her toilette had been hasty. She'd brushed her hair with her fingers the best she could.

Now, hurrying to the taproom door, she was stunned to see tables and chairs being tossed aside as they pounded away at each other.

Phillip was actually the more disciplined fighter. He belonged to that set of Corinthians who enjoyed training with pugilists. He was quick, clever.

Justin was not trained, but he held his own. He was stronger.

And might would win every time.

Charlotte let Justin get a good, meaningful punch in before she started shouting at them to stop. It was at this time the innkeeper also came charging in. He blinked in horror at the shambles they were making of his taproom and grabbed fistfuls of Justin's shirt to throw him off Phillip. Charlotte hurried to put herself between the two brothers.

"Stop this," she said to Phillip. *"Now."*

Phillip's eyes were bright with anger, but he pulled back.

She turned to Justin and was suddenly stuck by how similar his eyes were to Phillip's.

And she suspected they were going to learn they were more alike than either would care to admit before this day was done.

"What have you done to my taproom?" the innkeeper said. "Who's going to pay for these damages?"

"He will," both brothers said at the same time, pointing to each other.

"*I* will," Charlotte said. Upstairs, she'd tucked Phillip's coin purse in her bodice for expediency's sake. She hadn't wanted to leave it in the room alone. She now turned and pulled it out, handing it to the innkeeper. "This should cover the damage, and I'd like a pot of tea."

The innkeeper didn't take her word for it but poured the coins into his hand. The gleam of gold made him happy.

"Is that enough?" Phillip demanded, a ducal sneer to his tone.

"For that price, we should break a few more

chairs," Justin answered. Picking up a chair leg, he splintered it into pieces over the nearest table.

The innkeeper was not amused. "You shall leave after breakfast." He turned and walked out, the money tightly clutched in his fist.

"Did you notice he took your purse, too?" Justin asked Charlotte. "Do you want me to go fetch it for you?"

"You aren't going to do anything for her," Phillip flashed back, the heat in his temper surprising Charlotte. "Stay back."

Phillip's tone obviously struck a nerve with Justin. "Oh, I will," Justin informed him. "In fact, I'll stay so far away you'll never see me again."

"You said that last night," Phillip reminded him.

"I mean it now."

He started for the door, even as Phillip said, "*Good.*"

It was up to Charlotte to grab Justin's arm and swing him back. "You'll do no such thing. At least, not until after breakfast." She pushed him toward the lone standing table. "Sit down. And you, too, Phillip, while I see if I can order some breakfast."

"We've ordered it. And paid for it, too," Phillip said.

"You paid too much," Justin muttered, but he was lifting a chair that still had all four legs off the floor.

"It's my money," Phillip answered. "She can spend it how she wishes." He set a chair in place for her.

Charlotte sat and waited for the two men to do so also.

The innkeeper entered with her tea and the men's plates. "That looks tasty," she said, looking over Phillip's plate, more for the innkeeper's benefit than Phillip's. "I'd like to have that, too," she said to the innkeeper.

"See?" Phillip said to his brother. "She likes cheese."

"No, I don't really," Charlotte answered, a bit distracted. She amended her order. "I don't care for cheese."

"How can you not like cheese?" Phillip said.

"I'll eat it if you wish me to," Charlotte answered, "but I'd rather not."

"He has trouble understanding any desires but his own," Justin grumbled as he picked a tankard off the floor close to his feet. He rose. "I'm getting ale. Do you want one?" he asked Phillip.

"You'd drink off the floor—" Phillip started but was stopped by Charlotte's heel coming down hard on his toe.

He looked at her in surprise. She sipped her tea, giving him a "meaningful" look over her cup.

Leaning toward her, he said in a low voice

meant for the two of them alone, "I like your hair down. It looks lovely. But no one would suspect that such a calm and serene creature as yourself has just crushed my toe."

She almost spilled her tea laughing. He smiled back. "You are beautiful in the morning, with or without clothes."

Charlotte glanced to see if Justin overheard them. "This isn't the time."

Phillip frowned. "I don't want to deal with him," he confessed. "He's rude and obnoxious."

"Who is?" Justin asked, setting an ale he'd poured for Phillip in front of him.

"You," Phillip answered brutally.

He picked up his tankard, but his hand was stayed when Justin said, "I picked your cup off the floor and wiped it off on my breeches—"

"Stop it," she said. "Don't you understand? The more you do this, the more Laird MacKenna wins. I'd wager he isn't even looking for us. He's done his damage."

Justin gave a brittle laugh. "Exactly. I'm his revenge. Me with my big callous and hard ways. They are probably all sitting around the banquet hall table laughing at me right now."

"Then don't give them something to laugh at," Phillip replied.

"And what do you imagine I should do?" Justin lashed back. "Eat cheese?"

"Please," Charlotte said, wanting calm. "I know how you feel, or believe I do," she told Justin. "It isn't easy to be between and betwixt, but you have no choice. I thought I knew what I was doing when I uprooted my sisters from the Ohio Valley to come to London. I won't lie to you, Justin, it hasn't been easy. People are cruel there . . . but then, they've been cruel to you here. All I know is that one doesn't have any choice in life other than to go forward. Even when you aren't certain it is the direction you want to go, there is no other. And you aren't alone. Not anymore. You have Phillip."

"That seems to be the problem," Justin answered tightly.

It was on the tip of her tongue to tell him not to be so sensitive. She could understand Phillip's exasperation with him. But then she noticed a razor on the floor. She rose from her chair and went to pick it up. "What is this?"

"I asked the innkeeper for it," Phillip said. He rubbed his hand across his coarse whiskers. "I need to get this off. The soap is over there." He nodded to where a cake of shaving soap rested alone on the floor.

Inspiration struck. She glanced back and forth between the twins. Was blood thicker than water?

It always had been for her. She went over and picked the soap up, knowing of only one way that could bridge the gap between Justin's defensiveness, Phillip's disappointment, and her own curiosity. "One moment." She left the room, searching for and finding the innkeeper in his kitchen grousing to his wife, who apparently served as cook. "We need very hot water and some towels. Can you do this for me, please?"

The line of his mouth flattened, but he said, "Yes, mistress, I can. I'll be out in a blink."

"Thank you, and I'm sorry again for the mess they made."

The innkeeper grunted his response, busy pouring hot water from a kettle over the fire into a bowl. He carried it out for Charlotte, who had him set it on the table between Phillip and Justin. The two of them appeared as if they'd not said one word to each other since she'd left them. Nor had they touched their breakfasts.

This might be more difficult than she had imagined.

"Here we are," she said in her sweetest voice. "Who wants to be shaved first?"

"What?" Phillip asked.

"I'm not losing my beard," Justin answered.

She held up the razor. "I'm the one doing the shaving."

Phillip shook his head. "Charlotte, you don't need to do this. I can do it myself."

However, a crafty gleam had appeared in

Justin's eye. "Come to think of it, I wouldn't mind losing my beard. And I'd like to be shaved by a pretty lass."

Phillip's hand came down on her wrist before she could take a step. "Don't go near him."

Justin smiled. He had a crooked smile, one that caught a woman's attention. His voice turned honeyed. "Come here, lass. I won't snarl and bark at you."

Charlotte looked between the two men. "Actually, I *am* beginning to feel like a bone between two angry dogs," she said. "What is the matter with both of you?"

"You are not *between* the two of us," Phillip answered. "You are *mine*."

Justin snorted his thoughts on that. "Does she have your name—?"

He was cut off as Phillip rose up over the table, tipping everything. Charlotte managed to save the plates, but Phillip's tankard went flying, ale and hot water spilling onto the floor.

"See what you did?" Justin chided as if talking to a child and completely unintimidated. "Miss Cameron will be upset."

"I'm tired of you 'snorting' at everything I say," Phillip answered. "If you snort one more time, I shall pull your tongue out of your mouth and tie it into a knot."

Justin's response was to snort.

Charlotte threw her hands out to Phillip to stop him from attacking. "Please," she said. "Let's eat breakfast and be civil." To Justin, she said, "If you continue to be provoking, I won't give you a shave."

"I don't want you to touch the bas—" Charlotte cut Phillip off by covering his mouth with her hand. "Ale. Go get ale. And since it hasn't been mentioned, I'm not your servant. Nor do I have *your* name. You have no authority over me, Your Grace."

Phillip drew back in surprise. Had he thought she hadn't realized what had made him angry?

She also doubted if anyone had ever been so direct with him—and then realized there was one other. Justin. He sat watching them with interest, obviously enjoying the moment.

"I know you aren't a servant," Phillip said to Charlotte.

"Then understand that I shall make my own decisions," she answered.

His brows snapped together, but before he could argue, Justin started clapping. "Very good, Miss Cameron. You told him off good."

"Quiet, Justin," she said, and he was wise enough to listen.

Phillip picked up the fallen tankard and walked in the direction of the kitchen without saying a word.

"The ale is behind the bar," Justin called out to him.

"I won't drink out of a tankard off the floor," Phillip answered, and left the room.

"He's not one who likes to be crossed," Justin said. "You handled him well, lass."

"So, you know what you are doing," she said before hitting the back of his chair, a command for him to scoot away from the table. "I don't want to get hair in the food." She opened and closed a pair of scissors experimentally. They were sharp. She was going to need them to be.

"Lean back," she ordered.

He raised his hand as if to ward off the scissors. "You aren't angry at me, too, are you? I should know before I expose my throat to you."

"How's your wound?" she asked.

The humor died in his eyes. "Well enough."

"Lean back."

This time he did.

Justin had thick, shiny hair like Phillip's. She cut as much of the beard away as she could before lathering his face with the soap.

Phillip returned. He filled his tankard and sat by the bar, watching sullenly. She hoped he remained that way. If her suspicions were correct, it would reinforce the point she wanted to make. She'd just prayed the twins would react in the way she anticipated.

After his initial nonsense, Justin turned out to be good-humored about the whole thing. As they waited for the lather to soften his whiskers, he said, "You've done this before."

"I used to shave my father. He broke his arm once, and the task fell to me. It became so he liked it." She picked up the razor. "Don't say a word. Not while I have the razor at your throat."

He pretended to gulp his distress, and Charlotte laughed. She set to work. She'd never shaved anyone with such thick whiskers, but she didn't do a bad job of it. However, shaving Justin's lip and around his nose was difficult. When she nicked him a second time, Phillip surprised her by saying, "Here, let me finish."

Justin started to rise. "I don't know if I want *him* close to my face with a sharp blade."

The razor in his hand, Phillip pushed him back. "Relax. I haven't killed you yet."

"While you two bicker, I'm going to run upstairs." Charlotte didn't wait for an answer but went up to their room. She walked over to where the rectangular mirror hung over a washstand. Phillip would need this and, if her suspicions were correct, it would become very valuable.

As she reached for the mirror, she caught a glimpse of her own reflection. She looked tired, and, yes, a bit angry.

In the mirror she could see the bed behind her

and the crumpled bed linens. She'd already gone too far. Her only hope was to trust in Phillip's honor. Lowering the mirror, unable to stand the reflection of her own sad eyes, she left the room, plastering a smile on her face.

When she arrived back in the taproom, Phillip was done and starting to shave himself. He used her mirror to make quick work of the chore. Charlotte waited until he was done and then turned the mirror so the twins could see themselves in it side by side.

"Dear God," Phillip said, the words bursting out of him.

Justin was speechless.

And Charlotte was very pleased with herself. Her suspicions had been correct. "Do you understand now?" she asked Justin.

All he could do was mutely nod in wonder.

They weren't completely identical, but the family resemblance was astonishing. And any animosity between them evaporated instantly.

Chapter 16

*P*hillip looked to Charlotte with admiration. "You are amazing. How did you know when we couldn't see it ourselves?"

"Only because you didn't want to see it," she demurred. "My sisters and I often don't see how close we are in looks and action."

He and Justin were not mirror images. There were differences. The skin beneath Justin's beard looked silly it was so white and, because his hair was longer, he didn't have as much gray at the temples. And perhaps, he lacked some of the lines in his face Phillip had, lines received under the weight of his responsibilities to his title, his family, and his country.

Not that Justin didn't have his own characteristics of the life he lived. There was a scar on his cheek that was now noticeable without the beard.

He noticed Phillip looking. "Lady Rowena chased me with a hoe."

"She caught you."

"I learned to run faster after that," Justin assured him, and Phillip laughed before pulling out a chair for Charlotte to sit.

He took the chair beside her, setting the mirror aside. "Were they hard on you?"

Justin mulled the question before admitting, "I didn't know any better. It was my life."

"What had they told you about your parents?" Phillip asked. "Or how you came to be there?"

"No one claimed me, that was for certain," Justin said. "I knew I was a bastard. Lady Rowena was the one who called our mother a whore. After that, I stopped asking questions."

"They called *our* mother a whore?" Quiet rage shot down Phillip's spine. "She wasn't. Her family's one of the oldest in England. You have the blood of kings in your veins."

And that blood would tell. Yes, Justin irritated him, but there was much admired about him, too.

The innkeeper arrived with Charlotte's breakfast, and then stopped dead in his tracks. He looked from Phillip to Justin and back again. "I knew you were brothers," he mumbled, before hurrying to his kitchen.

"The resemblance is a bit unsettling," Charlotte confided.

"Except I'm more handsome than he is," Justin said with a wink, and Charlotte laughed—and Phillip was jealous, a jealousy he tamped down. He had no cause. Charlotte was his.

He forced a smile.

"So why did Lady Rowena kidnap me?" Justin asked.

"She's mad," Phillip answered.

"That's always been obvious, but the laird dotes on his sister," Justin agreed.

Phillip retold the story.

"It's terrible what your father did to Lady Rowena," Charlotte said soberly.

Phillip shrugged. "He wasn't a warm man." He'd never criticized his sire aloud, and it felt good finally to have those around him he could trust. It opened something inside him, something he'd not known had been closed.

He continued, "MacKenna feels Father took after her because of the family history. Apparently there was bad blood between MacKenna and Father in school. Those sorts of rivalries are hell, and I've met more than one man who carried a grudge from his school days. I'm also certain Father would have taken a bit of advantage of her. He knew how to abuse an enemy."

Justin spoke. "It was whispered that Lady Rowena had once attempted to kill herself. They said she couldn't have children. She was married once, but her husband brought her back." He touched the scar on his cheek.

Thoughtfully, Charlotte said, "I suppose it is a sort of rough justice. She couldn't have children, so she stole your father's."

"I find it difficult to pity her," Phillip answered.

"There is one thing I don't understand. When she came pretending to be the midwife, wouldn't your father have recognized her?" Charlotte asked.

"Father traveled," Phillip said. "He was rarely home, and we came before her term. He was on a special envoy for the king to the Netherlands at the time we were born. He always pushed the limits. When he received word that his heir was about to be born, he raced back to Darnal Abbey but, of course, he was too late. For that reason, I refused to go anywhere for Elizabeth's confinement."

"Elizabeth?" Justin asked.

"My wife," Phillip answered, and then seeing his brother's surprise, he said, "she died. In childbirth six years ago."

Justin noticed that Miss Cameron tensed at the mention of Phillip's wife, and he realized the lass's heart was involved. He knew the signs. He'd been that way with Moira.

He liked Miss Cameron. By the easy way

Phillip rested his arm on the back of her chair, he sensed she was important to his brother. But he sensed Phillip was oblivious to the depth of her feelings.

And it was very possible he didn't return them.

Justin was all too sensitive to the pain that lay in that direction. Moira had been the one person he'd believed loved him, and she'd played him false.

Almost brutally, conscious of Miss Cameron the whole time, he asked Phillip, "Did you love your wife?"

His brother acted surprised that he should put forth such a question. "Of course. She and I had known each other all our lives. She was Lord Lynnhall's daughter. Very well connected."

"Of course," Justin answered, mimicking his brother's English accent and realizing how wide the chasm between his life and Phillip's truly was.

Phillip didn't understand. He thought the mimicry was directed at him. With a heavy sigh, he said, "We come from different perspectives. There will be times when what I say sounds cold or indifferent. I don't mean it as such. It's just the way things are considered and evaluated by people of *our* class." He leaned forward. "You may have been a blacksmith in one life, but in your new one, you shall find the world's perception of you very different. Are you ready for this?"

Justin's concern for Miss Cameron evaporated,

replaced by his own challenges. "How can I be ready for what I don't understand?" He shook his head, suddenly overwhelmed by just the possibilities. "I can't be a duke. Look at these hands They've worked all their lives. You keep the title. I don't want it."

"Yes, but it is yours." Phillip leaned one arm on the table. "If you don't accept it, Charlotte is correct—MacKenna wins. He'll have made a mockery of you and our family."

"I'm no duke," Justin said flatly.

"You aren't alone either," Phillip returned. "I'll be beside you. There's two of us now. We can see our way through this."

Two of them.

Justin studied his brother a moment. He'd been alone all his life. An outsider. To be offered so much of what he could only imagine didn't make sense, not according to his experience of life. "Why include me in this? Why give up what you have?"

"Why would I not?" Phillip countered.

"Because you are the one who loses," Justin said.

"We've both lost," Phillip answered, "but now we have the opportunity to correct that wrong." Seeing the surprise on Justin's face, he asked, "What? Do you believe you were the only one to suffer all these years? Riding to Scotland, after

I'd received the letter, I often wondered what my life would have been like if you had lived. It isn't easy always being singled out and being evaluated and judged. Father was a hard taskmaster. He offered little advice but plenty of criticism. In the end, I tossed aside most of what he'd preached. I've tried to make right decisions, but sometimes it is hard. They come at you from all sides asking for favors, soliciting your endorsement, begging of your time. I've no true friends. But now, I have a brother."

"But you would give up the title?" Justin dared.

"Yes. To do less would be dishonorable. This isn't your fault any more than it is mine."

"How does one go about changing the title?" Miss Cameron asked.

"We'll ask to rescind the letters of patent that passed it on to me," Phillip answered. "It's a matter of signing papers. Nothing more, nothing less. There will be talk. A scandal." He looked down to where his hand rested on the table inches from Miss Cameron's and glanced up to her, his expression one of wry self-knowledge. "I've learned to weather scandals."

She pulled her hand back and crossed her arms against her chest.

Justin looked from one to the other, sensing an undercurrent.

Phillip answered his unspoken question. "I asked for her sister's hand, and she jilted me."

"Well, better to know before than after," Justin said.

"Not in London," Miss Cameron corrected him. "It's a tiger pit there, with everyone using gossip to destroy people."

"But you needn't worry," Phillip hurried to say. "We'll get through this."

"What do I care what a few wagging tongues have to say?" Justin said. "I'll be a duke."

His response appeared to shock his brother. Phillip's brows came together as if he'd not ever heard anything so outlandish. "What?" Justin asked. "You can't say that you worry about idle minds?"

Phillip opened his mouth as if to protest, then paused. "It's different," he said at last.

"Well, if you are imagining that I shall be taking stock of what gossips say, you're wrong," Justin said. "I had enough of that over Moira. My hide's thick, and you'd best thicken yours, brother. I shall not back down from anyone." He softened the words by adding with a smile, "And don't worry. I'll not be tossing you out of the ducal mansion."

That made Phillip laugh, as he'd hoped it would. "I have no fear of that. After all, I will expect a very handsome recompense for my advice, brother. I have no desire to be the penniless sibling, not after I built that fortune."

"I thought all dukes were wealthy," Justin said.

"Not the ones who game money away like our grandfather did," Phillip answered. "Or who sank it into every investment scheme he could. Father did not have a good financial head."

"But you do," Justin noted.

Phillip nodded, "Helped by my wife's substantial fortune that came to me upon our marriage."

"Are you saying I'm a *poor* duke?"

"I'm saying that we are family now, and we shall work together toward our mutual success. I shall become Lord Phillip and respected because I am well connected to my brother the duke. The only one with regrets might be our cousin who had stood in line to inherit. But *I'll* be free to do whatever I wish."

He said this last as if it were a new idea.

Miss Cameron glanced at him. Justin knew she wondered where she would fit in his brother's schemes. However, he was struck by a new idea, one beyond wealth and titles. "I will sit in the House of Lords?"

"Yes," Phillip said.

"I'll have power?"

"You will."

A sense of purpose filled Justin, expanding with a growing awareness of power. "I can change the Clearances."

"What?" Phillip said.

"I will talk to the House of Lords. I will explain what they are doing to people's lives."

"You will do no such thing," Phillip answered. "In fact, what we are going to do is leave as soon as we gather our things for Edinburgh. I'm going to the garrison commander there and report to him on MacKenna. We'll stop his insurrection before it goes any further."

"We'll not do anything of the sort," Justin said. "I know those people. I grew up with them. If you tell the Sassenachs, they'll march up there and destroy everyone."

"Perhaps they deserve to be destroyed," Phillip replied.

Justin was stunned. "Are you really that cold? Are you saying that the children and the families deserve to be hurt more than they have been." His brogue was stronger. He could hear it, but he'd not hide it. "Those are poor people and not guilty of the laird's schemes. It's harsh times for us all. And why should they not want to fight for their rights to live on their land? You English have created the problem. A man will fight for what is right. Isn't that why you came for me?"

"You don't understand," his brother said. "The question is more sophisticated. The land wasn't theirs. I don't care to hear about old codes and how matters were handled in the past," Phillip said, holding up his hand to stave off Justin's argument. "This is a modern age. It's the rule of law that matters, and the land belongs to the landowners. I don't agree with what they are doing, or what our father did, but the law must be honored. Nor can I let an insurrectionist build his army and attack the Crown. And neither can you. Remember the responsibilities of being a duke."

Justin had heard him out, his temper growing with each word. With surprising restraint, he said, "Well, then, perhaps I don't want it." He stood and stomped out of the room.

Phillip looked after him. "Was I better off without a brother?"

"He's a brother, Phillip, not a lapdog," Charlotte answered, knowing how difficult this was for both men. "Family will say to you what the rest of the world is afraid to speak. Do you think my sisters are any easier to manage?"

"At least the three of you started off together, Charlotte. You have common values. What if I've opened a door I might want to close? I've been trained since birth for what I owed my title. He doesn't have an idea."

"He *has ideas*, Phillip," she answered, not bothering to hide her exasperation. "And they may be different than yours. After all, he does have an understanding of the opposite side of this Clearance question, one that perhaps you should listen to. People can't be chased out of their homes without wanting to turn around and fight. I saw enough of that on the frontier."

"But they aren't *their* homes," he answered with a touch of impatience. "The landowners are merely claiming what is theirs."

"But if people have lived for generations on a piece of property, if they think of themselves as family, then they believe they have rights. And they do, don't they? Didn't you just say as much to your brother over his right to the title?"

Phillip rubbed his face in his hands as if he were tired. "I don't know anymore. That was Monarch's argument—" He stopped. "Monarch," he repeated as if just discovering something in his mind.

"The king?" she asked puzzled.

"No, Lord Monarch. He's from Edinburgh. He wanted to talk to me about the Clearances the same day I received Nanny Frye's letter. We will go see him," he said decisively. "He told me he was heading home. He can explain to Justin what is right. He knows more about the situation than I do, and he'll be able to advise us on MacKenna." Phillip clapped his hands together.

"The problem is solved. Monarch can help Justin understand. The three of us can come up with the correct solution."

He kissed her forehead. "You are a source of inspiration. We'll set off for Edinburgh within the hour."

"Should we send a messenger to this Lord Monarch and warn him we are coming?" she asked.

"We will arrive before any messenger we send. Don't worry," he said in answer to her look of concern. "He'll be happy to see us. He wants to curry favor. And his house would be the perfect place to spend some time and give Justin a bit of polish before taking him to London. We'll go shopping for you, too. After all, I've lost your entire wardrobe with all of this," he said, before dropping his voice to an intimate note. "Not that I don't prefer you in absolutely nothing." His hand at her waist pulled her closer.

Her pulse quickened. He had that power over her. He wielded it effortlessly. But before she could answer, he was already turning away. "I'll get the horses ready. You prepare yourself."

"What of Justin? Are you going to speak to him?"

Phillip hesitated before saying, "He needs a moment to consider how much his life is changing. I don't believe it wise to discuss this with him now."

As if he'd passed an edict she must obey, he left. A moment later, she heard the door to the inn open and close.

She looked down at the remains of cold food from their mostly uneaten breakfast and wondered just how far she was going to follow him.

"He can be a bastard, can't he?" Justin's voice said from the kitchen doorway.

Startled, Charlotte turned to him. He leaned on the doorjamb. "How long have you been there?"

Justin made a self-deprecating sound. "From the beginning." He straightened. "I went storming off in the wrong direction and found myself in the kitchen with an innkeeper who is not fond of any of us."

His honesty made her smile. "I understand why."

He moved into the room. "Aye, I agree. What I don't understand is how matters are between you and Lord Phillip."

She heard the mockery in his voice over his brother's new title. "He's a good man."

"He is. If he can get his head out of his—" He stopped, a gleam of mischief in his eye. "I should mind my manners. Not be so coarse."

"You aren't a blacksmith anymore," she agreed.

The light in his eyes died. "What am I? A fool? A puppet?"

Charlotte pushed a chair into the table. "You are what you wish to be."

"Will *he* let me?"

"Does he have a choice?"

"He could slit my throat and be done with me. No one but you would be the wiser."

"And you'd believe I would keep silent?"

"Women do many foolish things for love."

"Not I," Charlotte answered, offended.

Justin's face split into a grin. "I've got your back up, haven't I?"

"Are you saying you are deliberately being provoking?" she countered.

"Aye."

Charlotte leaned back, considering him. "To what purpose?"

"Perhaps for my own, Miss Cameron."

She nodded. "And what purpose could that be, Mr. Maddox?"

The line of his mouth flattened. "I'm no Maddox. Mayhap I'll be the duke, but that name has been burned in my soul as one of shame."

"Phillip said there was no shame. He defends his family's reputation."

"Phillip and I disagree on many matters. We've only scratched the surface. You were right, Miss Cameron. I'm not a lapdog. Not anymore."

She believed him. This past week had changed

all three of them, but he more than her and Phillip. "What shall I call you?" she asked quietly. "Are you ready to be referred to as the duke?"

"Call me Justin."

Their gazes met with understanding. "You like the name."

"Aye, the man I was is dead. I'm no fool, Miss Cameron—"

"Charlotte," she corrected.

He smiled. "Charlotte," he said, testing the name. "I'm no fool although I realize I've been played one for years. The laird is a sly one. He knew from the beginning what he was doing. I see that now."

"What do you mean?" she asked.

"Moira. He arranged my marriage to Moira when we were both too young to know better, and I was happy to stay right where he wanted me."

"And then he took her away."

Justin shrugged, his expression hardening. "I don't know if he was that clever. Once Bruce noticed her, she changed. It's hard for a man who suspects his wife is being unfaithful. If he loves her, he wants to pretend ignorance."

Charlotte heard the pain of experience in his words. "Why would you want her to stay if she didn't love you?"

His gaze slid to hers. "Now you sound like the MacKenna. That was his question to me before he ordered me to divorce her. It's all a game to him, and she is a prize. Bruce loves her as much as I did. Now she shackles him to the laird."

"But you'd go back to her."

He shook his head. "No. Never. Every time I look at the scar her knife will have left in my shoulder, I'll remember she'd wanted to bury that dirk into my heart. Some things sober a man, Charlotte."

"It's a pity it had to go to that extreme," she agreed.

He smiled, the expression bitter, before saying, "Don't feel sorry for me, Charlotte. You love him, don't you, lass? Ah, you don't have to answer. I know the look. The first thing you lose is your principles. I begged for Moira back, Charlotte. I embarrassed myself. But I learned a valuable lesson."

"What lesson?" she asked, almost afraid to breathe until she heard the answer.

He stepped closer, his words for only the two of them to hear. "I learned that you don't settle. That you have the right to expect your lover to be as honest and open as you are. It doesn't work when one has nothing to lose, and the other has everything."

Dear God, it was as if he'd read her fears and doubts.

But before she could speak, Phillip's voice

came from the hallway door. "Am I interrupting something?"

Both she and Justin turned away while heat surged to her cheeks. She hated blushing. It made her look guilty.

"We were discussing my divorce," Justin said, easily.

Phillip walked into the room. Charlotte could feel him studying her. She met his eye.

"I've been thinking about that, too," Phillip said, returning his attention to his brother. "What conclusions did the two of you reach?" There was a challenge in his voice, a challenge Charlotte didn't quite understand.

But Justin did.

"We've no conclusions," he said. "Not yet."

"You won't," Phillip assured him.

Charlotte looked from one to the other. There was a current flowing between them. They understand without words what was being said. She didn't know if it was because they were twins, or men.

Justin caught her confusion. "It's fine, lass. All is well between us."

"Thus far," Phillip amended with his customary caution. But then, he shifted his mood. "I've been thinking about the divorce."

"And?" Justin queried, the word testy.

"We should follow it up with an annulment.

I'll make the arrangements. Divorce is a sticky problem in England. I know you Scots are more lenient—"

"We're not lenient at all. I know it cost the laird a pretty penny and me my pride."

"Well, it's not done in England. Not done at all," Phillip said decisively. "But if we put through an annulment, there will be no questions in the future."

"My marriage was consummated, well and good," Justin declared. "I'll not stand before any man and say I could not take care of my wife."

Phillip frowned his impatience. "You don't have to stand before anyone. We'll leave it to the lawyers. They will find a reason, and once they do, the clergy will agree. It will all be done very quietly."

"There is no reason. We were married right and proper."

"Leave it to the lawyers," Phillip pressed again. "For the right price, everyone will agree, and we'll not need to worry about this matter."

"Why do I sense that you are rather happy to be giving up this ducal kingdom?" Justin asked.

His shrewd insight caught both Phillip and Charlotte by surprise. Phillip's twin was no fool. In some ways, he would make a more dangerous enemy than Phillip.

"I'm doing what is right, brother," Phillip said,

using the word "brother" with deliberate intention. "And it is for that same reason I shall insist on an annulment."

Justin appeared ready to argue, but then capitulated. "Do as you wish."

"I usually do," Phillip answered briskly. He clapped his hands together. "Are we ready to travel?"

Charlotte realized she'd not done a thing to prepare. "Give me a moment," she promised, and started out of the room toward the staircase.

"Let me help," Justin said, coming after her.

"No, that's fine," she said. "I'll only be few moments."

Phillip waited until she was gone to tell Justin what was *really* on his mind. "Stay away from her. She's mine."

Justin walked over to the corner where he'd leaned the Sword of the MacKenna. He picked up the weapon before answering, "You have no claim on her, brother."

"And stop calling me brother in that tone of voice," Phillip added.

"What tone?" Justin asked, sounding innocent.

Phillip couldn't help but swear. "If I'd known a brother would be this much of an irritant, I would have left you where you were."

"I understand," Justin said easily. "However, let us be honest with each other. Charlotte is not only beautiful but courageous. She deserves better than being played the doxy."

"I could call you out for that," Phillip answered.

"Call me out?" Justin lifted an eyebrow. "For what? Speaking the truth. You can go to the devil." He started out of the room, the Sword of the MacKenna in his hand, not even bothering to choose a different direction. Instead, he walked right in front of Phillip.

Phillip blocked his path with an arm across the doorway. "She's mine," he said.

"She is yours," Justin agreed. "But be careful you don't lose her. After all, every woman wants to marry a duke." He pushed his way past and went down the hall and out the door.

Phillip stared after him, unable to move or think as he realized the truth in Justin's words and exactly what he'd given up. Up until this moment, he'd been willing to hand his title to his brother. It was the right and honorable thing to do.

However, it might cost him Charlotte.

He'd not considered that possibility—not until he'd walked into this room and found her and Justin so cozy. The jealousy that had surged through him had been alarming, but he'd managed to keep appearances intact.

Charlotte wanted to marry a duke . . . and he no longer was one.

In fact, he no longer was sure *what* he was, a realization that shook him to his soul. For the first time, he realized he was going to have to be considered as a man, not a duke.

A Cameron had already jilted him once. The scandal had humiliated him, but it had also prepared him for accepting his brother.

However with Charlotte, his heart was involved.

Footsteps warned him she was coming down the stairs. He turned to greet her. She smiled and his heart seemed to stop.

It was then he also realized that his love for Charlotte Cameron wasn't going to be a static thing. It grew and had been growing from that first kiss.

If he wasn't careful, she could crush him.

She immediately sensed the change in him. "Phillip, is something wrong?"

Yes, everything.

He shook his head, more to clear his senses. "No, everything is fine," he said.

"Good. Is Justin waiting outside?"

Justin. A man Phillip had pitied because he'd been willing to trust a woman he loved, a woman everyone but he could see was mercenary.

"Yes, he is," Phillip answered, sounding more curt than he intended. She was so beautiful . . . but what if she really wanted a duke? It had been her purpose, her dream.

"Are you coming?" she asked.

"Yes, I'll be out in a moment," he answered, wanting to put his jumbled thoughts together.

"I'm going ahead," she said with her customary independence.

And watching her go, he knew he must be careful, or he could be played for a fool as his brother had been.

He might not be a duke much longer, but he had a duke's own pride . . . and a man's realization that Charlotte was the one woman who could expose all his vulnerabilities. She could destroy him.

And for that reason, Phillip would keep his heart secret. The risk was too great. Let her be the one to speak first. Then, and only then, would he allow himself the freedom of his heart.

When he went outside, Justin and Charlotte were already on their horses and laughing companionably . . . and once again, he was the outsider.

"Let's go," he said curtly. "We don't have time to dawdle." He didn't wait for an answer but kicked Homer into a trot.

Chapter 17

*C*harlotte sensed a change in Phillip, but she couldn't understand why. He'd become distant and yet, more protective. He kept himself between her and Justin and frowned anytime either of them laughed.

It was as if they traveled with a Puritan.

"He's jealous," Justin whispered to her.

"Of what?" she wondered.

"Me."

The idea was so outlandish, she laughed. They'd stopped for a moment on the road. Phillip had stepped away for some privacy. Otherwise, she could not have spoken to Justin at all.

"It's true," Justin said. "I told him he didn't deserve you."

Shocked, Charlotte asked, "Why did you say that?"

"Because he doesn't. You love him, don't you?"

She nodded, upset to realize how transparent she was . . . and how weak. She was now defenseless to the world, her reputation in tatters, and yet, she could not help herself. "He and I really don't know each other."

Justin gave a bark of laughter. "What does that mean? That you haven't formally been introduced?" He waved a dismissive hand. "It's all rot. If a man wants a woman, he should say so. Until he does, she's fair game."

Her eyes widened. Was he saying he wanted to court her?

He smiled, the expression sly. "You are a beautiful woman, Charlotte," he said, his voice warm.

She stumbled backward. "Oh, no. No. I'm not some game. If this is nonsense between you and Phillip, leave me out of it."

This time, Justin's smile was genuine. "Come along, lass, you can't expect me not to want to tweak his nose a bit."

She shook her head, uncertain. Justin was completely different than his twin. Phillip was straightforward. He said what he believed. She wasn't so certain Justin did.

However, before she could ask questions, Phillip returned. He took in the scene of Justin and Charlotte, and his scowl deepened.

"Mount up," he ordered, and practically manhandled Charlotte up on the back of her bay.

Justin caught her eye and gave her an "I told you so" smile.

However, for as difficult as Phillip was being to her, he and Justin actually started to become better acquainted. She and Phillip were both surprised at how quick Justin's mind actually was. He told them about the priest's teaching him to read. He didn't know Greek, but he had a smattering of Latin and a head for figures honed by years of running his own smithy.

That night, they stayed at a widow's cottage. Justin and Phillip paid for their board by doing chores.

"Which one of those bonny men are yours?" the widow asked Charlotte. "Or does it make a difference with them being twins?" She chuckled over her own humor.

Heat rushed to Charlotte's cheeks as she realized what the woman had *really* assumed.

Charlotte prayed to God that Constance never learn of this escapade. In fact, her big worry was Constance.

Constance must marry and marry well. Charlotte would be mortified if her sister had such a relationship as the one she now had with Phillip.

However, that evening, up in the widow's hayloft, when Phillip held out his hand for her, she went. She couldn't help herself.

As for him, he made love to her as if this night was their last. He turned her inside out. In his arms she became a creature of passion . . . and yet, he never spoke of a future between them. When he talked about anything beyond the moment, it was his plans to stop MacKenna or for Justin's future.

He didn't mention her and him together. No talk of love, and so she kept what was in her heart secret, where it would be safe.

The next morning they were up at dawn. Phillip readied the horses. "Where is Justin?" Charlotte asked.

A beat later she found out when the cottage door opened. Justin came swaggering out, tucking his shirt in his breeches, the Sword of the MacKenna hanging from his belt and a cloth sack in his hand. He'd not taken a step or two before the widow came hurrying out and gave him a passionate kiss.

Phillip and Charlotte could do nothing but wait. At last, the widow had her fill. "Godspeed, my bonny man," she said in her musical burr.

Justin gave her a pat on the rear for remembrance. He mounted his horse, a grin on his face from ear to ear.

Phillip waited until they were out of sight of the cottage before he said, "Did you enjoy yourself?"

"Aye and so did she. Enough to feed us break-fast." He held up the sack. "Bread, cheese, and a jar of cider."

"I thought you didn't like cheese," Phillip said.

"I like anything that woman offered," Justin said, and set his mare Butter off at a happy trot.

They stayed the next night with a Presbyterian family. Again, Phillip introduced them as Mr. and Mrs. Smith.

And so, living hand to mouth, they made their way to Edinburgh. After that initial morning, Phillip and Justin didn't fight. Not once. And it was sounding more and more like they had known each other all their lives. The most amaz-ing moment to Charlotte was when they had a belching contest, and Phillip won.

"Never, not even in my wildest imagination, would I have imagined you making such a rude noise," Charlotte said to Phillip.

He laughed, sounding more carefree than she'd ever heard him. "It's schoolboy nonsense, Charlotte. I've had my share of that."

And yet, she sensed that he hadn't. Justin was proving to be more outgoing than Phillip, more willing to play the clown and entertain. Perhaps because he had not ever had the weight of expec-tation on his shoulders. She wondered what he would have been like if he'd not been stolen from his parents. Would both the twins be somber and serious?

At last, they reached Edinburgh. Phillip had no trouble discovering where Lord Monarch lived. His family was an old established one and, although not wealthy, they owned a yellow limestone home in the heart of town.

"I wish to see Lord Monarch," Phillip announced to the butler who answered the door.

The servant looked at Phillip, who stood in shirtsleeves, breeches, and scuffed boots, up and down and didn't like what he saw. "He's not at home, sir."

Charlotte and Justin would have gone down the steps, but Phillip didn't budge. "He is at home, and I wish to see him now."

He hadn't raised his voice, but the servant heard the tone of authority. He reconsidered and opened the door wider. "Please come inside."

Once they were in the foyer, the butler said, "If you will excuse me, I shall announce you—"

He paused for a name.

Phillip smiled. "The Duke of Colster. He knows me."

The servant looked from Phillip to Charlotte and Justin, the three of them looking the worse for their travels. "Very well . . . Your Grace," the butler said, and backed out.

"He doesn't believe you," Justin said.

"He believes me," Phillip answered.

A minute later, Lord Monarch himself came to greet them and recognized Phillip immediately, or thought it was Phillip. He first walked over to Justin with his hand out, and then stopped when he realized there were two of them.

Before Phillip could make the introductions, Lord Monarch noticed the sword at Justin's side.

His face under his red hair went pale. He turned to the butler. "Harris, go speak to Cook. Tell her we shall have three guests for dinner." The moment the butler was beyond earshot, he demanded, "How did you come by that sword?"

"You know the weapon?" Phillip asked.

"I've heard its history," Lord Monarch answered.

Phillip moved close to the young lord. "Are you loyal to the king?"

"What has MacKenna done?" Lord Monarch asked.

Without answering him, Phillip posed the question again.

"Aye, I'm loyal," Lord Monarch said, sounding irritated. "MacKenna is a fool."

"Then let's talk," Phillip answered. "I've got quite a story to tell. But first, let us see to Miss Cameron's comfort."

Lord Monarch went rigid. *"Who?"* he asked, the word shooting out of him.

"Miss Cameron," Phillip said.

"Cameron?" Lord Monarch repeated in amazement. *The* Miss Cameron?"

Phillip enjoyed Monarch's reaction although it discomforted Charlotte. Well, they might as well become accustomed to this. "No, not *the*," he said, adding to his brother, "He's talking about Miranda, Charlotte's sister, the one who jilted me."

Justin nodded, noticing Charlotte's surprise. "He told me."

"When?" she asked.

"We talk."

"This is what I mean about the gossip in London," Phillip instructed him. "Although I'd not imagined you, Monarch, as the sort to take part in tongue rattle."

"I'm not," Lord Monarch assured him.

"Good," Phillip said, "because I have a story to tell and must rely on your ability to keep a confidence. By the way, do you have brandy? It's been a long week."

"Why, yes, I do, Your Grace."

"Good," Phillip said. "Lead us to it, and you don't mind if we stay a day or so? We need clothes and to get this MacKenna matter settled before returning to London."

"Yes, Your Grace," Monarch said, a bit befuddled as if still in shock that the Duke of Colster had come knocking on his door. He led them into a reception room with a several decanters waiting a thirsty visitor.

While he poured drinks, Phillip explained in a low voice to Justin and Charlotte, "I'm not correcting him because I believe he is in enough shock. It's a taste of what we shall meet in London. But don't worry," he added cheerily. "Being a bit of a scandal broth isn't the worse thing that could happen. This will make them all forget about the jilting."

And he was happy, Phillip realized. A week ago, the idea of being the subject of anyone's gossip would have set his teeth on edge, but today, he didn't mind. In fact, he really didn't care what others thought.

It was such a radical notion, it made him pause, amazed by the transition in himself.

Accepting a glass of sherry for Charlotte, he realized as he handed it to her that she was the reason. Charlotte and her direct, practical response to the world and situations around her.

She wasn't afraid to confront him, to let him know her mind or tell him when he was wrong. He was also beginning to realize there were some things more important than his pride.

"Your brandy is good, Monarch," Phillip said. He caught a glimpse of the cautious way Justin was approaching the wine. Just as his brother started to take a swig, Phillip shook his head and demonstrated how to "taste" it.

"I actually prefer whiskey," Monarch said.

"I do, too," Justin agreed quickly.

A hint of a smile appeared on the mild-mannered lord's face. "Would you like one?"

"If it wouldn't trouble you," Justin answered.

"No trouble at all. I was going to pour one for myself." Monarch poured two glasses, and then like the Scotsmen they were, he and Justin sampled them without airs and with relish.

"I wouldn't be standing if I drank like that," Phillip said.

"That's because you are a lily white Sassenach," Justin answered, and helped himself to another one.

Monarch looked between the two brothers, a charmed expression on his face. "This is amazing. Amazing."

"You're surprised? You should see how we feel," Justin said with his blunt wit, and all of them, including Charlotte, laughed.

"My wife is in Glasgow," Monarch said, apologizing. "That's why she isn't here to greet you. I know she will be saddened to miss your visit. I'll have the guest rooms made up." He rang a bell, a signal for his butler. "I'm certain Miss Cameron is anxious to relax."

"That's kind of you," Phillip answered, and

then almost casually mentioned, "Put her in my room."

If he'd hit Monarch over the head with a board, the man would not have had a different reaction.

Phillip would not apologize, or look at Charlotte. She slept with him. That was what he wanted, and that was what would happen. He couldn't give her up.

He also knew Monarch would not challenge him. If there was an uncomfortable silence, Phillip didn't care. She belonged with him.

Charlotte felt betrayed.

It took all her courage to sit calmly and sip her sherry. Her ruin was complete. Lord Monarch, a very capable and earnest young nobleman, knew she was Phillip's mistress ... and there was nothing she could do about it.

She sat, pretending to listen as Phillip told their story. She dared not look at Lord Monarch. If she did, she'd crumble.

Justin knew how she felt. And Phillip did, too. He knew, and he'd humiliated her anyway.

"We have to stop MacKenna," Phillip concluded.

"Or?" Lord Monarch asked.

"Or Scotland will go up in flames," Phillip answered.

Lord Monarch glanced at Justin. The two understood each other as Scots.

It was Justin who said quietly, "Phillip, if the laws don't change, we'll go up in flames anyway."

Phillip set his brandy glass down and hit the arm of his chair with his fist. "I will not let MacKenna keep an army up there. More lives will be lost."

"Chances are, he's gone," Lord Monarch said. "If he hasn't chased after you, he's been busy moving his people."

"He didn't chase us because we burned his barn," Phillip answered.

"With all due respect, Your Grace, we Scots are more canny than that," Lord Monarch answered.

Charlotte thought he was right.

In the end, the gentlemen decided to invite the local British authorities to dinner the following night. Lord Monarch knew these men and felt they could be trusted.

It was done. Their adventure was finished.

Phillip rose and offered Charlotte his arm. She felt as if she moved in a dream. She could have refused. She didn't. They followed the butler up to their set of rooms. The bedroom was of modest decoration in a very relaxing blue. It overlooked the garden. There was warm water to bathe with in the basin, clean towels, and a bouquet of flowers on the dresser.

Someone had even been kind enough to provide a brush for her use.

Charlotte washed, taking her time and not quite wanting to meet Phillip's eye. She could feel him watching but still, she was surprised when his hand took her arm and he swung her around.

Before she could speak, he kissed her.

She wanted to resist. She tried. But she couldn't. Her body always responded to his.

And even though she knew she had to give him up, that her pride, her sense of decency demanded it . . . she wanted one more night in his arms.

He moved her toward the bed, and she let him. Sex, the intimacy between a man and a woman, was the finest sort of communication. Words involved pride, but here there was no place for pride.

Charlotte used her body to let him know what she feared to say. She used it now to let him know she loved him. Inviting him into her, she held him tight, not wanting to ever let him go. He was her mate. A half of her soul.

But then, she grew angry. Why couldn't he love her? Why did he not speak to her of what was in his heart? Or was she just a distraction?

She let him know what he was missing. She became demanding and furious and wicked— sliding her tongue across his skin, nipping him with her teeth.

Phillip didn't stand a chance. He met her every step of the way. He thrust deep and hard . . . and brought to her eyes tears of pure, savage joy.

It would not be like that with anyone else. Ever.

And yet, he would not love her. If he did, he would have spoken of it by now.

Later, when all was done and the house was quiet because everyone else had gone to bed, she held her sleeping lover in her arms and waited for the sun to rise.

The adventure was over. Charlotte knew she had to return to the true world. She prayed she had the courage.

Lord Monarch was an early riser, much like Charlotte herself. The met in the breakfast room overlooking the garden. Phillip was still asleep upstairs.

His lordship greeted her pleasantly enough and offered a cup of tea. "Or do you prefer coffee?"

"Tea is fine," she said. She'd dressed the best she could in what she'd been wearing for the past three days and had pulled her hair back in a modest and demure braid.

He set her tea by her place on the table while she helped herself to hot rolls on the buffet. Charlotte sat down.

There was a moment of awkward silence. She was just getting ready to frame the request she'd been mentally rehearsing all night when he blurted out, "I don't wish to insult you, Miss Cameron, but you seem a sensible young woman, and I must beg your indulgence a moment."

"Yes?" she asked, stirring her tea.

"My wife and two children are expected to return home today."

Shame rolled through her. She set her spoon down, dropping her eyes to her hands in her lap.

"It would be awkward if you and the duke are sharing the same room when they return."

"I know."

"Thank you," he said, sounding as if it had been as difficult for him to bring up the subject as it was for her to hear it. A long silence stretched between them.

She knew what must come next, what decent people would expect—and the weight of her decision was lifted.

"We were thrown together unexpectedly," she admitted. She took a sip of her tea. Her hand was surprisingly steady, a sign her decision was right. "I did not anticipate the turn of events."

"How could you?" He had hardly touched his breakfast and she pitied him this awkward moment.

She reached over and lightly touched his hand. "Please do not feel poorly. I appreciate your honesty. You've helped me realize, I'm not good mistress material." She glanced away, not daring to meet his eyes as she said, "I do believe he cares for me . . . but not enough."

"Then he is a bloody fool," came Justin's blunt voice from the doorway. He too was wearing the breeches, shirt, and well-worn boots of the last several days, but he'd combed his hair, and she was surprised to see that he had shaved, something he'd done every day since she'd taken off his beard.

She smiled, appreciating his support. "You're right." Reaching her decision, she turned to Lord Monarch, her head high, "My lord, I don't want to move to another room."

He paled. "What do you wish to do?"

"I want to return to London." She should see Constance at Madame Lavaliere's boarding school, especially since she was so close, but a visit to her sister would have to wait. She needed to return to her friends Isabel and Michael's house. She wanted to know if there was word of Miranda and Alex. She had to return to *that* life and peace of mind. The one she'd had before she'd accepted Laird MacKenna's invitation.

The one she'd had when she'd thought hers the most pressing problems in the world. "Life takes strange twists, doesn't it, gentlemen?"

"Are you *and* the duke leaving?" Lord Monarch asked.

"I don't believe he is," she answered.

His Lordship set his elbow on the table and buried his face in his hand. "He will not be happy if you leave alone."

"Well," Justin said cheerfully, "sometimes each of us has be a little unhappy. You go, lass. Leave my twin to me."

"I have no money," she confessed. "I shall need a loan. I will pay it back as soon as I arrive, but right now I'm without funds or very much clothing."

There, she'd said it, and she felt completely exposed.

Lord Monarch looked as if he wished she hadn't spoken. She understood. She'd placed him in an awkward position.

"Give her help," Justin growled. "I'll be the new duke, and you and I will be the best of friends."

"I suppose I don't really have to worry about him," Lord Monarch said.

"No, just worry about me," Justin said, grabbing a warm roll from the basket on the sideboard. "If you can loan her the money, Monarch, give it to her. There's no honor in loving someone who holds all the cards. And if he doesn't come for you, Charlotte, he isn't worth it."

"Will he come for me?" she dared to ask, hope in her voice.

The light of a thousand devils danced in Justin's eyes. "I could guarantee it. But first, let's give him a scare, and then you won't have problems in your future."

Within two hours, and while Phillip still slept, Charlotte found herself wearing one of Lady Monarch's dresses and crammed on top of the stage for London.

The first thing Phillip did when he woke was reach for Charlotte. It had become his habit.

She was not there.

He sat up and looked around the room, listening. The house was quiet. A glance out the window told him he'd slept unusually late.

She was probably downstairs.

Phillip washed, using the razor they'd purchased in the inn, and dressed. He was growing tired of these clothes. He looked forward to taking her shopping. Edinburgh was known for its tailors, and he planned on sampling several.

The hallway outside his room was silent.

He went downstairs. Breakfast had been cleared from the dining room. Voices could be heard farther on down the center hall.

Phillip followed their sound and found his brother and Monarch in a companionable game of chess in the library. He looked around the room, expecting to find Charlotte tucked in some place.

She wasn't there.

"Oh, hello, Phillip," Justin said, and moved his pawn to take Monarch's bishop.

Monarch pounded the game table. "I just taught you this game an hour ago, and now you are beating me."

Justin smiled. "It's not that hard."

"It's torture," Monarch countered. "I've studied it for years."

"Do you want me to put your game piece back?" Justin offered.

Phillip interjected himself into their discussion. "Where's Charlotte?"

"Gone," Justin answered, not bothering to look up at him.

"Gone where?" Phillip asked with undisguised impatience.

"Gone to London," Justin said.

"*She left?*" Phillip couldn't imagine such a thing.

"Aye," Justin confirmed. "She said she wasn't good mistress material. Isn't that right, Monarch?" He grinned up at Phillip as if he'd just performed a trick. "Did you admire the way I spoke to him? Very ducal. *Monarch.*"

Phillip wasn't amused. "You let her go?" The tension in his voice sucked the air out of the room—but Justin appeared unbothered.

"Monarch, would you give my brother and me a moment alone?"

He didn't have to ask twice. Monarch shot up and left, shutting the door behind them.

"What is there about you, Phillip, that makes some people so afraid? Is it because you are the duke?"

"Or because they *should* be afraid?" Phillip suggested tightly. "You let her go. You probably encouraged her."

"No, brother, *you* let her go. I just didn't stop her."

Phillip doubled his fist. He could have hit Justin right in the face. His brother knew it. "Go ahead. I know a bit how you feel."

"If you did, you'd not have helped her."

Justin didn't deny it. "Helped her what? Protect her heart? Phillip, you didn't give her a choice. You haven't made an offer."

Phillip looked around the room, not seeing anything. "She's not given me a choice either. I don't want to be like you."

"Like me?"

"Charlotte. She could own me."

"She could hurt you," Justin amended. "Aye, Moira hurt me. But at least I let her close. I doubt if you've ever done that. What is it, Phillip? Have you been alone for so long, you can't take a risk?"

"Would you risk it?"

His question made Justin pause. "I don't know." He shrugged. "I won't know until I meet someone who makes me feel the way Moira once did. But Charlotte's no Moira. You know that."

He did know that.

"I've been an idiot."

A smile sprang to his brother's face. "Aye."

But he spoke to the air because Phillip was already on his way out the door, where he paused long enough to say, "Handle that MacKenna business, will you?"

He didn't wait for an answer.

He *had* been an idiot. It was pride that made him so. Pride that had caused problems between them in the beginning when he should have been thanking God he *hadn't* married her sister. And pride that was almost going to cost him Charlotte.

He loved her.

There it was. No more hesitation. He should have said the words last night. He prayed he wasn't too late.

Monarch was only too happy to loan clothing, money, and have Homer saddled and ready. He even knew which coach Charlotte had taken. Within the hour, Phillip was on his way.

Charlotte refused to cry although she was tempted several times. She tried to focus on anything but Phillip. Sitting in the middle of a row on the roof of an overcrowded coach, she struggled to muster the enthusiasm and sense of adventure that had led her to cross an ocean and meet her future head-on.

Instead, she was exhausted. It would be a long time before she would recover her spirits after this. She wasn't one to fall in love easily and, next time, she vowed, she'd be more guarded with her heart.

Her seat on the coach was situated with her back to the coachman and guard. The dust from the horses made the man beside her sneeze repeatedly. On her other side, two women chattered about very personal problems that were a bit embarrassing to overhear.

Charlotte would be very happy when this trip was over. Maybe then, in the privacy of her guest room at Michael and Isabel's, she'd have a good, hard weeping session—one that would last a month.

The coach had just rounded a sharp bend in the road when it suddenly came to a screeching halt. The passengers fell all over the top of each other.

It took a moment for Charlotte to right herself. Their driver was furious. "What are you doing standing out in the road, man? I could have crashed into you."

"I'm glad you didn't," a familiar voice said.

Phillip.

Charlotte didn't dare to turn to see him. She ducked down, wanting to become invisible and yet secretly thrilled. *He'd come.*

"I'm the Duke of Colster, and you have a passenger who is needed by authority of the Crown," Phillip said. He tossed a coin purse to the driver, who caught it with one hand.

He opened purse and said happily, "Your Grace, you can search them all, but please make it quick."

"I shall," Phillip answered. But he didn't move forward. Instead, he stayed on the ground and said in a loud, strong voice, "Charlotte Cameron, *I love you.*"

Charlotte swallowed her breath, and then bolted to her feet. She faced him.

"I shall always love you," he admitted. "And if you come down from the coach, I shall carry you off to the closest village and marry you posthaste . . . if you will have me as not a duke, but as a man."

Tears filled her eyes. She stood, feeling windblown and jostled and so much in love it had to radiate from her.

He saw her and smiled. "I love you, Charlotte. I love you."

The two biddies that had been sitting beside her gave her a shove. One said in her brogue,

"Well, go down to him, missy. If you don't, one of us *will*."

All the passengers laughed. Charlotte joined them, laughing with happiness through the tears.

Phillip came for her. He leaped up the ladder and offered her his hand. "Will you marry me, Charlotte?"

"*Yes*." The word burst out of her, and being said once had to be repeated. "Yes, yes, yes. And I'll even take you for better and worse."

The passengers started cheering as she climbed down the ladder with him. He swept her up into strong arms with a kiss that stole her very breath.

With a crack of the whip the coach was on its way, leaving a trail of dust.

"You came," she said when she could speak at last.

He held her close. "Charlotte, I knew I loved you, and yet, I—" He paused as if words failed him.

"I know," she said. "I understand. I had those same fears and yet, I felt worse without you. Please, let us never let go of the other."

And she realized that it was true. All her fears and doubts had been laid to rest. At last, she understood. Love was what gave life meaning.

It was what her mother had searched for, what Miranda had run for, and what she'd found.

She prayed Constance would be as fortunate.

"Come, love," Phillip said. "Let's find us a parson without fanfare, titles, or nonsense."

And that was just perfect with her.

*If you loved this Cathy Maxwell book,
then you won't want to miss any
of her other delicious Avon Books!*

*Following is a sneak peek
at some of Cathy's
other amazing love stories . . .*

The Price of Indiscretion

The granddaughter of an earl must charm the ton
and secure a good match for herself and her sisters.
But her true love is a renegade
and a most improper marriage prospect.

The dark room opened onto a deserted area of the terrace that had been set up for privacy. There was no light save for the moon.

Large pots of conical junipers, gardenias, and tiny trailing flowers shaped like white stars lined the edge of the lattice wall that separated this part of the terrace from the rest of the house. Red roses climbed up the trellis against the support columns. Their heady scent mixed with those of the gardenias.

Beyond the lattice came the music and conversation and laughter from the party. No one would hear them here.

It was the perfect spot for what Alex had in mind.

He could feel her coming. She walked quietly, but he could hear her kid leather dancing slippers move quietly on the tile floor. He stepped into the shadows and waited.

Miranda came out onto the terrace. Moonlight turned her hair to silver and her skin to alabaster. Her eyes were wide and dark. She looked around the terrace, her gaze stopping when she saw him.

Alex stepped forward into the moonlight. "Having a good time this evening leading all those men around by their noses, Miranda?"

Veral Cameron's daughter took a step back before

pulling herself up as regal as a princess. "Is that why you wanted me out here? Is that what you wished to say?"

Oh no, there were questions he wanted answered, and this time there was no one with a horsewhip to protect her.

"Men must come across as fools to you," he continued conversationally.

"You don't." She took another step back. She *should* be afraid.

"I should," he said, answering his own question, letting her hear his anger in the depth of his voice. "I was the biggest fool of all."

Almost defiantly, her face pale, she demanded, "What do you want, Alex? An apology? Would one erase what happened between us?"

No, nothing could do that.

And it made him angry that even now, after all these years, the sound of her voice made his heart skip a funny beat. She had no right to still have control over him. He should leave.

Instead he walked toward her.

She took a step for the door, but then stopped as if rooting herself in place. Miranda was many things, but she was no coward

How much he had once loved her . . .

He stopped in front of her. With a will of its own, his hand came up to rest on the trimness of her waist. Time might have passed, but some things had not changed. Memories rushed through him.

Alex went hard with a force he'd not experienced since last they'd met. He caught the scent of her hair. "You smell of the forest and of the spring wind in the valley," he whispered. "I'd forgotten how sweet it was."

He hated having her in his blood. She was a curse, a weakness that had almost destroyed him, and he'd best remember it—

Miranda leaned toward him, her shoulder against his chest. Her lips formed his name.

Pulling her closer, he let her feel how aroused he was. Her lashes dropped seductively over her eyes. Her nipples hardened . . .

But the innocence they'd once shared with each other was lost. He brushed his lips against her ear as he said, "And I think you are a pert tart to be dangling for a husband, when the man you married is standing right here next to you."

Miranda's eyes flashed. She pushed away, trying to free herself from his hold at her waist, but he kept her close. She attempted to strike out with her other hand. He captured her wrist in an iron grip. She had always been a fighter—in all matters save confronting her father.

She lashed out with words. "We were never married."

Alex gave her a little shake before pulling her closer. "Why?" he demanded. "Because you don't believe promises between yourself and an Indian carry weight?"

Her breasts pushed against his chest. "There was no church, no preacher—"

"There was *us*, Miranda." Alex was all too conscious that her curves had grown more womanly over the years. Their bodies fit together well. He focused on his anger. "*We* were all that mattered back then, or have you forgotten? Do you not remember that night? How we stood beside the river and followed the Shawnee way? Do you remember what I whispered to you?"

She shook her head, refusing to look at him. She tried to wrest her wrist free, but he held fast.

"You are lying," he accused quietly. "You can't forget."

"How do you know?" she threw back at him.

Alex smiled. "Because I can't," he admitted sadly.

Temptation of a Proper Governess

A governess should be mild, modest and keep to herself. And she must never attract the attention of any male in the household . . . but Isabel Halloran is too beautiful for Michael Severson to miss!

Michael watched the woman walk to him, her expressive eyes wide with apprehension—and longing.

Yes, this is what I need. Mindless sex would relieve the tension and frustration that had been building in him ever since he'd returned to England.

Elswick had shut him out. For close to five months, Michael's every effort to reclaim a place in Society had been thwarted to the point he'd had no other venue to pursue than the likes of Riggs, the profligate nephew of a duke whom few people accepted, and the drunken, fawning Wardley.

Not even his brother returned his calls. The butler, whom he had known since boyhood, seemed to enjoy informing him they were "not at home."

Michael knew Carter was there, and his wife Wallis, too. He could feel them watch him as he left their doorstep. They wanted him to stay out of their lives.

Meanwhile, Alex had returned from a profitable trip to Spain. Their shipping venture was already returning their investment fourfold. He had suggested Michael go with him on their next trip. Michael refused.

There had been a time, before Aletta's death, when he would have taken the easy route, when he would have forgotten the past. Now, he was a man who got what he wanted.

And at this moment, he wanted this woman.

She offered a much-needed diversion—and an excuse not to return to feigning drunkenness with Wardley and his ilk. He'd had enough.

Nor was Michael unaccustomed to women presenting themselves to him. He wasn't vain about his looks, but he knew their power. Furthermore, money was a potent aphrodisiac. In spite of the rumors swirling around his name, women in London eagerly sought him out. But the incident with Aletta had taught him discretion. He'd not taken what was freely offered. Even in Canada, he'd rarely had lovers. He'd been too focused on building his fortune and preparing for the day when he'd return to clear his name.

However, this woman attracted him in a way he'd not felt for a very long time. Her shining hair hung in a loose braid almost to her waist, reminding him of the proud Indian women back home. She was tall, her straight back and high cheekbones giving her an aristocratic air. A most unusual woman for a servant . . . but then, in Canada, he'd met many who had been bold enough to carve a place for themselves in the world. He'd just not expected to find such pride under Wardley's roof.

The woman stopped as if unable to take the last step toward him. The flickering candlelight cast dancing shadows around the room. Her skin was smooth and without the artifice of the cosmetics that so many women used in London. Her full, black lashes framed apprehensive sherry gold eyes. Seductive eyes. The sort that lured a man with their innocence.

His mind warned she could be a trap. His instincts didn't believe it. She was as leery of him as he was of her . . . and yet as caught up in the moment as himself.

He lifted his hand toward her hair. She drew back. He held still.

"I want to touch your hair," he whispered. "I want to know if it is as silky and heavy as it looks."

This time, when he raised his hand, she didn't flinch. He took his time, slipping his fingers into the clean, shining mass. She smelled of soap, fresh air, and woman.

Just this light touch was enough to make him hard with a force that was astounding, and he knew he was going to have her. She shifted away, shying from him. He brought his other hand to cup her face. Her skin was softer than he had anticipated.

"Don't be afraid," he whispered. "I won't hurt you. I'd never hurt you."

Her gaze held his. "I shouldn't be here," she said, her voice so low he could have almost imagined her words.

"But you are," he responded just as quietly.

She nodded.

"What is your name?"

She wet her lips, the movement almost bringing him to his knees. He wanted to smell, touch, and bury himself in her.

"Isabel."

"Isabel," he repeated. Even the sound of her name was magical.

A pounding began in his ears. It was the beat of his blood propelled by the force of that blessed need that made him a man.

Go easy, he warned himself. *Take care.* But he could not heed his own advice. "I want to kiss you."

She didn't reply, her gaze solemn, and he took that as permission, placing his hand on her waist and gently bringing her closer. She didn't balk . . . or turn away when he lowered his mouth to cover hers.

His mind registered a moment's resistance, a hesitancy, but as he fit her to him, her lips softened. She sighed her acceptance, and he could finally kiss her properly.

Elswick, Riggs, Wardley, *the world* disappeared. For too long he'd kept his guard up, his drive for vindication taking precedence over other desires. Now, the urge for release pushed him as it never had before.

He could tell she'd not kissed many men, but she was an apt pupil. As their kiss deepened, her own uncertainty vanished. Her arms came up around his neck.

Adventures of a Scottish Heiress

Miss Lyssa Harrell longs for love,
but knows her duty lies in marriage . . .
she is promised to a lord, but does the unthinkable—
and ends up in the arms
of fortune hunter Ian Campion.

*D*umbfounded, Lyssa stared after the Irishm—
Her mind stumbled over the appellation as she
broke off the thought. *Campion.* He wanted her to call him
Campion.

She frowned. The pride in his voice nagged at her conscience. The man had saved her life, but he was too high-
handed by half. And at this moment, he was walking away
as if he didn't care if she followed or not.

No. He *expected* her to obey.

Which she did, because she had no other choice.

She picked up her skirts and followed, but rebellion
brewed in her mind. Think what he may, she was *not* returning to London.

She would *not* marry Robert or go through another hu-
miliating Season of idle, patronizing chitchat from those
who only pretended to like her to please her stepmother or
even her father. She was too old for such nonsense.

She wanted purpose in her life, and she knew she would
find it here, in Scotland, the birthplace of her parents.

In the meantime, she would contrive to be everything a
proper, biddable young woman should be. After all, when
they reached Amleth Hall and she refused to return to London

with him, the Irishman would be cheated out of a great deal of money, and he wasn't going to take it very well.

So, Lyssa did her best to "march," but keeping up with him was a challenge. He had a long stride and moved as if he planned to cram the two days of travel inside this one night. She wasn't about to complain. Living with her father had taught her it was best not to pull on the watchdog's whiskers, and this man was definitely a watchdog.

Of course, it didn't help that her stockings were wet from their dash through the stream, and that water had seeped into her tight shoes, causing blisters to form on her feet.

She ignored the increasing pain each step caused her, and focused on placing one foot in front of the other.

She stumbled over a root growing over the path.

For a second, she was in midair, heading for the ground. But Campion turned, with that uncanny ability of his to know everything that was happening, and in the next instant, her cheek was against the solid wall of his chest. He set her on her feet. "Are you all right?"

"I'm fine." She took a step away from him. He wasn't the only one with pride. "I'll be better when we arrive someplace where we can hire horses."

"We won't be hiring horses."

Lyssa almost stumbled over her feet again in surprise. "You don't mean to *walk* all the way to Appin?"

"How else did you think we would travel?"

"With Charley and Duci, I had the wagon."

"There is no money for a wagon either, unless you have some."

She didn't. Her money had been hidden in the wagon that was burned to the ground. "You came after me without a shilling?" She'd never imagined herself without money.

"What little I have can be better spent than hiring horses."

"I doubt that."

Her flat reply startled a laugh out of him. "Oh, come now, people walk the distance across Scotland and back all the time, Miss Harrell. We shall manage."

"But not with my—" She stopped just in time. She'd been about to complain of her blisters, but she wouldn't give him the satisfaction. She'd heard the touch of satisfaction in his voice over having the power to make the rich man's daughter walk. Oh, no, like the noble Joan of Arc, she vowed to keep her personal sufferings private.

"Not with your what?" he prompted.

"Not with the present company," she improvised. "I'm certain walking is more pleasant with better company." He didn't like that response one wit, and she liked getting a bit of her own back—even though each step was agony.

And yet, she kept on, refusing to complain. She was her father's daughter for a reason.

The Irishman led the way, holding back low-hanging branches that would have swiped her in the face or helping her scramble up the often steep climbs in the forest path. She hid her suffering. Behind his back, she would hobble like a troll, but once he turned, she forced herself to walk upright.

In truth, the longer they traveled, the friendlier he became. As the first rays of the sun signaled the approaching dawn, he appeared ready to smile—until he caught sight of her limping.

"What's the matter?" he demanded.

"I've a blister. Nothing more, nothing less." They had come to a smooth road which she hoped would make the walking easier. She attempted to pass him, her head high . . . but parts of her feet felt like hot coals.

He held out his arm, blocking her path. "Sit down on that rock and take off your shoes."

"I have no intention of doing any such thing." And she would have ducked under his arm and continued on her way, except he hooked his hand in her elbow and swung her around to face him.

Lording his height over her, he asked, "What? You'd rather walk until you have nubs instead of feet?"

"That won't happen," she said.

"It will and it has," he shot back. "I've seen grown men lose *all* their toes because they didn't take care of a blister."

Lyssa frowned, slightly unnerved by his accurate diagnosis of her problem and yet not believing such a preposterous statement. "You're hoaxing me."

He shook his head. "Sit on that rock. We've been walking most of the night and the time's come to take a breather."

Her pride tempted her to nobly wobble on in spite of the pain. She wondered if he would be more contrite if she *did* end up with nubs instead of feet.

However, what won her over was the idea of sitting. He was right. They had been moving all night. Letting down her guard, she gratefully sank onto the round, flat stone half buried in the hillside beside the road.

Who would have thought "sitting" could be such heaven?

He dropped to his knees in front of her and reached for her shoe. She pulled her foot back. "What are you doing?"

The Lady Is Tempted

When a well-bred lady, Deborah Percival,
becomes stranded at a country inn,
the Earl of Burnell tempts her with the chance
to fulfill all of her dreams . . . in his arms.
She knows she should say no—
but how can she resist?

*D*eborah's mind went blank. She should protest, proclaim her innocence.

But then, another part of her, a part born from curiosity and unfulfilled lust, wanted to mew like a hungry kitten for more. Mr. Aldercy's kiss was a far cry from her husband Richard's perfunctory pecks. This was a full-lipped, on-the-mouth, real-man-behind-it kiss.

Lust won out.

What harm could a little taste do? After a marriage to a man who'd been more of a father figure than a lover, she was more than a touch curious about what she had been missing.

With a soft sigh, she let down her guard.

Mr. Aldercy's hand went to her waist and pulled her closer.

The kiss changed. His lips became more searching, insistent. She hesitated, uncertain . . . and then decided that if she was going to experience kissing properly, she must throw caution to the wind. She kissed him back for all she was worth.

But—

Something was wrong.

He broke contact. She would have pulled away, but he held her near, his arm still around her waist. The light of a thousand devils danced in his eyes. "Mrs. Percival, what are you doing?"

Hot embarrassment flooded her cheeks. She wasn't sure how to answer. "I thought you knew what we were doing," she replied stiffly.

A low hum in the back of his throat was his answer. "If that is all you know of kissing, then, with all due respect to your late husband, you have been sorely neglected." He took her hand and pulled her toward the door. "Come."

Apprehensive, she asked, "Where are we going?"

"To a place where I can teach you to kiss properly."

Deborah hung back. "I don't see why you can't show me here."

He turned. He was so tall, so strong, so overpowering, and yet his reassuring squeeze on her hand was gentle. "I don't want Roald or Mrs. Franklin to walk in. Not if we are going to be after a proper kiss."

That would not do.

As if to lend credence to his words, a footfall sounded behind the pantry door. It started to open.

"Come." This time she didn't hesitate but hurried behind him. She couldn't help herself. Her hand felt safe in his . . . and she did want her kiss—if for nothing more than to satisfy her curiosity.

After all, she couldn't very well ask anyone in Ilam to teach her. Mr. Aldercy was providing an excellent opportunity.

However, she did have second thoughts when he started for the staircase. She balked. "Why not the sitting room?"

He paused, one foot leading up the stairs. "Too public. At least for the kiss I have in mind."

She shouldn't.

Upstairs were the bedrooms. She wasn't so naïve that she didn't suspect his intentions—

Roald's low voice came from the dining room. "They've left the table. I'll clear it now."

Deborah panicked. What if he looked out in the hall and saw the two of them standing there in this ridiculous pose like she was a reluctant mule Mr. Aldercy had to coax forward?

They could dash into the sitting room—but then, she wouldn't get her kiss. And she wanted one very much.

With a glance over her shoulder to ensure no one saw them, she charged up the stairs. Mr. Aldercy fell into step behind her, and they hurried like schoolchildren afraid of being caught in a prank.

However, at the top of the stairs, games stopped. He whisked her up the last step, twirled her around until her back was against the wall, and kissed her.

*And don't miss these other
amazing love stories
by Cathy Maxwell*

*The Seduction of an English Lady
The Wedding Wager
The Marriage Contract
A Scandalous Marriage
Married in Haste
Because of You
When Dreams Come True
Falling in Love Again
You and No Other
Treasured Vows
All Things Beautiful*